Night Fires in the Distance

By

Sarah Goodwin

ISBN 978-1-326-81603-2

Cover Illustration: Bo Moore (bomoore.net)

Prologue

Laura

I threw another dress on the fire and watched the flames take it. Black smoke rose up from the wet fabric and the smell of burnt cotton mixed with those of urine and blood.

I scooped a stained bed sheet from the pile at my feet and threw it on the fire. There were grasshoppers caught in the cotton, and I watched them burn. All around me the ground crawled with them. Some jumped stupidly into the flames, some were crushed under my boots, the rest just scavenged for anything not yet eaten.

The smoke made my eyes run. I wiped my face with my hands, picked up the rest of the clothes and fed the fire. I'd always worried about our fires and the long grasses of the prairie. A prairie fire was the definition of hell – nowhere to go, flames all around and acres eaten up in a minute. But now, there was no grass, summer had baked the earth bare. No corn, wheat, beans, nothing green anywhere. Just the dust blowing across the ground and the brown bodies of the grasshoppers. This was hell.

I heard, over the whirring sound of the insects, one of my daughters crying. They were all hungry, like I was.

I stamped over the grasshoppers, away from the fire. The rifle was just inside the soddie door and I took it and the patch box. Before I closed the door on my family to keep the insects out, I wondered if it would not be better to shoot them now. Spare them the end that was coming, slow as it was.

It was getting hard to think. No water. No sleep. The grasshoppers weren't leaving. The rain wasn't coming. It was only for them that I'd kept on. I could give my own life up but I had to fight for theirs. It was all I knew how to do.

With the rifle in my hands I went around the fire and towards the barn, where the oxen lowed hungrily. At least today I could feed my family. Even if it meant fighting the grasshoppers for every bit of the ox meat.

Outside the barn I looked up, as I had for so many days, but there still wasn't a cloud in the sky.

Chapter One

Laura

By the summer James arrived I hadn't seen a tree in two years.

Sometimes I tried to remember what a tree sounded like. I could see the damn thing – the trunk, the branches, the roots. I could feel it. But I couldn't remember the sound of leaves moving in the wind or the way rain sounded on them in a storm. You wouldn't think that was something a person could forget, but somehow I could never fix it right in my head.

There were no trees on the western prairie. Practically the only things we had out there were grass and sky.

I was sitting in the shade of the house, my back to the sod wall, peeling early potatoes. The dry grass on the sod prickled against my neck and the sun beat down on me. I wasn't fit for most work, being only a few weeks from having my seventh child, though of the previous six, only three were still living; Rachel was taking care of my youngest Beth, and their brother Thomas was out with their father.

I filled the iron kettle with water and the potatoes, then hung it over the bare circle of ground where I made our fires. I'd twisted up some hunks of prairie grass and dried them out in the sun as kindling. To keep the fire going I stacked up buffalo chips, they smelled no worse than horse dung and burnt clean, cleaner than coal.

The potato skins were destined for the pig, along with our other scraps. Our winter side of bacon was already forming nicely within its hairy hide. While the hog ate I scratched its back with a stick, watched the flies scatter as its skin twitched.

In the soddie I wiped the paring knife with a cloth and put it away. I wiped my forehead with my hand. Though the two windows let in some of the hot air that baked the ground outside, the thick turf walls and roof oozed damp and cool into the room.

The girls were on the corn husk tick, where they slept, by the far wall. Beth looked ready to start fussing. Rachel had given up on trying to entertain her, she didn't

4

have her brother's patience. Rachel was very like her father, quick to anger and slow to let go of a grudge.

Beth stumbled off of the tick and crossed the room, little fists out, clasping. I steadied her as she clung to my skirts.

"Ma, I'm hungry."

"You'll get your supper soon, if you let go of me so I can get on with making it. Why don't you play with your sister?"

She tugged at my skirt, starting to cry. I knew there'd be no shaking her off. I poured some of the water out of the heavy bucket into a jug, covered it with a cloth. Rachel picked up her sewing with her face turned from the door. I petted Beth's hair but she only clung tighter, like she knew I had an idea to pull her from my skirts like a burr.

"Take your sister please, Rachel. I've supper to look after."

Rachel's face was a black blur of pure temper. She had her father's dark hair and muddy complexion, somehow she always looked dirty, angry and uncared for. I had my eye on her, but she didn't move.

"Now, Rachel," my voice was sharp, my back aching. Why couldn't I have just one obedient daughter?

"Yes Ma," her voice was sullen, but she put down her sewing and came to take Beth, who struggled until Rachel pinched her fat little leg. I pretended not to see. Beth popped her thumb into her mouth and sucked.

I went back into the heat to tend supper. Rachel carried Beth out and set her on the grass while she spread a blanket and set out plates and utensils for everyone.

Supper was salt-risen bread and potato hash. Back in England I'd made such fine loaves with my mother and sisters, plaited, golden loaves shaped like ears of corn or baskets of fish. There's only one kind of loaf you can make with that salt-risen dough – brick shaped.

I filled the coffee pot and put it on the fire, stirred the hash and cut up the bread. What I'd have given for a cup of cold water, a piece of my mother's light, white loaf, and a bit of butter.

Will, his dark hair thick with sweat, came around the ox shed with Thomas, carrying his scythe. They'd been cutting and shocking the corn, getting the harvest in.

"Pa!" Beth called out and Rachel ran out to meet them, passing Thomas by to hug her father.

Thomas looked the most like me, with my mulch brown hair, the same freckles and turn to his nose. He sat down right away on the edge of the blanket. He may have been the eldest at ten, but I ached to see him so worn down and tired. He looked up at me, his mouth twisting upwards in a small smile.

Will cut his eyes in Thomas's direction. "Go wash up."

Thomas got to his feet slowly and went into the soddie to wash his hands and face for dinner.

"You shouldn't boss him so, he's tired."

"And I suppose I'm not?" Will raised his thick, dark, eyebrows and unwound Rachel's arms from his waist. "I've done the larger share of work."

"He's only a boy."

"I was helping my father at six years," Will turned from me to the fire, "is that coffee ready?"

I poured a cup, still wanting to argue. He took it from me and sat down, hands unwashed. Thomas came back with wet shirt cuffs and I handed out bread.

The sun was going down, the light still yellow, but with shadow creeping in behind the ox shed and the sty. The grass kept up a steady beat against the wind. Only the girls had energy to speak and one look from their father reduced them to bowed heads and silence. It was like eating with a damn bear, not knowing when you were about to get your head ripped off.

After dinner was finished I scraped the plates and wiped them clean. As darkness came down on the prairie, we took up the blanket, put out our fire and went inside. William drew the bar on the door.

I herded the girls behind the canvas that was draped across one corner and helped them into their nightgowns.

"Ma, when will Pa be going to town?" Rachel asked.

"Soon, when the harvest is done." The thought of that harvest tallying up against our long list of needs put a snake in my belly, coiled tight. For a second I couldn't breathe.

"And will he buy us candy?"

"If you're good, and mind me. You may even have new shoes for when the snow comes."

Rachel smiled and I wondered if she remembered England, where we'd always had shoes for winter and the market had been only just over the hill, rather than a full day's journey away in a town Will never took us along to.

William settled in one chair, I in another and we shared the last of the coffee while the children drifted off to sleep. To anyone peaking in the window- and who was there to do that this far into Indian Territory? - we might have looked happy, content with our lot.

I wanted to scream.

With the children I had to lie to about candy and better things to come. With Will there was just silence or meanness. If there'd been any hiding place on the prairie I would have gone to it and screamed until there was no air in me. I would have screamed 'damn' and 'hell' until my throat bled, instead of keeping all those curses inside.

"Looks like we're doing alright, as far as time's concerned," Will said after a long silence. "Tomorrow we can finish up on the corn, get that wheat in. I should be clear to get to town end of next week, pick up bottling supplies, trade for the rest."

"Good," I was thinking of all the salting and pickling and preserving to come, of another winter living on cornbread and chokecherry jam. "When I made the bread for dinner, I noticed we were low on cornmeal and we've used the last of the molasses."

"I'll take care of it, but you could stand to make things stretch further."

I lowered my eyes. "I just worry about the baby.' I touched my belly. 'It needs fresh greens, a bit of meat. Make sure it's born strong."

"You'll have it, at the end of the harvest."

"I think it might come soon. Is there a woman in town, someone to help when the baby arrives?"

A frown drew in between his brows, "Not much in town but the store and a few houses, mostly men setting up for their wives to come join them. Unless you want a whore to play midwife for you."

"I thought you might know some decent women."

He snorted. "I don't think I've ever met a decent woman."

I looked away, took my sewing from its bag under the table. I could hardly see it in the feeble light of the lamp.

"It's just, this one will be my first away from the help of women," I said, hoping he'd soften at seeing me afraid.

"Well, you had that doctor in Ohio with Beth and he was no use. Barely earned his fee," he scratched the coarse hair on his jaw. "Besides, you have Rachel."

"She's only eight. What does she know about birthing, aside from what she's seen of barn cats? There's things *I* don't know."

"You'll be alright," Will said, draining his cup of sugarless coffee. "It's what women do, isn't it?"

I bowed my head over my sewing. It was what women did, but Lord, how many times in our months of travelling across the country had we met men with wagons full of children and a sack of old dresses? Men with wedding rings around their necks on strings? How many small stones had we passed on the trail? How many trees notched and carved with names, Flora, Susan, Martha, Patience?

I looked at my children, at Rachel and Beth, and Thomas sleeping in a ball. What would become of them, if I died? I couldn't imagine William coping. They'd be parcelled off to settler families while he found himself a new wife, or took off with a saloon girl and left them to grub someone else's farm for charity.

My sewing shook so hard I couldn't make a stitch. I knew I mustn't die. For their sakes.

We only had a short period of lamp light, the kerosene was too dear. I put on my nightgown and got into bed, and Will took off his trousers and laid them by the bed. He got in with his shirt on and left the rifle in easy reach.

Will turned out the lamp and settled under the quilt with me. It was the quilt I'd stitched myself, during our courtship. If I looked hard at it, in the right light, I could still find the patch I'd sewn on with the wrong colour thread when my patience was wearing thin.

The darkness was total without the lamp. The windows were shuttered, but even if they'd been open there were no lights on the prairie. No other soddies or dugouts had been built nearby and we had no neighbours yet. The night was cold, I kept as close to Will as the baby would allow. A wolf howled, and a handful of cries rose up in response. I kept my eyes closed and thought of the rifle.

Chapter Two

Laura

The next day I was up with the sun. My back ached badly, and my stomach was a mess of cramps. Luckily there was leftover bread for breakfast; only thing I had to make was the coffee. The blackened pot stood in the flames and I rubbed my belly and back, looking over at the edge of the prairie where the sun was showing like a heated flatiron.

Will and Thomas left for the fields. Will had the rifle slung across his back. I hated being alone in the house without a weapon. There were too many dangers to count in Indian Territory, far from the reach of law and a day's travel from town – the closest trading post. It would take only one passing Indian or lowdown trapper to leave me in the dirt with my children, the house a bonfire around us. Only a week before Will'd seen Indians riding their horses south, plain as day. We were living in a tinderbox of animals and savages.

Still, work wouldn't wait for the rifle's return. We were in need of more fuel so I took the girls with me to collect chips on the prairie

I should have known, really, that it didn't matter whose hands were on the rifle. I was carrying danger inside me. A settler I could beg for mercy, Indians might take tobacco or supplies for our lives – but I couldn't bargain with the baby in me. If it came awkward, or made me bleed too much, I'd be subject to a worse end than an Indian could give me.

On the wide plain a brisk wind tried to steal my shawl, it whistled and moaned and tossed the grass to and fro. The line of the prairie was unbroken in all directions, none of it still. It was maddening to see miles in every direction with nothing to hold your eye. For a moment I thought I saw a narrow blot on the edge of the world, a man or woman against the empty sky. Then it was gone.

I kept the girls close while we picked up the large, dried out buffalo chips. The pail I'd brought filled quickly. It was a good thing too, as the cramps in my belly were getting sharper and more familiar. I rubbed at my stomach, tried to ignore it. I'd had the trick labour before, this had to be the same thing. It was too soon.

"Ma!" Rachel said, pointing into the long, brittle grass. A snake lay only about a foot from her. I snatched at her shoulder, pulling her further back. My eyes went to Beth, but she was behind us, away from the snake.

"What is it?" Rachel asked.

"Rat snake," I picked up the pail and continued shooing her away. It wasn't a dangerous snake, but my God, I would never be used to seeing the things in the grass, long and black with their flickering tongues and unblinking eyes.

The open plain was working on my nerves. I took the girls back to the soddie. The pail I put by the hearth circle, gasping as a new pain cut through me.

While Rachel took up her dusting and Beth played with her cleaning rag by the supply crate, I went to the table to lean and catch a breath. The chairs were just too uncomfortable, I seemed to be all bulk and bone in the wrong places. Lying down on a tick of course was out of the question, it was hard enough to get up from it once a day.

I gasped, gripped the edge of the table, bit my lip as the pain came, stronger. It wasn't time but it was happening anyway. I put my hand on my belly, trying to still the squeezing cramps. Panic hit me, I needed my mother, a neighbour, a friend. Someone, anyone to help me. What was done for babies that came early? What if it was backwards like Thomas'd been?

"Ma?"

"Damnit, not now," I couldn't feel my mouth move, I was too scared. "Please not now."

Another slice of pain cut me in two, my nails bit the table top.

Beth tugged my skirt and I whimpered, reaching out to push her away. She wouldn't let go.

"Ma!"

I twisted and saw Rachel, frozen by the back wall, rag in hand.

"Rachel..." I held out my hand, "help me to bed."

She came forward slowly, her eyes very wide, and took my hand. "What's wrong?"

"The baby's coming, early," I tugged Beth's hand from my skirt, harder than I meant to, managed to get to the bed with Rachel helping me. My heart wouldn't slow down, I kept remembering the stories I'd been told each time I'd borne a healthy child – the stories of backwards births, bleeding that could not be stopped, babies that stuck fast in their mothers and had to be pulled out. Who would do that for me?

Beth started to grizzle, low at first, but getting louder every moment she was ignored. I gulped air, tried to think. I couldn't send Rachel after Will, out on the prairie where anything might be lurking. I fisted the tick's scratchy material as another wave of pain crested, drew tight, and left me.

I gritted my teeth. I had borne three healthy children, though each time I'd been scared and hurting, though each time I'd faced troubles, I had come through it. Even the ones that filed to thrive, I had survived. I would not die. I would not beg. I would not allow myself to be afraid.

You'll die alone, fighting until you can't anymore. You'll die begging for mercy, for forgiveness, something in my head whispered. I couldn't force the fear out any more than I could stop the labour that was tearing through me like a rabid dog.

"Rachel, stand at the door and call for your father. Loud as you can. Please."

She hurried around Beth and grabbed the frame of the door in one hand. "Pa! Pa, Ma's having the baby! PA!"

I knew it was pointless, he'd never hear her from the field.

"Rachel, find the shears and make a small fire outside, warm some water. Stay close to the house now, don't wander off. You're going to help me."

Please God let it come. Let it be well and whole and if it can't be that, please let it be over fast.

She brought me the shears but her little face was scrunched up with fear and her eyes were wet. Beth started to wail.

"Don't cry," I patted Rachel's hand and tried not to grimace as pain went through me again. "It's alright. You'll be alright."

Rachel hurried outside and I heard chips being heaped on the scorched earth, the clang of the kettle against the crossbar. Beth began to shriek but I couldn't bring myself to get up and comfort her.

"Beth," I called.

Her face was red, mouth a gaping black hole in her face.

"Beth, stop crying."

The sound of it was ringing in my ears.

"Elizabeth Deene, shut your mouth right now, or I'll give you such a hiding!"

I caught my breath as the pains squeezed me, Beth's shriek cut off in sobs and whimpers. The pains came steadily, growing more urgent with each passing minute. I struggled to breathe deep and even. When Rachel returned a particularly bad one caught me off guard. I gasped through it, felt my skirt grow sopping, the waters soaking the tick under me.

"Keep watch for your Pa, from the door," I told her, "and take Beth outside to the ox shed." The shed was safe, but out of hearing.

I gripped the tick tightly in my hands and shifted my legs apart, feeling the aches go up my spine, the pains running through my belly. It would come soon, I knew it. My labours had never been long.

I fought to breathe even. The boy after Thomas, born stone dead. A little girl only a year after Rachel, who barely filled my cupped hands. Another boy the year before Beth, blue-grey as flint. But I would live, I would come through it. I had before.

I arched my back, unable to keep my keening inside. With my knees wide apart I panted, dress plastered in sweat. Flies came to buzz around me, landing on my skin, crawling on the sheets. My body cramped, forcing me to push. I groaned. I was going to be torn in two.

Rachel didn't return. In between gasps for air I screamed for her, but no sound came from outside aside from the sizzling of crickets. The waves of pain came closer together. I couldn't remember whether I should be pushing or holding back. There was no one to tell me what to do and I was terrified of doing the wrong thing.

The pressure in me became unbearable and I pushed as hard as I could, crying out as I felt my body tear. My baby was born, part way. I couldn't see over my belly, couldn't twist my aching body to see whether it was the head or buttocks or legs that had left me. It could drown if the legs came first, I knew that, or be strangled by my insides.

The need to push came again and I did, sobbing, straining to end it, to get the baby out and staunch the trickle of blood that I could feel, hot and sticky under my thighs. The flies buzzed there, their crawling the only sensation that wasn't pain.

William appeared over me; his unshaven face stuck over with harvest dust. He knelt down and took my hand between his cracked and dirty palms.

"Laura?"

I squeezed my eyes shut, couldn't talk, exhausted. Again I felt the need to push, fought to expel the weight of the child from me. I felt it coming, and the rip of my flesh had me sobbing as I pushed and pushed, an awful sound coming from between my jaws.

When I opened my eyes, Will was gone. The door stood open.

I felt the child slip free, lay, my legs limp, fighting for breath. Everything was silent. I eased myself up, shaking as I looked down at the wet sheet, peeled my stained skirts from my thighs. She was there, red and small and wet. She snorted damply, and then opened her little mouth and let out a mew that fast became a cry.

I shifted, my body screaming, picked up my shawl, and wrapped the baby in its dark brown wool.

My belly was shivery with more squeezing, the other matter would come soon. It must.

"Will?" My voice came out raw. "Will, we have a girl."

He came in, carrying the kettle of water, white under his coating of dust, he knelt beside me again.

"Well, look at that," he said, reaching out and touching the edge of the shawl. Nose wrinkling at the blood. He cast an eye over the wet sheet, the cord.

"I'll send Rachel in."

He went out and a moment later Rachel appeared in the doorway, pale and big eyed and trembling. Her eyes were red rimmed and there was a mark on her cheek. She'd been struck for crying and carrying on. I wanted to hold her, to shake her for leaving me. I wanted to tell that it wouldn't be like this for her, but I couldn't.

"Here, hold your sister." I held the baby out gently and Rachel took her, looking as awed as if I'd just given her a china faced doll. "Clean her off and put her in the cradle."

The cradle was an old goods crate lined with a little tick all its own and a quilt I'd made for Thomas when I was first expecting. Rachel placed the baby in it, and while she was getting the water I rubbed my belly and grimaced through the passing of the slippery mass that followed the baby. Before, my mother had looked it over, checked to see if it was alright. I didn't know what to look for, hadn't ever really seen it myself before – it looked like offal, veined and bluish-purple, the rest of the cord hanging from it. I couldn't let Rachel see that, which left it to me to dispose of it. I dragged a gunny sack inch by inch from where it lay under the tick as protection from the damp. Folding the mess into it was the best I could do.

I had Rachel open the windows to air the room, putting the shutters back and opening the screens a little. William sent Thomas to bury the sacking bundle out at the corner of the field.

Once the smell of blood was fading on a prairie breeze I showed the baby to the girls. I was still bleeding a little into a folded rag, but I felt lighter, knowing the danger had passed me by, as though Indian riders had stampeded past without sparing me a look.

I never failed to feel proud when I held my babies and she was no less beautiful to me than the others had been. Relief made my eyes run, tears mixing with the sweat and dust.

"She's got hair like Pa," Beth said, winding the little spring of dark hair around her finger.

"She'll look like you I suppose, Rachel," I said, "you're the spitting image of your Aunt Caroline, Pa's little sister."

Rachel looked into the little bundle. "She has a mark, on her neck."

I had noticed the birthmark, of course, a pinkish brown thing, about the size of my thumb. I hadn't said a thing to William, but now he came to see.

"So she has," he said, regarding the baby, who stared seriously up at him, "almost like a scar."

I lifted the baby and kissed the little mark. "She's perfect."

William did not look convinced, "I suppose we should name her as soon as possible, even if we can't have a baptism," he looked against at the small bundle, "Let's name her Nora, after my Mother. I never did like Caroline."

Rachel had been named for his other sister and Beth for his grandmother. Thomas he had named for his favourite uncle.

"It suits her," I said. After the pain and fear of the birthing, I was tired and leaning heavy in the chair.

Thomas came in from the field, washed his hands and stood by me.

"Can I hold her?"

I passed her to him. "Her name's Nora."

He glanced at William, "Like Grandmother Deene?"

I nodded.

He pressed the tip of one finger into her little pink hand, smiled as she gripped it. I reached out and stroked his arm. My gentle little boy.

"A few days, then you can help us with the hay making," Will said, filling his pipe from the tobacco tin on the shelf. "We've a lot of grass to cut."

I nodded, and took the baby back from Thomas as she began to mewl. I took her behind the screen used for changing, and put her to my breast. I stroked her little cheek and thought of the camomile cream that my mother had made for me, to soothe the pain feeding caused me. I knew I'd miss it.

Once I'd fed the baby and laid her down in her cradle, Will took Thomas back off to the fields, I was left with the girls and a dinner to prepare, as though nothing had happened at all.

Chapter Three

Laura

With the baby I was tied to the house and couldn't go far. Even picking chips was difficult, I didn't like to take Nora under the hot sun.

The fifth day I knew I would not heal sooner for lack of outside air. If I was going to be sore, I'd be sore with a belly full of prairie hen.

"Would you leave me the rifle today?" I asked Will as we ate outside on the grass. "We're so short on things, I should find some game."

"I don't like you being alone with it, you might have an accident. Shoot your goddamn foot off."

"Jacob taught me to shoot in Ohio," I said. Fact was I could shoot better than him and he knew it. I had the steadier hands.

He grunted, not liking the mention of his brother, but he left the gun.

Rachel could take care of Beth and Nora for a short while, just long enough for me to find a hen and bring it home. With Will's patch box and bullet pouch, I set off on the prairie.

The clean, hot air smelled of baking bread from the parched grass seeds. Though it pained me to walk, I was glad to be outside where there was no smell of milky shit and no bleating cries to cut through my head, no mouth to latch onto my sore nipple. I loved them but it felt like they all wanted pieces of me, pulling at me and crying or just needing me. Alone I could be myself.

I was almost disappointed when I saw a brown hen a little way off. I crouched and lifted the rifle, had to get the bird with my first shot, reloading would give it time to fly off.

My shot was straight and it took the prairie hen to the ground. Jacob would've been proud. I went to the spot in the grass where the hen was lying, picked it up by the feet and started back for the soddie, but a shadow made me turn my head.

For a moment I was sure it was a trick of the sun and the wind in the grass. Then he stood up.

He had on an old, wide brimmed hat and a patched coat. Travelling clothes. I could only see his eyes, the rest of his face was covered by a no-colour scarf of raw wool. He pulled it down and held up a hand in greeting.

"Good morning, Miss. I hope I didn't scare you."

His voice was low, carrying an accent that I hadn't heard in two years, that of a born American.

"I've been travelling a while, haven't seen anyone around since the last town. Quiet out here, isn't it?"

I could only stand there, holding the dead bird. It was so strange to hear a new voice where there had been only those of my family and the sound of the wind before. I couldn't remember the last time someone had wished me a good morning, or asked a question of me that required more of an answer than handing over the salt or listing the groceries we needed.

"There aren't any other families out here yet. Can't imagine all those politicians in Washington'll waste too much time opening this territory for settlement though."

He smiled when I spoke and his teeth were white and small, none missing. It was only then that I thought to worry. The rifle was empty, I'd forgotten to reload. Had he seen me shoot? Did he know the gun wasn't loaded?

"Is your husband around here?" he asked.

"Yes," I said, "he's at the house," it was still within screaming distance, perhaps that would deter him from trying anything – there was no telling how long he'd been on his own.

The man considered me. "I saw a man and a boy out harvesting wheat...were they not your family?"

"My son and brother-in-law."

"If you wouldn't mind taking me back with you then. I need to ask a favour, you see, I've come this far for a place to settle, and I was hoping your husband could help me build before winter."

"A soddie? Might just get one up and stocked before winter sets in."

He nodded. "I could help him and his brother finish your harvest, as payment."

"You're alone then?" It was the longest conversation I'd had in two years and I could feel the unused hinges and joints of my tongue loosen. "No family following after you?"

He nodded. "No wife, no children. I've come to seek a living, then I shall build my family." He spoke strangely, as if he was putting on a show like a farmhand in skit who was really a young clerk under a smudge of soot and an old hat. I guessed he was from some city back east, wanting to seem experienced.

With him being so green I felt more secure in talking. We'd met a few such men on our journey out west, men who'd never farmed but who were intent on getting out to Indian Territory before it was opened for settlement, though the railroad companies had been trying like devils to get congress to buy the land from the Indians so they could lay their tracks and Americans could build homes legally on the good flat farmland. By law Will and I, and every white man in the territory, were squatters. We kept our land by working it and warding the Indians off, not by having deeds on paper. He didn't seem like he had the belly for that. I couldn't imagine him making a living hunting and trading furs either, or getting a claim in gold country on the west coast, all the way out in Coloma.

Watching me closely, he said, "I'm not a man to be afraid of, Mrs..."

"Deene."

"Mrs Deene."

"Where have you come from?"

"Ohio," he said.

I nodded. "I recognised the accent. We were in Ohio, before we started west."

He raised his eyebrows. "Really? And what did you make of it?"

"My husband thought it crowded."

"The reason I myself am all the way out here. Men think alike, it seems."

He seemed harmless and now that I had begun to speak to him I didn't want to stop. "It was my husband you saw. I'm sorry for the lie, just not used to seeing anyone out here. He'll be back soon, would you like a drink of water from our well?"

"I would appreciate that, it's difficult to find out here."

We walked back together. There was a bit of chain over the heels of his boots and it chinked on the hard sole as he walked. The jug of well water was inside the soddie, where Rachel was wiping dust and the baby was sleeping. With a mug of water in my hand I went outside to him.

Up close he was slighter than I'd thought, though a head and a half taller than me. The large coat was long in the arms and slack across his shoulders. The skin around his eyes was smooth and he had soft hands. I pegged him for a man just approaching twenty.

"Thank you." He drank deeply, handed me back the drained mug. "I'd hate to inconvenience you further, would it be alright if I waited by the house for your husband? There's no other shade about."

I nodded, and he sat down with his back against the wall.

I went back to the door and Rachel's blackberry eyes found mine. "Ma, who's that man?"

"We've a new neighbour," I said, then realised that I hadn't heard his name. Somehow I'd thought he'd told me, or that I already knew it.

"Does he have little girls?"

"He doesn't have any children." I couldn't tell if this displeased her, or if she found the news agreeable, she only nodded and went back to her cleaning.

I was lost, should I go back outside to speak with the stranger, or stay with my children and load the rifle in case he turned nasty? Then the baby began to cry, and my choice was made for me.

She was at my breast when Will came in, storm-faced.

"You let a stranger near the girls?" he snatched up the rifle, "and the gun not even loaded. What if he'd tried to steal the oxen?"

"He wanted to speak with you and I couldn't see that he posed a threat," I said, even though I had been afraid of him before, I had more anger than fear in that moment.

Will curled his lip at me and shook his head, went back outside.

I took Nora from my livid breast and adjusted my dress, patted her back before laying her down in her cradle-box. With the water jug and a half-pan of cornbread for the midday meal, I went outside.

Will was sitting with the stranger, Thomas was lying on the grass, looking up at the sky. I set the dinner things down and took Beth on my lap while Rachel found a seat on the grass.

"I'd be happy to get some help," William was saying, friendliness all over his face.

"Then I'll come to the field with you when you return." He looked at me and nodded his head, "forgive me for not introducing myself Ma'am, James Clappe, pleased to meet you."

"Welcome to Indian Territory, Mr Clappe," I said. "Will you have your meal with us?"

William scowled at me, but Clappe shook his head and said "I need to fetch some poles to put up my tent for the night, once I've rested myself a little. Mr Deene, would it be alright if I pitched it by your barn?"

"That'd be fine."

"Where's your wagon?" Thomas asked, sitting up as I offered him cornbread.

"Oh, well, I sold it," Clappe said, glancing between me and Thomas, "I'll use the money to replace some of the things I left back in Ohio."

"Not all?" Thomas asked.

"No, not all," he shrugged, "some things are sadly out of my reach."

There was a quietness over us then and I watched William and the children eat their cornbread, managed to eat my own portion while Clappe sat with empty hands, watching us with his warm, green eyes.

"Why don't you take Beth indoors and get out the wash tub?" I said to Rachel.

"Can I play outside afterwards?"

"If you stay where I can see you."

She took Beth by the hand and hurried inside.

William stood and shook crumbs from his shirt. "Thomas, fetch the whetstone to sharpen a scythe for Mr Clappe, I'll hitch the oxen to the wagon." He shot me a warning look as he left, he was still angry with me over the empty rifle. If I only got a few hard looks it'd be a miracle.

Clappe stood at my elbow while William went out of sight behind the barn.

"I'm sorry to trouble you but...do you have any scraps I could take for myself? I can pay you."

I was surprised, not many settlers were fool enough to travel without keeping their supplies up. He was greener than I'd thought. There was a small piece of cornbread left from lunch, which I'd planned to thicken a soup with. I spread it with some syrup and took it back to him. His gloved hand offered me a tarnished coin, but I refused it.

"You can pay me back when you've got your own harvest in."

"Thank you, Mrs Deene. But, I want to pay my way, and you could use it, with winter coming."

I was taken aback. "We'll get by, we have to."

His smile was uneven, a small scar cleaving his lip in a thin white line. "Seconded." He stuffed a hand into his pocket and produced another coin. "May I count on you for something tonight?"

I took the pennies to spare his pride. "There'll be the hen and cornmeal mush."

The coins were warm when I tucked them securely into the waist of my skirt.

"Thank you again, Mrs Deene."

"Laura."

He looked surprised, but it was strange to hear 'Mrs Deene' after all this time. Only the preacher that married us had ever called me it. "Laura. I'm James."

We shook hands, and then he was on his way to cut his poles, eating the cornbread as he went. I watched him go. It was good to watch a man so easy in his stride. I found myself admiring the shape of his lean body and made myself turn away.

Stupid, to think of him like that when his was young, what with me years older and plain as a boot. Besides, I'd learnt in Ohio that no matter the man, it was always the same.

*

As if he'd read my mind, or seen me looking at Clappe's fine stride, Will started at me that night.

We'd had our supper with the children. I'd given Clappe a plate of chicken and some mush while Will was in the outhouse. The girls and the baby were sleeping. Thomas was turned away from us with the blankets up over his head. Even Clappe must have turned in, there was no sound from outside. Will lifted himself up over me in the dark, pawed at my nightgown.

He'd chosen a bad night for it, for me anyway. I'd yet to heal up and it'd hurt all day, making water was like passing lye. I moved away from him, pretending I was asleep, but he only tried harder to wake me up. In the end I turned to him.

"I'm not healed yet."

He pulled me over, as if he didn't understand plain English and pushed up the nightgown. I closed my eyes and turned my face away from his. If he gave me another baby, I knew it would be the end of me. I was lucky to have survive one birthing without a woman to help me, I couldn't take the fear and pain on my own again.

It hurt like a hot iron but I bit my lip and let him do it. He was careless, held me down, pushed hard and deep. When it was over he lay on top of me for a while, breathing tobacco over my face, then he rolled over and lay on his back. I had to get up and find a rag to clean away his mess, the blood. I hid it under a corner of the tick so I could wash it in the morning.

Lying down on the tick again, I could still smell him on my skin, in the quilt and all over the tick itself.

Will and I, we were never a love match. Will was handsome and he came from a good family, his father and my father knew each other in England. I'd never had a man chase me for my looks, or my heart, so I'd never thought about marrying for love, though he was sweet, back then.

The first time we'd lain together I'd been scared, not knowing really what he was doing, what I was supposed to do. I was afraid to touch him while he got on me, and when he got going I'd lain there and let him. It'd hurt, but he told me it was supposed to. At the time, I never questioned how he knew. It wasn't until after we'd been married a few months that I found out about the string of young girls he'd flattered into his bed. There was more than one'd been forced out of her family home and off to some relative or another. Plenty of Deenes growing up in other men's homes I didn't doubt.

I slept poorly, waking twice in the night to go to Nora, Will grumped on the tick but only turned over and ignored the crying. The children were so used to it they slept on through. I woke in the morning, just before dawn, stepped outside onto the dew covered grass to start the fire for breakfast.

Clappe was standing by the cold bones of the fire, the prairie behind him grey in the pre-dawn. He tipped his hat at me when I came closer. It was good to see him but I was thinking of my tangled hair and stained dress. He smiled, took off his gloves and offered me another penny.

"I'd be much obliged for some breakfast," he said.

I had a pail of chips for the fire but he took them from me, squatted down on the scorched earth and started stacking them together. I went for the coffee pot and the breakfast things, my hands shaking as I tried to be as quiet as possible. It was like I was a girl again, blushing around some boy doing a few jobs for my family.

Outside the fire was smouldering and I put the pot on. Sitting on the ground I shook flour into the bowl I'd brought out and mixed in water. Inside I shook myself and tried to stop acting like a fool.

"What are you making?"

"Hot cakes."

"Like pancakes?"

I nodded. "My mother made good hot cakes. Always fried them in bacon fat. That's my favourite way with them." I took the spider and stood it on its metal legs in the fire. Into the pan I dropped a small amount of the grease from the roast hen, fried the hot cakes fast. Clappe poured the coffee out into cups.

"We don't have sugar, or any more molasses," I said.

"I think it's fine as it is," he said, though I noticed he grimaced as he sipped it.

I flipped the cakes and offered him one. He held it with his fingers at the edge, changing hands when it began to burn him. Once he'd finished he wiped his fingers carefully on the cuffs of his trousers.

The door of the soddie opened, and I heard Will come out and stop short. I turned to him.

"Morning, I've got the coffee ready."

He looked at Clappe, nodded, then went to the outhouse. I could tell from the set of his shoulders that he was angry.

My hands were trembling as I ladled more batter into the spider. Clappe took the bowl from me, setting it on the ground before I could drop it.

"I expect he thinks it doesn't pay to be too trusting of strangers," he said quietly.

I watched the hot cakes turn brown and furrowed at their edges, where the grease had them crisping. I wanted him to stop looking at me, but the way he talked, like he knew me, that made me feel good and embarrassed at the same time.

I served the cakes as William returned, saving me from those eyes. He sat down between Clappe and I, took a tin plate from the stack.

"You should wake Thomas, or he'll be late out," he said.

I got up and went to the soddie, aware that I was being watched. Thomas was still asleep on his pallet, I knelt beside him, touching his shoulder gently.

"Breakfast, everybody up and outside."

Nora was still asleep in her cradle, but the girls woke, and Thomas blinked his eyes open, slowly, then rolled sharply onto his side to get up.

"Girls, put your shawls on over your night things, I'll dress you in a while."

William was alone at the fireside. "I sent Clappe on ahead, to carry the tools out," he stretched and I heard his spine crack like a knot in a piece of firewood. "The thresher should be here tomorrow."

Chapter Four

James

I awoke at the side of the road. I say road; it hardly deserved the name, being but a track in the grass. Before going to sleep I had wrapped myself in a sheet of canvas, and found myself already stifled by the heat of the day. Under the sharp sun I ate some stale bread and drank water from my bottle. All around me was a blustery nothing, only grass and dust, it lowered my spirits just to look at it. How many days of it had I endured? Too many, with no clock, no newspaper by my plate of a morning and no chiming church bells to ring the hour.

There was no way back for me now, on foot, alone in the wilderness. The weeks of rude travel by stage and wagon, the latter filled with buckets and wheels, seemed then a great luxury. I half wanted to pull my canvas over myself and never get up again, but the rest of me was crying out for fresh water and civilisation. Civilisation! As if that could be found this far west.

I walked into 'town' around midday; a collection of wooden buildings in a crooked row, surrounded by packed earth worn bald by the feet of men and beasts. The railways weren't here yet, neither was the town itself, officially. According to every map and every man in Washington, I was standing on Indian land.

It was only my second time in such a place and it was certainly the meanest settlement I'd visited. My stomach shivered with nerves as I tried to remember to walk the way my brother did; striding out with a straight back, head up and eyes straight ahead.

I bought myself a meal of biscuits and molasses from a woman selling food from her window; food I wouldn't have given my dog a month or so ago. Reluctantly, I also used my dwindling funds to buy more ammunition for my rifle, having wasted too much on clumsily shooting a hen out of hunger. I had to keep myself from walking primly past the saloon and row of sheds – the so-called 'cribs' that fallen women kept. I was a lone man after all, it was expected that I would drink and associate with low females. I went in and bought ale from the barman, sweating under his gaze. I kept my eyes on the table after that, too scared to look around me. The ale was disgusting and the cup was dusty.

When I had bought the last of my supplies I walked on into Indian Territory, glad to leave the eyes of strangers behind me. As much as I longed to be surrounded and safe, seeing what passed for urbanity in this part of the country was a wrench to my heart.

Around midday on my third day since leaving the town behind me, I came over a rolling rise in the grassy plain. If I'd walked on, instead of stopping to look about me, I would never have seen her and she would not have noticed me.

She was a tall, brown woman, scorched by the sun. Her long brown hair was twisted into an out of style braid and she had on a stained dress of sprigged cotton, made over and over. In her hands was a rifle.

I was tempted to remove my hat and explain, tell her she didn't need to fear me.

Then the moment was gone and I introduced myself - James Clappe, homesteader.

*

She had a husband, of course. He seemed a decent sort, unshaven and overprotective, but he accepted an honest trade of my labour for his, and for that I was grateful. I knew nothing of farming or building and would need his help. I had no tools with me and would need the loan of his, as well as the use of his plough and wagon.

I watched her, though I tried not to. I watched the new baby she carried with her like a heavy parcel she longed to pass off to a maid. It hurt to see those small arms and legs waving, but I looked all the same. How Laura could carry that child like she was anything less than a treasure I did not know. Didn't she know how lucky she was?

There was less time to watch Laura after work began in earnest. Deene showed me the process of cutting and 'shocking' wheat, then when the thresher arrived. It took the two men who'd brought it to drive the horses around and feed the crops into it. I helped Thomas fill the bags with the grain that spilled from the incredible machine. I tried to act as if I'd seen one before, when in fact it was a marvel to me.

At a little after midday, when we had threshed the last of the grain, we stopped to eat. The men with their machine hitched up their horses and carried on towards the next farm. In their wake they left silence and a trail of gold.

"I'll head to town soon," Deene announced as we sat on a blanket in front of the house. "Once I've cut the hay, you can handle the animals for a couple of days 'til I'm home again."

Laura nodded. Her braid caught the sun like oiled rope.

Deene turned to me. "Will you be helping with the hay tomorrow? Got to get to it while the weather's with us."

I nodded, inwardly cringing; my whole body ached already and my skin, which had been fair, was red and flaking wherever the sun had reached it. The need for a cool bath was almost maddening. My body screamed for me to lie down on the grass and close my eyes.

As we ate I watched Laura's children, dark Rachel, little Beth with her clasping hands, and Thomas, so wide eyed. I'd seen, of course, how his father bullied him in the field; how he shouted at him for the slightest clumsiness. He was a child still, and clearly tired to his bones.

Deene stood and dusted the crumbs from his trousers. "You need water hauled?"

Laura answered no, and so Deene set off for the field, with me and Thomas in his wake. My feet were so sore that the effort of walking took up all my concentration; I couldn't let my pain show on my face.

Deene didn't speak to me as we dragged the sacks of wheat and corn to the lean-to by the house. The work was hard, but I paused in order to help Thomas with his sacks, despite my own exhaustion, as he was not equal to the task. He didn't shake me off and that pleased me. I liked having my help accepted, though I was careful to offer it out of his father's sight.

At last darkness drew in over the prairie and it became too late for work. Deene gave me a nod as he picked up the last sack and took it around to the lean-to. Thomas went after him without looking back. I straightened and eased my back once they were out of sight. My shoulders and spine were needled with hot pain.

I looked up to the sky, where the stars were winking. At times like that, in the darkness, the prairie seemed small and felt downright snug. Darkness all around like a quilt drawn tight against world. The cool night air was a balm against my skin. I was almost asleep on my feet.

I turned to find Laura staring at me. She'd started her fire, the kettle was buried in flames. The scents of smoke and baking met with those of parched summer grass and sweat.

"The corn is in then," I said, "soon as I have my house, the weather can do what it likes."

"Don't tempt it, last winter we had snow to the eaves, blizzards so thick we could hardly find the barn."

"I'm sure I shall survive."

"I'm sure you will," she stirred the flaming buffalo dung and I thought of that hot, fresh cornbread. Before coming to Indian Territory I had never thought I'd ever be so hungry for cornbread. But I had no money to give her, only stolen jewels, hidden in a cloth, and buried under my tent.

"Ma'am -" I started, then stopped, I couldn't beg, she'd already given me enough. It was my own fault for not bringing more supplies with me. I'd thought to travel straight on, not to settle so soon.

The light of the fire gave her face back the glow that I imagined it had possessed when she was young.

"Help yourself to supper. Call it a gift," she said, "for helping Thomas."

"Anyone would've done the same."

"It was kind."

We were still looking at each other when Deene, washed up for dinner, came outside with the coffee pot. He put his arm around her waist and squeezed.

"Are you ready to cut the hay tomorrow?"

She nodded, looking away from me.

Deene's grin was very white in the approaching darkness. "Then we can get all those things you've been on at me about, sugar and meal, coffee and pork, cloth for a new dress." He looked up and caught my eye. "Maybe then I'll have a moment's peace."

Deene released her and pressed the coffee pot into her hands.

"I invited Mr Clappe for dinner," she said.

He looked at me, and I could feel the crackle of his disapproval. "We've hardly enough for the five of us."

Laura opened her mouth, but I cut in first. "That's fair. I was about to say, thank you for the kind offer, but I have some beans back in my tent that are waiting for my attention." I let my face bear a cocky grin, the one our governess had slapped from my brother's face when he'd done something particularly naughty.

Laura looked at me, an apology evident on her face, but I just nodded a little, and went back to my tent. I cursed myself for not rationing my food better, though when I'd left the previous town I'd thought only of reaching a settlement further south where I could have resupplied. It had not been my plan to settle, but I'd been so happy to find a friendly woman for a neighbour that I decided to stay. Hardly my rashest decision. I told myself that one night without food was a small price to pay for keeping the peace. I would have to try my hand at shooting game again to keep me fed until Deene took me to town. Perhaps Laura would cook it for me if I could only shoot something.

My tent was a sheet of canvas with pockets sewn on the inside and loops to hold the entrance closed at night. I'd bought it just before I'd set out from the wagon on foot. Whenever I had to stop to make camp I cut poles from nearby trees or else slept wrapped in the canvas. On the prairie, I'd had to travel to a creek that ran through a ravine some miles from the house in order to find wood.

Inside I had my spare clothes, a shaving kit, with the scissors I used to keep my hair short and a pamphlet on the sort of farming I intended to do. I'd never known anything about grain and livestock, about ploughing and reaping. My family were in the fur business; though I'd never had to know anything of that either. It was astonishing to think; soon I would plough strips into the soil and sow seeds that would feed me for a year.

It was too dark to read, so I undressed and lay down on the blanket that lined the ground. My rifle was next to me. I'd heard wolves in the distance and shivered, knowing that I couldn't go forever without seeing one. Even looking at the gun gave me a chill.

A shush against the grass outside startled me, I could hear steps, the flicker-flack of grass on skirts. I pulled my other blanket up to my chin.

"James? It was Laura. My hand tightened on the blanket.

"Mrs…Laura?"

She opened the slit in the tent and looked in on me. I could hardly see her in the dark, but for the lantern she'd set on the ground outside.

"I came to feed the oxen, but, I've a bit for you as well."

I sat forward to take it, her rough hand brushed mine and I took the chunk of cornbread from it. Her hand vanished and then returned, a baked, ashy potato in its palm.

"It's probably cold now," she said.

"That's very kind of you Ma'am," I said, remembering my manners. I wanted to hug her and offer my deepest thanks, but propriety held me back.

"It's only what I promised," she moved a little, looking around my little tent. "This is quite a set-up - cosy."

I snorted. "It won't be if I'm still here come snowfall."

I felt her hand on my blanket covered shin. "Well, Will promised and I'll do my best to keep him to it."

"Is he the kind given to breaking them?"

She was quiet a moment. "He don't promise much."

Then she was gone and I heard her skirts sweeping against the grass, the creak of the stable door and the hard sounds of the expectant oxen.

The potato was still warm in the centre and the cornbread was a good weight in my empty stomach, but still I felt cold and uneasy. Perhaps I had been wrong in making a deal with William Deene.

Chapter Five
James

I took my scythe out onto the plain with Deene and his son, Laura followed after us with blankets and a basket of food, it was almost like one of our picnics at home, save that she had the baby with her in a box she called her 'cradle'.

Whenever I paused to wipe my forehead, I'd glance at the girls and often found Rachel and Beth clapping rhymes, or squabbling over the rag dolls they'd brought out with them. Laura looked their way often and called out for them to put their bonnets back on whenever the girls pushed them back.

The effort of watching the blade and fretting over whether it was too close to my feet soon exhausted me. I envied the ease with which Laura did the work. Her hands were as large and calloused as her husband's, square fingered and sure on the scythe handle. She swung the blade easily, keeping it free of her skirts; her braid was draped over one shoulder, her brown skin like a smooth, dry stone. I was sweating hard before the grass was stacked to knee height, the muscles in my arms and back still complaining from helping with the harvest of grain.

"You keeping up Clappe?" Will called. "Don't need to sit a while? Little sup of water and a rest in the shade?"

"I'm doing fine," I called back, and heard him laugh, a thin, nasty sound.

The sun gradually reached its height and we lay down our scythes and sat with the girls in the shade of the growing haystack. Laura unwrapped an ugly loaf of bread, and cut it into pieces to have with cold prairie hen.

I'd breakfasted on the small amount of cornbread I'd kept by from the previous evening, but my stomach ached for more. I saw her glance at me, looking sorry. I was permitted to drink from the water jug and that helped to fill my stomach a little, though I was scared I'd need to relive myself if I drank too much. Deene and his son didn't go back to use the outhouse when we were in the field, they only stood off away from the women. The idea of having to relieve myself that way filled me with dread.

As if my worry prompted him, William stood and went behind the stack to pass water. Thomas followed after. Laura was watching me, as if waiting for me to go. I stood and stretched, then wandered back to my scythe, hoping we'd be done in the field before it became necessary for me to creep off to the outhouse.

When we began to work again, Laura started to sing. Perhaps she had done so before, but I had been unable to hear her. It was not a familiar song, which I thought strange as I had been to many performances when I was younger.

But leaves are scattered not more wild,

By autumn's winds unhurled,

Than all that group of faces bright

Upon the wide, wide world.

But still on memory's page in light,

'Gainst which there's no resistance,

Stand out those scenes, that home and tree,

Like night fires, in the distance.

Her voice was plain, but she could carry the simple tune. I noticed that William had his mouth set in a firm line as he cut the grass. I wondered if she sang often where he could hear her; whether she kept it to herself and her children, the sound of her almost-pretty voice.

It was late afternoon by the time we had the grass cut and stacked. I desperately needed to relieve myself.

"It'll be getting on for dark soon, better get the oxen watered," Deene said, and clapped me on the shoulder as he passed me by, on his way to the barn. The impact of his hand made me stagger. Thomas collected Laura's scythe and followed after his father. I watched them go, Thomas's back stooped in exhaustion.

I turned and saw Laura plodding to the place where her daughters were sat in the shade of the new haystack, playing with dolls and a small 'house' of loose straw. She stooped and lifted her baby into her arms.

"Rachel, would you bring the cradle?"

The girls followed their mother past me. I picked up my scythe and trudged back to the barn to return it. Thomas was standing at the door, in the process of taking a bucket to the well.

"Long day today," I said.

He ducked his head.

"I'm not so young as you," I said, smiling, "it will take more than an hour's play to unknot my spine." I reckoned I was only about seven years older than him. I'd taken pains to appear a little older though, and I thought I could comfortably pass for twenty.

I realised immediately that I'd misspoken. I'd meant it to be kind, but I knew that Thomas already had no time given for play. He nodded, ducked past me and went on around the house to the well.

Through the half open door I could see Deene forking the old hay from the manger onto the floor for bedding. I started to creep away.

"All set for winter now," Deene said spotting me. "At least until it's time to dig the potatoes," he grunted, turning and taking my scythe from by the door, setting it up on its wooden peg. "Then there's turnips, still got to get the wood corded, and I'm looking to have a stove put in before it snows." He rubbed the back of his neck, "Can't go another winter without. Made do with a bake box of embers last year."

"I guess you'll all be warmer with it," I said, desperate to get away.

"When we first got here in the summer, year before last, she wanted one then. She's too rarefied to deal with a fire out of doors."

If there was a word less apt for that keen eyed woman, I could not think of it.

"With the snow, it must be hard," I said, though I'd barely cooked on a fire, inside or out.

"I'm worried about the first fall myself. I suppose you'll be expecting that hand with your house tomorrow?"

"Yep, tomorrow it is. Night," I said, ducking out of the barn and fleeing to the outhouse. Once I was done I crawled into my tent and lay down. It was too dark to shoot any game and too much to hope that Laura would bring me supper again. I could only pray that she offered me something in the morning, before Deene and I began work on my home.

I couldn't help but think about my home, the real home I'd shared with my parents and my older brother, Franklyn; with the fine porch and the sitting room and my bedroom on the second floor, with my four poster bed. Lying on the dirt, cushioned only by a blanket, I remembered that feather mattress with a pang.

I wondered at Laura. How had she been raised? To be so worn out and marked like her dresses that she no longer cared that she was soaked in sweat under the sun, doing the work of a man. That she cooked outside over a hole filled with burning dung. How could she not care? Watching her it seemed as if she'd been born to live that way, like a rabbit living in its little hole. I'd thought England was a place for neat homes and dainty manners.

I prayed that she would never know how low she was.

Chapter Six

James

I woke when the first rays of sun reached the canvas over me, wishing as usual that a basin of hot water and a laden breakfast table awaited me. I put on my dirty clothes and crawled out of the tent. The air was curiously clear; where Laura's morning fire usually burned, only a cold, dark circle stood out. It was early, yes, but usually she came out to cook almost as soon as first light. My stomach complained over its lack of food and I went around to the front of the Deene soddie to gauge their wakefulness. Perhaps, like me, Deene had succumbed to exhaustion. The thought cheered me greatly.

The soddie was quiet, not a sound from the baby, or the scrape of a chair leg disturbed the silence. I went around to the window, peered through the gap in the wooden shutters and saw that the tick nearest to me was empty, the blankets folded neatly at the end. With a hitch in my chest I went to the barn and listened. Utter stillness. The oxen were gone. So was the wagon box that usually sat behind the barn, under a canvas.

"You no good..."

Even alone, I could not bring myself to swear at that moment. I just stared at the empty stable and knew that I'd been duped.

Deene had promised me a fair day's labour on that day to start building my soddie and now he was nowhere to be seen, had taken his family off to town. I knew he was making a point. I thought of confronting him when he returned, but what could I do? We had no contract, so I could not seek justice and though I could walk, talk and act like a hard-nosed, westering man, I couldn't fight like one; I knew when I was beaten.

I didn't have the tools to cut my own sod, or to make my roof. I had been hoping to use Deene's, but now I would have to find some other way. A man who would cheat you of honest work was not a man who would lend tools to be neighbourly.

There was nothing for it but to move on, to go back to town and then settle elsewhere. I'd have to sell the jewels to afford the tools and supplies that I'd been relying on Deene to provide in exchange for all the work I'd done for him.

With an aching stomach I packed my things and took down my tent. I left the tent poles on the ground. Perhaps Laura would find them and use them to feed her fire.

Laura. She had warned me about her husband, had told me he was a man to watch. She'd been right, and I knew should have listened to her. I hadn't believed he would cheat me. My face grew hot with humiliation. God, she probably thought me a complete fool.

With my bare hands, sore and aching from my work with the scythe, I dug up the jewels in their kerchief. I would have to sell them further afield than the closest town. There was no way on earth that I would willingly lead Charles to my door. The thought of him finding me turned my skin to ice, despite the sun.

I filled my bottle from their well bucket, hoping it would be enough to get me to the creek, then I hung the rifle over my shoulder and began to walk.

The day was already getting hot as I started out and the sun only grew stronger. The prairie unrolled ahead of me right up to the horizon; grass, waving and rippling like an ocean. No rise or fall in the land for miles. In all directions it spread, so that I felt I was in the very middle of it and would never reach the edge. It was hours before I was out of sight of the soddie.

Eventually I let my tears fall. I cried all the harder for the spectacle I was making of myself, crying like a little girl. I wanted my mother and father, my brother. I wanted my old home with a longing that made me sob harder.

As the sun beat down on me, sinking its teeth into the exposed skin at the base of my neck, I swore that if ever I returned to that particular circle of stamped grass, to that soddie, I would go only to seek my revenge on the man who had duped me; I would buy his land from under him with my own money. I would see Deene and his whole family walk over the prairie, as hopeless as I was then.

That night, as I wrapped myself in my canvas and laid down to sleep on the ground, I almost cried from hunger. My water bottle was almost empty and my mouth dry as dust. I listened to the scurrying of animals in the grass, bending my ear constantly for the cries of wolves. Fear licked up my spine and all around the grasses hissed like snakes.

The second day I shot and luckily, managed to kill, a prairie hen and I built a fire to cook the thing. I was no expert at plucking and gutting, but I tried my best and the result was grizzled, but not inedible. I ate with my fingers, until grease ran over my chin. Nothing had ever tasted so good. I was out of water and thought about lemonade constantly.

I walked, missing the nearest town, to which I guessed Deene had taken his family, heading onwards to the larger town beyond.

On the third day the land showed some variety, finally, and instead of endless, flat grasses, I found a ravine with a creek running through it. I guessed that it was the same creek that ran closer to the Deene house, but I'd been walking towards a more distant part of it, as it disappeared across the prairie. Since my water had run out I'd thought of nothing else, fearing that at any moment I might lose the strength to go on, and that some traveller would come across my parched body in the months to come. I was so thirsty by then that I bent over the water like a dog and drank with my face in it, flies and water skaters prickling against my hair.

It was there that I found watermelons growing on a thick tangle of vine. God only knew how they came to be there, some settler must have sown them where they would get the best of the water and rich, cooler soil. I'd never seen them growing before, in fact, I couldn't remember having seen a whole one, only the slices that sometimes appeared at dinners.

Having never cut a melon before, it took several tries, holding the thing between my knees, before I broke it open with my knife. The fruit inside was crisp and cold. Even the creek water had been warm on my tongue, but that melon was like snow and far better than I remembered it tasting at dinner parties.

After hiding for months, fearing that my secret would be discovered at any moment, it was a balm to my nerves to be alone and unobserved, away from other travellers and off of the flat plains on which there could be no hiding. I stripped off my disguise and slid into the water, letting it cover me and take the dirt away.

For a while I had felt as though I'd left part of myself behind when I escaped, something I'd never get back, which had been taken from me. I thought I'd always be running and hiding, looking over my shoulder, scared of the dark and the sound of every footstep. I was exhausted from jumping at small sounds, from sleeping in fits and starts. Just keeping up with my act and the work I had to do on the farm had almost broken me.

I lay back in the water and looked up at the endless blue sky, trying to pull the sense of freedom into myself, into my bones, where I could believe it.

"I'm free," I told myself, quietly, almost losing my voice in the flow of the creek and the sizzling of the insects.

"I'm free!" I said slightly louder.

In the water, far from anyone that knew me or who might be hunting for me. I could stop pretending to be James Clappe and be Cecelia. I told myself, with every wave that broke over me, that I was leaving it all behind. I wasn't his wife, his property, his prisoner. I was myself, Cecelia, a free woman.

*

The fourth day I left the creek behind me and trudged on through dusty grass that sizzled with insects and swam with the heat. It was only the day after that I reached town and allowed myself to smile. I was no longer clean, but this was the place to buy food, clean clothes and the tools to build my home. I would buy a mount to take me further into the country; having money would mean not going hungry again.

It was a slightly larger settlement than that closest to the Deenes' land, but still much the same; a store and an inn made of boards, hastily nailed board walks and board fences. With the wood and the dust, the whole place was brown and grey. There were no women around, men walked this way and that on the boardwalks, wearing the pants and suit jackets of clerks, or, more popular, the homespun trousers and old shirts of homesteaders and farmers.

I took a moment, no more than that, to tighten the bonds between me and my disguise. I'd let it slip a little while walking the prairie with no soul around to watch me. In town, with all the men milling around, was a place for James, not for Cecelia.

I made my way to the bank, a smaller building tacked onto the store. Inside was a single, small room, fronted with a wooden counter. Polished bars separated me from the little clerk on the other side, behind him I could see the safe, lock boxes and two desks piled with papers.

"Afternoon," I said, for I judged it to be after twelve, "I've some jewellery to sell, where'd be the best place in town to get a good deal on it?"

The clerk, a man with grey in his oiled hair, considered me.

"Are you settling around here?"

I knew I looked like a homesteader just arrived in the west, but I couldn't sell my jewels and tell this man I planned to stay nearby. Charles might trace them and find me too easily, the chance of that was worse than all the wolves and privation the prairie could offer. The territory wasn't officially open to settle, so I wouldn't have to sign my name on a deed, only chose a place and claim it. It was the perfect place to hide.

"Not just at the moment, sir," I said, in my Clappe voice.

"We can make purchase of them, the only other place would be the broker who deals out of the saloon, and he would not offer you a fair price." He motioned for me to produce the jewellery.

"These were my mother's," I said, eager to give him the story I'd worked on. "She died last year and my elder brother got the farm. This is my whole inheritance."

I took out the kerchief and unknotted it. Without looking I could have described each piece easily; my gold wedding band, the engagement ring with the opal in the centre, flanked by tiny diamonds, the gold chain my parents gave me on my wedding day, which had belonged to my mother and had a tiny pearl on it, and lastly my pocket watch, which was only silver, but had a real emerald in the middle of its face.

Charles had told me the rings alone were worth five hundred dollars. I knew they were precious and vital for my survival, but just looking at them made my heart thud fearfully. I felt, irrationally, as though he could see me selling them, and that he was more angry with me now than he had been before.

"Seventy dollars."

I couldn't stop the sound of angry dismay that burst out of me, mingling with Clappe's rough voice, "They're worth five hundred if they're worth a cent."

He shrugged. "It has to sell to make the money, and I'll be honest with you Sir, whoever sold your dear mother these trinkets was a shyster, the rings are more copper than gold and these are glass," he pointed out the diamonds, "only thing real is the emerald, and the pearl, but that's small, not a costly gem."

Of course, it never occurred to me to think that the clerk was lying.

I was so hungry I couldn't find it in myself to argue. I only nodded. The clerk counted out notes and put them in a pile.

Standing there, in the dim interior of a country bank, holding that slim bundle of notes, I felt so small and stupid as the clerk gathered up my fake jewels. I'd travelled so far from home, knowing nothing of the world. I had only the vaguest idea of what I needed to buy with my small supply of money, let alone what to do with a plough if I could get the thing to a plot of land somewhere.

I realised that I needed Laura, for her help as well as her company. The journey to town had reminded me of the terrible silence of being by myself, the emptiness of the prairie, without a kindly or familiar face to great me in town. I wasn't strong enough to go somewhere else, live without my one almost-friend. Even if I had to lie to her, to everyone, for the rest of my life.

The weight of my deceit was almost as suffocating as the heat. Every day stretched out before me, days where my choice would be loneliness or lies, and act or the silence of my own memories. Was it so different to what I'd left behind? To Charles and the locked doors of his house, the public engagements where I was never out of his sight, never more than a few steps from his side, my mouth unable to utter more than the most frivolous of pleasantries.

I had to believe that there was more for me here than with him. That even if I was limited and not completely free to be myself, even if my poverty and need for aid would force me back to Deene's who had wronged me, I would never again be under Charles' thumb.

I would rather perish alone under a lie than be imprisoned with him by the truth.

Chapter Seven

Laura

The clerk was reckoning up with Will while I kept half an eye on the children. Our sacks of wheat and corn were carried by the store owner's sons into the shed around back. We were making out good on the trade. Not as good as we could've, the crop was probably worth more, but there was only the one store. Their price was the only price.

The store was also where the letters and parcels were delivered by passing riders, and I'd expected to receive something from home. Will usually brought back a letter when he returned from town, but this time there was nothing. I worried that my family had forgotten me, now I'd been gone for so long. I left my letter with the clerk anyway, to send out with the next rider.

That morning I'd seen the creek for the first time in two years, with the shrubs around it and the birds in them singing. I'd been half-ashamed to find my eyes wet. Will hadn't taken me to town before and it was the first time I'd been back over the prairie since we crossed it to where our house now stood.

There was almost too much for me to take in, like I was seeing some king's treasure trove instead of a line of buildings and a market half the size I was used to. People were selling silk ribbons, rose sprig calico, sturdy boots – all from a wagon. There were barrels coming off a cart, chickens scratching, men eating fried bread and drinking coffee at a porch rail. The air smelling not just of grass but like cigarettes and pipes, frying bacon and dough, boiling broth and greasy dumplings.

The general store was full. It'd been a long time since I'd seen so many things all jammed into one place; broom and axe heads, barrels of crackers, candy and salted meat, nails and tacks in big boxes, bolts of cloth, shoes, boots, sacks, flour in its various grades, packets of paper, baskets of eggs, bunches of pencils, and over the counter, hung in pride of place on the wall, three ploughs.

I looked long and hard at the new sod cutting plough. We had one already, an old and rusty thing that Will had traded from a family on their way back east. We'd put up a sack of cornmeal and Thomas's old shoes for it.

How would Clappe cut his sod? Will wouldn't loan our plough, Clappe would have to buy one, but how? He didn't seem to have anything to trade, and though he'd given me pennies for food I didn't think he had much coin left. Not enough to buy a plough at any rate, or a wagon to get it home. I'd thought he'd meant to borrow our tools and set himself up properly when he brought in his first harvest, living on game 'til then, as we had our first year.

"Rachel, mind you don't mark those," I said, noticing her as I thought gloomily on Clappe's fate.

"You said we'd have candy when we came to town," Rachel said, turning from where she'd been stroking the toe of a new pair of boots.

Beth pulled at my skirt and pointed to the jar on the counter that held red and green striped sticks of candy.

"Ma, look!"

I picked her up. "Yes I see them, would you like one, sweet pea?"

Will turned a little and I caught the shake of his head.

"If you wish very hard," I said, trying to keep the disappointment from my voice, "you might get one for Christmas. Why don't you pick out the buttons for your winter clothes yourself?"

Rachel glared at me with Will's sloe eyes.

I'd been stupid to promise them candy, but the year before when he'd gone to sell our harvest, Will'd brought some back with him. I'd thought we'd manage again, the crop had seemed as good. Maybe what we'd grown wasn't as good as before, or maybe the store owner had decided to widen his profits. Either way, we were short for it. The hope of the day dried up. Just once I wanted Rachel to smile at me and make my heart float, just like when she was a baby showing me her pink gums.

Thomas was looking at a Winchester rifle that was hung on the wall. I knew he wanted a weapon of his own, but he was not yet old enough to shoot. His eyes were very round as he looked at it, fingers curling and uncurling at his sides in want. Still, when Will clapped his hands together and said it was time for them to go outside, Thomas went without a word.

While Thomas watched the girls and the wagon, William picked out stove pipe lengths to go with the little iron range. It was a two holed stove with a bake oven cast of lumpy looking iron with sharp edges. It would be a fine thing to have it heating the soddie, and to be able to cook indoors. I pointed out sacks of cornmeal, the cheapest flour they had, brown and flecked with split kernels, Lord knew if I'd ever get it to rise.

"We'll take some of that as well," Will said, pointing out a brown calico and a darker brown linsey woolsey. "How much'll you need to make yours and the girls' dresses?"

I told him, watched the store clerk cut out lengths of goods for us. Brown to match the dirt. First new cloth we'd had since we came to the territory.

Outside I helped William pile the wagon with our goods. Soon we were on our way back to the soddie. I hoped Clappe had found the piece of muslin with the bread inside it hidden by the house. He'd have been starving when he woke up, after having almost nothing the day before.

I was vexed with Will, had been all day, not that he noticed. That morning Will had told me to get the children ready for a trip to town. I'd asked him what he thought he was doing, hadn't he promised the day to Clappe? Will hadn't seen fit to argue with me, he'd just gone out to get the wagon ready.

Arguing with Will never came to any good. I'd packed up some lunch for the journey, helped get the harvest onto the wagon and shushed the children as I helped them into the box beside the sacks. Clappe'd proved himself a heavy sleeper.

I only hoped I could count on Will to get around to helping out our neighbour. I didn't want things ruined between us. It'd been pleasant the last few days, having a new face around to see, a new voice to hear.

The ride home was long and hot. I had my bonnet on, but the back of my neck burnt fast. With Nora in my arms and Beth close at my side, I was desperate for a cool drink and a breeze. Rachel sulked on the other side of me, thinking of candy sticks no doubt. Her new shoes were in the wagon, next to the goods for her dress, but what were warm clothes and sturdy shoes to her when she wanted candy? I didn't know how she'd grown up so spoiled. Even when she was a baby and we lived with Will's family, there had been no sweets or treats apart from Christmas.

It was finally getting cool as we reached the soddie. For miles I'd been able to see that the tent was gone. Will'd grunted as he noticed its absence, but said nothing. The oxen pulled us on home.

I climbed down to help Beth and Rachel on to the grass. Thomas went straight to the barn to start fetching water for the beasts, and I unloaded the wagon, giving Rachel her shoes to carry. With Will's help I took our purchases into the soddie, stocking the supply chest and putting the new fabric and trimmings away. Rachel had chosen gilt buttons for her dress, a whole two cents dearer than plain metal. Will, his bottle of whisky already paid for, let her have her way. You couldn't predict who he'd favour or what he'd do with the promise of drink to cheer him. Rachel got her buttons and the rest of the children got nothing, not even a stick of candy to share.

I'd be reusing the chipped buttons from an old frock, the make up the cost.

The stove went into the corner, where it would stand once Will fitted the stove pipe. That night I would cook my last meal outdoors.

"Would you look at that," I said, running my hand over the sun warmed metal, "did you ever see a finer thing?"

"It's just a stove," Rachel said, already shoving her dirty, summer tough feet into her new shoes.

"Get your feet out of those shoes," Will ordered, cheer lost on the long drive home. "I don't want to see you in them 'til there's a foot of snow on the ground."

She pulled them off and stuffed them away by the door.

"This stove'll be keeping us warm long after those shoes have passed to Beth and are worn to holes," I said. I could see that Will had found his bottle and was taking a few nips from it.

"Tonight we'll have a proper dinner," William said, catching Rachel up and spinning her around while she squealed, his good mood restored. "Salt pork and cornbread and beans, that's what we'll have, my little hen." He held her in his arms and scratched her face with his dark whiskers until she struggled, laughing.

"But what about our candy?" she asked. "Ma said to me and Beth that we'd have candy when you went to town."

"Well, you see," he said, lowering his voice a little, "Ma needed this lovely cook stove, so there was no money for candy – but you shall have some at Christmas."

My hands tightened on the bundle of wicking I was poking into a tin can. The lies tripped easily off his tongue when he spoke to the girls. The cook stove was as much for them and him as for me, wouldn't it keep them warm come winter? Wouldn't it heat water to wash them, dry their clothes, bake their goddamn bread? What would his bottle of whisky do for them, for me? Nothing.

While the girls soothed the ragdolls they'd left behind, I fed Nora, trying not to let tears fall as she drew on my cracked nipple. Oh for some salve, I would have walked to town for it if I'd had the money. I'd asked Will for some coin as we'd passed a house with a sign in the window, offering medicines and balms. He'd only grunted that he didn't have money to waste on 'every little whim' of mine.

Once I'd patted Nora's back and laid her down in her cradle box I tried to arrange my dress so as to stop it rubbing on my chest. Then I went to start a fire.

Stacking buffalo chips and knotted grass, I struck a light to it and poked at the tinder until the whole pile caught. Beans and salt pork and cornbread he'd said. It was already growing dark. I was tired from the jolting of the wagon and my back ached with carrying Nora around the store.

"Rachel? Come help me with supper," I called. When there was no response I tried again, "Rachel? Come now, I'll let you make the bread."

I went to the door of the soddie and looked inside. Rachel was sitting on her tick, dandling her rag doll by its yarn hair. Beth dozed on the tick, her thumb lodged in her little rosebud of a mouth.

"Didn't you hear me call?" I said, "I need your help with the supper."

Her mouth twisted in a set pout. "Why?"

"Young lady, get up and get the cornmeal from the chest before I lose my patience," I warned. My back tightened in pain. I could feel the milk on my raw teat sticking to my shift.

Rachel dragged herself from the tick and flung her doll away, it slapped against Beth's face, waking her. Her mouth opened, the wet thumb slipping out as she began to wail. Nora started to grizzle in her cradle box.

I took two strides across the packed dirt floor and grabbed Rachel's arm, hauling her out of the soddie. With one hand I lifted the skirt of her dress, with the other I slapped her sharply across the backs of her thighs, twice. I pulled her dress back down and spun her around. Her mouth was a thin line, but her eyes were large and wet like a dog's.

"Don't you ever pretend you don't hear me, Rachel Deene, when I tell you to do something, there's a good reason for it. Now go quiet your sisters."

Her little face bunched up and she tore away from me, off towards the barn, "I'm gonna tell Pa!"

"You come back here right now, or I'll spank you again, with a wooden spoon this time!"

She rounded the soddie and disappeared. I kicked out at a chunk of firewood in the grass. "That goddamn child."

51

Never had she failed to mind me, though she had a habit of being contrary. I hadn't had to raise a hand to her since she was a tiny child. Then I'd struck her only to keep her out of the hearth, or from eating buttons or stones, the way children will, as if they're born with the determination to die as soon as possible. A child who wouldn't listen to me was a child in danger. If a wolf or band of Indians should come to our door and she didn't pay heed I shuddered to think what would happen.

I went into the soddie and lifted Beth, holding her though it pained my back. Nora had snuffled herself to sleep. I took Beth outside and put her on the grass a little way from the fire, took out the bowl and the skillet, the cornmeal and salt pork and carried them outside as well. I showed her how to stir while she wrapped her pudgy hand around the spoon handle.

"One day soon you'll be doing this all on your own." I hoped that she would be more of a help than Rachel, or that my eldest daughter would mellow soon. It was hard to have no one. Sometimes I almost wished Thomas had been born a girl. He would have been a great help.

Thomas appeared at the edge of the circle of firelight, carrying a bucket of well water. It was as though he knew I needed him. He set the bucket down and went to the soddie, brought out the plates, jug and the bundle of knives and forks.

"Rachel's crying by the sty," he said, face lowered as he filled the water jug.

"Why?"

"Pa slapped her."

I felt a twist of vicious satisfaction in my belly, followed by the ache of shame. I stroked Beth's hair and bobbed her on my knee. Why couldn't they grow like wheat? Fingerlings one month, full stalks by summer's end? Why this slow rearing? My children as much use on the dry, empty prairie as a fistful of flower heads.

"Take your sister," I said to Thomas, "and watch the beans don't burn."

I poured the cornbread into the skillet and went to find Rachel. She was by the sty, leaning on the sod wall.

"Come on back to the fire now, it's not safe out in the dark, you know that."

I put my hand on her thin shoulder, my shame lessening when she didn't squirm away from me.

"Ma." She turned her face up to me, pointing at the pig in its pen. "He's not moving."

Chapter Eight

Laura

"It was that fucking Clappe bastard."

"Will," I hissed, holding the lantern high and watching him as he crouched in the sty with his butchering knife. The girls were in the soddie, our dinner getting cold outside.

"He can't take a little disappointment, so he goes and he kills my goddamn hog?" He jerked the knife down the belly of the beast. "If I see that bastard cocksucker again, I'll kill him."

"It wasn't him," I said, "it must've been an animal, or an Indian." If there was one thing Will hated more than other men, it was Indian men.

"Savages, just left it here to rot like it ain't worth nothing, a whole year of scraps and hauling water, spoiling." He handed me the knife so he could lift the carcass.

I was the one who'd fed that pig, shovelled shit from its sty for the garden. I said nothing. Will was already roaring mad, adding to his temper wouldn't improve our lot any. The pig was almost spoilt, the day had been hot, the flies had already been on it, but, if we got it into brine and soaked it there was a chance of saving the best part of it.

Thomas was filling the barrel as we carried the carcass, he'd poured the salt water in, and we sank the pig into it and sealed the lid on tight. Only time would tell, but if in a month I was hauling up green pork, stinking and dropping maggots, I too would be kicking at walls and shouting for all the world and the Almighty to hear.

As we took our half-cold dinner inside out of the dark, I noticed a white shape by the door. It was the muslin wrapped bread I'd left for Clappe. He must have missed it in his hurry to break camp, or else left it as an insult. I couldn't blame him. I doubted that he'd killed the pig, but still, William had something coming to him for welching on their deal. I had something coming for letting him.

By the time I had the girls dressed for bed and Thomas had settled onto his tick, the whisky bottle was out and Will's mug was half drunk up. I left him to it, changed into my nightgown and put myself to bed. I lay praying that he would drink enough to have him sprawled out on the tick rather than sprawled out on me.

When the morning light found me untouched and William asleep in his chair I caught myself smiling. A piece of luck, that's what that was.

I shook Rachel and Beth lightly. "Time to get up girls. You too Thomas."

As I ushered them out I heard William groan, the chair creaking with him. He was in for a mighty sore head and I had no want to be the first thing he laid eyes on. Will went to the outhouse and returned sour and grey-faced to drink coffee and shun food. I was grateful to have things to do out of doors, while he set about fitting the stove, his head full of bees.

It was the day for bottling our fruits and vegetables, now that I had the sugar, vinegar and jars for it. If the pork went rancid we would be relying heavily on the preserves.

Rachel was peaceable, whether from the slaps she'd received, or from seeing the hog butchered in its sty. She helped me to build up the fire and tended it while I hunched over the pot, taking the stems out of chokecherries. Beth was on a blanket by my side, playing with her rag doll.

"I'm sick of these," Rachel said, screwing up her face, "why can't we have plum jam?"

"There aren't any that grow around here, we'll have to go and try and find some before winter." I would be doing no such thing, mostly because we'd been on the prairie two years and I hadn't ever seen a plum tree anywhere nearabouts.

Rachel huffed, but it was her usual kind of sourness and she kept the fire going without being told. Once I'd prepared the berries I put the pan over the fire and charged her with stirring them until they broke down into pulp.

"Thomas, why don't you come and boil these jars, I can pick the onions then."

Thomas had been cutting lengths of stove wood, but he looked so tired, I thought a lesser chore would be better for him. I could always chop the stove lengths later. It was only one small tree that William had hauled for kindling.

The garden was a square of hot, dry earth in the waving grass. I'd planted rows of onions, beans, squash, chokecherries and some herbs. I clenched my fist on a spray of silver sage leaves. The smell was like my Mother's roast chicken, like the attic where she'd hung her herbs. Like home. It was good to have it nearby.

I set about filling my basket with onions, pulling hard to separate the thick stems. My hands were a private shame, rough and red-knuckled as they were, but they could pick or shuck, chop and chink as well as Will's.

Around the rail fence that kept the animals out, the prairie grass moved to and fro, brown and dead as anything, jittering in the wind. I looked to the flattened place where Clappe had made camp, saw the small holes that had held up the tent's poles. Where was that tent pitched now? There was precious little time until winter came. The grass was already dying back, the sky growing distant and cold at night. I hoped he'd have food and shelter by the time snow came to the prairie and not one of those line shacks with the tar paper walls either. I wouldn't let a dog winter in a line shack, and a dead dog at that. Perhaps another woman would give him cornbread and beans, maybe a blanket for his bed. Maybe he'd marry her for her trouble.

From inside the soddie came a wail, a crash and a burst of cursing from Will. He stormed through the open door and glared at me. His eyes were red, his patchy beard standing out on his pale face. As he came close the smell on his breath told me that hair of the dog was not having helping him, though not for want of application.

"Your damn baby's crying, get it out of there so I can work," he mopped his face with a shirtsleeve already soaked in sour sweat. "Would it kill you to bring a man a drink of cold water when he's laying in a stove for you?"

"I'll get you some once Nora's down," I said, and went to get the baby, who was howling bitterly for a feed.

"And you, boy, get back to chopping that wood, or do you want your sisters to freeze to death?" I heard Will bark behind me, his shouting woke Beth, who started to fuss, and I came to the soddie door with Nora in time to see Rachel picking up her sister and shushing her. I'd never been more thankful for my eldest daughter.

William turned on his heel and came back to the soddie. I flinched as he passed me. There was, I saw, dirt all over the floor from where he was making a place for the stove. He had moved the ticks away at least. The table had a series of sticky rings on it from the whisky bottle.

He saw me looking and brandished a length of pipe. "Don't look like that, if you'd had the harvest I've had, you'd take a drink too. Not to mention that Clappe bastard killing our pig and running off."

I could've done with a swallow of whisky. The pipe and his wild eyes were frightening me. He'd never struck me with anything before, but there was always time for him to start. I didn't say anything, just took a seat and set Nora to my breast. Her little rosebud mouth stung like a bee, but I didn't let it show on my face. When Nora was done with her feed I laid her back down, but she started to fuss. I swear if babies had their way no work would ever be done.

"I'll get you that water."

Will harrumphed to let me know he'd heard.

I picked up the cradle box and the jug, took Nora outside. Nothing was worth getting on Will's bad side, and a crying baby with mess in her napkin was a sure way to make him fly off the handle again.

"Here, take her," I said to Rachel, who was flapping flies away from the cooling jars on the grass. "Why don't you play house?"

House was a game Rachel always loved, usually she parented a doll and played at being a fine lady, with Beth as her spinster sister who lived with her as a domestic. Rachel was ever making up stories like that. Make believing she was an orphan sold to a poor family, or that she was a secret princess exiled to life on the plain.

At the well I hauled on the windlass, making my back ache, dipped a jug-full out of the bucket. In the sun, away from Will and the smell of whisky, I felt myself start to calm. It would be alright, once he calmed down a little.

I put the jug on the table. Will was focused on finding a knife to cut the sod and I left him well alone.

Outside in the glare of the sun I picked up my basket of onions and took it to the side of the fire. Behind me I heard Will cursing the knife, and didn't anyone else have the sense to sharpen it?

"You can't take my baby away!" Rachel cried, clutching Nora closely while the little one tried to pull her bonnet off by the strings. Beth, the unwitting villain, stuck a confused fist into her little mouth and frowned.

"Rachel, Beth, keep your bonnets on, you'll catch the sun."

Rachel straightened hers and Beth pulled hers up from where it had been hanging around her neck.

I gave them a spoonful of jam on a plate to keep them quite, and Beth instantly put her fist in it and made a big rose print on her dress.

"Oh Beth," I left her in the soiled dress, she would only make another dirty if I changed her.

She smiled at me. "Pretty."

"Yes it is, a pretty mess."

A glance across the sun soaked grass showed me that Thomas was in the garden, picking the rest of the onions. The stove wood was chopped and stacked neatly. Thank God for days when the chores got done easy. Not that Will wouldn't complain, but it was best to leave him with little to rant over.

The jars were still warm, the jam was hot as hellfire, sticking to my fingers as I ladled it in. By the time I had all the big jars full there were a few new scald marks on my hands.

"Fuck this piece of shit," I heard William holler and looked to the soddie in time to see him fling the knife from the roof. The blade hit the hard turf and bounced off. Atop the ladder, clutching at the soddie's roof, William glared down at us.

"One of you bring me up a sharp blade."

Thomas ran for the barn to find the other knife. I prayed it'd be sharper. Or that the ladder'd break.

With the jam jarred up I could take Nora to the outhouse, escaping Will's glare. Rachel came with some jar-washing water in a bucket and a clean napkin, she looked set to stay with me, away from her father.

"Rachel, keep watch by the fire for your sister."

"Why can't I stay with you?"

"Because someone needs to watch Beth and Thomas's going to be picking."

She gripped the flat grass with her dusty toes. "Pa's awful angry today."

I reached for her and squeezed her shoulder. "He's not going to be angry with you if you watch your sister like a good girl." Nora, red faced and screaming by this time, grabbed my sleeve in her pink fist.

There came a crash from the soddie, and I saw that Will had climbed down and was draining the water jug, but had tripped on a pail left there to hold dry dung.

"Go quickly, and if you get scared, bring Beth back to me."

She scampered like a frightened rabbit. At least she didn't know that there was no way I could protect her from her Pa, any more than I could protect myself from him.

I laid Nora on the flattened grass. Under a layer of crusted shit her little backside was hot red and flaking. As I wiped her up she started to kick her small legs and cry harder.

"Can't feel good can it? Especially in this heat," I rang the cloth out, scraped the used napkin into the outhouse hole while I waited for her to dry off.

Once she was in a clean napkin I poured the dirty water onto the vegetable garden and washed my hands by the fire. Rachel was sitting there with Beth, both of them quiet and playing with Beth's grass dollies.

William, now with a sharp knife, was hacking at the soddie roof, whistling. He'd put the fear of God into us all, even sweet Beth, and now he was working without a care, as though he were the loving father in a children's tale.

By that night, the stove pipe was fitted and the pig iron box glowed cherry red with fire. Beth and Rachel had stripes of sunburn on their faces and Thomas was helping them braid the onions into ropes to hang and dry for winter. It was the first meal I'd ever cooked on a stove by myself. In Will's mother's kitchen I had hardly been allowed to lift a spoon before she tutted and took it from me. As it was I proved his mother right by burning myself several times, but the beans and pork were cooked well enough.

By that time, Will was so lit on whisky that he hardly seemed to notice the food. He was leaning against his chair back, tipped a little to one side.

The soddie was hot and stuffy from the stove. I left the door open as long as I could to try and air it out. In the heat of my little home, I thought of Clappe, and wondered whether he had found shelter from the cool night.

"Do you think," I asked of William as we sat by the table, listening to the children settled down to sleep, "that Clappe'll come back here?"

Will, full of pork and beans and looking for all the world like a decent husband again, sniffed and filled his pipe. "I shouldn't think so. Lanky city boy, soft handed, he probably had his fill and took the first stage back east."

I had noted Clappe's soft, long fingered hands, clearly meant for some finer work than farming. Perhaps he'd take a position as a clerk, or a banker, counting out notes and writing drafts and important letters. He didn't have the look of a man who'd stand much outside work.

"Seems almost like you're sweet on him," William muttered, "asking after him. Don't you go thinking I didn't see you slipping him the food I worked damn hard for."

"He gave me money for it."

"Food right out of you children's mouths," he muttered and I knew there was to be no talking to him. I sat rigidly in my chair and tried not to excite his anger any further. I'd been a fool. Inside, Will was still burning up with whisky, he wouldn't be happy 'till he'd put his fists to someone.

"Bet you wanted him, like you wanted Jacob back in Ohio," he said, standing up and taking an unsteady step towards the board shelf where I'd put the whisky bottle.

"I don't want Clappe," I said, trying to calm him.

He laughed a little, and I glanced to where Thomas was lying stiffly in his bed, so stiffly that he could only be listening. "Bet you'd fuck him."

The back of my neck burnt up. This was what William carried around under his skin all the time, and with enough whisky in him to bolster his male pride, he never failed to throw it in my face. I'd only done it because the thought of going off west with Will made me feel so miserable. I wasn't proud of myself for betraying my husband, breaking my vows worse than he'd broken his. When he'd gone with other women they'd been strangers to me, whores for the most part. I'd humiliated him by going with his brother. Coupling with him in the cowshed. It made me ashamed just to think of it. It'd been Jacob only because he'd flattered me, trying to get at Will for sheer meanness. He'd taunted Will with it, and only stopped when Will threatened to spread word of it about, losing Jacob his wife's love and his good name.

I looked at Thomas, still pretending to sleep. The girls were loose under their blankets, truly asleep, but Thomas, Lord he could hear every word.

"What did I do to deserve a wife like you?" Will said, slurring.

I kept my mouth shut, but it did me no good. He took two steps to me and belted me across the face. It took me off my seat. I hit the oiled dirt with my cheek and palms, legs tangled with the chair. He kicked me, once, twice, as I tried to hunch over. My breath left me in harsh sobs.

Over me, I heard William huff and a moment later he kicked off his boots, the tick rustled as he sprawled himself over it.

I glanced up, twisting my aching back, blinking tears away. Found Thomas's eyes glittering wet as he looked at me under a fold of his blanket. I raised my finger to my lips. My hand was shaking. Crawling from the fallen chair, I went to Thomas's side and patted his shoulder through the rough blanket. As quickly as they had come, my tears dried up.

"Get to bed," Will slurred, "work tomorrow, not getting out of it."

I went behind the canvas screen and took off my dress, which was heavily scented with sweat, stewed cherries and Nora's shit. The fastenings were hard to undo, my hands wouldn't work. Once I'd jerked the hooks open and peeled the dress from my sweating skin, I left it on the floor and slipped into my nightgown.

As I eased myself down onto the tick, smelling his whisky soaked breath and the sweat in his clothes, I wondered if he remembered how he had pursued me, courted me. To hear him talk you'd have thought I trapped him into it, but he was the one who'd brought me cherry blossom and walked with me to church.

All the work that'd roughened my hands, the prairie that took so much and brought only enough for us to slide by on, what had it taken from him to make him hate me? Was it just what I'd done with Jacob, or had Will found as little to love on our claim as I had?

Chapter Nine
Laura

I guess every couple has their bad nights. Lord knows my parents did, my father could make my mother cry with a few well-chosen words, and he'd raise hell if his dinner was late coming to him. I'd never known him to hit her, but then I hadn't been glued to her side. There's a lot to marriage that takes place behind closed doors, if you have doors to close.

The bruise on my face wasn't bad, by the day after it had faded some. He'd given me worse. After he'd found out from Jacob just what he'd done with me, he'd split my lip, blacked both my eyes and half choked the life out of me. Then my face had felt like a piece of bloody meat. For over a week I'd been unable to swallow, or speak without husking my words. Even now the thought of William in a temper brought an ache to my jaw and a twist of fear to my gut.

For a few days after he'd struck me down, William was the soul of good grace. I knew to take the good after the bad, if only because you never knew when you'd get it again. I tried to keep my thoughts on the matters at hand and not on long healed wounds, or fresh bruises.

I had Rachel help me rinse ashes for lye, and I made myself a good store of hard soap from the fat I'd been keeping by in a crock. The days after a run to town were always busy, I had green coffee to parch, supplies to jar and store. It was a week before I had all the vegetables canned, or sorted away into sacks to hang.

The soreness from the birth was mostly gone by then, but for my breasts which were still suffering from the feeding. A good thing too, as Will's good mood made him eager in bed. The night after I was done with the soap making he touched me in the dark and pressed whiskery kisses to my cheek and neck. It was one of the rare times I felt part of it with him, felt anything other than fear and dislike. I touched his back and pressed up against him, feeling the hair on his chest against mine, the heat of his skin, why, it was almost as it had been after we were married, when I'd gotten used to him a little. I felt the building of that wondrous thing that Jacob had shown me, and which Will had managed to cause in me a handful of times since we were married. Though I didn't make a sound I closed my eyes and held him tightly, gasping. I was halfway to enjoying myself when he finished with me. He pulled away roughly, leaving stickiness to spread on my thighs.

I almost reached out to him, almost, but my wanting for things made him angry. That night I was just like his other women, to be used and left. At least they didn't have to get up and brew his coffee come morning, wash his shirts, plant his fields, or the hundred other things I did for him, for no money and a bed on the hard ground.

I never thought I'd be jealous of a whore.

*

I was up the next morning, doing a wash with Rachel after breakfast. Will was gone to look out more winter wood, Thomas was inside with Beth and Nora. Though he said nothing on it, I knew Thomas loved taking care of the baby, he was always finding new things to dangle over the cradle to amuse her.

"Why do we put dresses on Beth?" Rachel sulked as we worked the mess of brown clothes in the washtub, "she should wear a sack until she's old enough not to spill or mark up her clothes."

For once we were in agreement. "Now Rachel, both you a Thomas were young once, and you made twice the mess that Beth makes."

Rachel didn't look as if she believed me. "But you had Grandmother Deene to help you wash."

Oh, and what a help she was, taking over every task and calling me useless to my face, while talking of my laziness when she thought I couldn't hear.

"Well, you're here to help me now, aren't you? And you're doing a fine job." I lifted the crock of soft soap and added a little more to a tough cherry jam stain. Rachel scrunched the sopping clothes in her little fists.

"Why's everything brown?" she said. "'Member Lettie had that blue dress?"

Her cousin Lettie had many dresses. Jacob could afford the best for his two little girls and his wife Anne. He had also been able to afford the fifty dollars Will demanded to keep our coupling a secret from them.

"Lettie and her mother and sister don't live or work on a farm, so they don't have to have working clothes."

"Where do they work? I want to do work where I can have a pretty dress."

Whores came to my mind, in their gauzy, unwashed, frocks. In the light of day I couldn't believe I'd envied them their leisure. "They don't work, because your uncle makes a lot of money sending American things back to England, where your grandparents live." I wrung out a shirt and spread it on the hot, dry grass. "Your new dress'll look lovely though, and they're saying in town that soon there'll be a proper store out our way. There's already work being done on a church, so you'll be able to wear that lovely new dress to meet our neighbours on a Sunday."

Rachel wrung out one of her own petticoats. "I still think Beth shouldn't have a new dress. You could use her cloth to make a winter cape for me."

I looked up at my vain little daughter, her dark hair shining where it spilled from under her bonnet, lips as small and smug as berries. Beyond her, like a ship sailing through the grasses, came a little prairie schooner. I stood up and shielded my eyes. About a half mile away the rig stopped, the solitary figure on its seat climbed down and began to take things from the battened pile on the back.

Rachel turned to look too. "Are they new neighbours?"

"I think it's Mr Clappe," I said, for I could see the familiar shirt and trousers, and the copper of his hair even at a distance. What was he doing back? I felt my heart leap in sick dread. Will was away at the creek bottoms, a good four miles in the direction of town, but he would be back soon enough.

"Will Pa shoot him, for killing the pig?"

"Rachel! Your father would never shoot a man over a pig. It was probably not even Mr Clappe who killed it." I wished I believed in Will as much as I did in Clappe.

"Pa said he did."

"Pa was angry when he said that." I put my hand up to my bruise, God, what would Will do to him?

I looked towards the schooner again, the small covered wagon so unlike our heavy rig. The sunlight struck the blade of a new sod cutting plough, forcing me to turn my face away. A plough meant he intended to stay.

"Let's get this wash done, then we can see about getting some chips for the stove," I said. I had to see Clappe before William came back. If nothing else I had to apologise, and warn him.

Rachel put her hands in the water and started wringing out clothes with a will. Soon we had the whole wash spread on the dry grass, baking under the sun. The wind toyed with the cuffs and bonnet strings.

I took my basket and we got up to the schooner in time to see Clappe, for it was him, unhitching the two mustangs and tying them to a wooden post he'd driven into the ground. They were dun coloured, sturdy things, far speedier than our oxen. Clappe had come into money, the schooner was groaning with goods.

"Mr Clappe," I said, half-watching Rachel scoop up tough, dried buffalo chips from the grass a few feet away. "You've had a profitable trip to town."

I was surprised by the hardness in his eyes when he turned to me, holding a basket of tools. He was still a boy, maybe twenty, with a smooth face and soft hands, but his eyes were frost split flints.

"I did. Though it was a lot quicker coming back than in setting off."

I felt at once the shame of what William had done, a shame that was mine for being married to him. "It wasn't my aim to leave you. I warned you about him."

"So you did, but I thought you were a decent enough woman not to go along with it, and leave me stranded." He thumped the heavy basket down on the ground and crossed his arms.

"I left you some food but it was still here when we came home. I worried for you."

"I never saw any food. But, I fared as well as could be expected. I happened upon some melons in the creek bottoms, otherwise I might have starved."

"You've been gone a fair while."

"I went further afield, wanted to see what the bigger stores had to offer," he turned and rubbed a hand over the solid wood of the schooner, which I saw was flaking paint, revealing another colour underneath. Third hand then. Not so much money as to afford a new wagon. "I intended to leave but when I reached the next town I changed my mind."

"The land here's good," I said, knowing it was a powerful good reason for one just starting out to remain on the prairie.

He fixed me with his eyes. "I've come far enough to know that I never want to run before a man again."

I wondered what it was his father or master had done to send him across the country.

"It'll be good to have you as a neighbour," I said, meaning it. It was lonely on the prairie in winter, with only the snow banks and the sky for company.

He turned back to me, and I saw he'd taken something from a basket at the front of the schooner. "I decided I wanted to be a good neighbour, even if your husband wronged me. I don't want to be the kind of man who holds a grudge, not against someone who hasn't harmed me through fault of their own." He held out a small clay pot, sealed with cork and wax. "I had this made up at the pharmacy in town."

I took it and read the little label that had been pasted to the clay. Chamomile salve. My face burnt and when I looked up, I saw that Clappe looked uncertain, his cheeks painted a lively shade of red.

"I didn't mean to insult you, but...my sister, when she was nursing, she went through this as fast as it could be made. I heard it helps with the pain."

The thought of the cream easing the cracks and soreness of my nipples with chamomile and beeswax, had me almost feeling faint under the hot sun. I'd borne the pain for weeks and I was almost at the end of my rope with it.

"Thank you, Mr Clappe," I held the precious jar carefully between my hands, "you must accept my fullest apology for the way you were treated by my husband, and..." I thought what gift I could give him, "you must also take a jar of my chokecherry preserve, and join us for supper."

He shrugged his coat off and slung it over a box on the schooner. "I don't think your husband would take kindly to me sitting in his home, eating his food, any more than he would me talking to you." His gaze was fixed on mine. "What reason did he give for that?"

I touched my cheek, where the bruise was a yellow-green reminder of William's whisky drinking. "Our pig was gutted while we were in town...William didn't take kindly to it."

"I suppose he blames me."

I nodded.

"Well you can tell him, there were two cows stolen and a pig killed within a few days ride of here. I heard about it in town. I would no more kill your pig than burn your house." His face cracked a smile. "Can you imagine me, creeping into that sty and cutting up your hog? I've never set foot in a sty, let alone slaughtered anything before."

I could believe that and knew it showed on my face. "William isn't at the house right now, how about a meal with me and the children?"

He looked past me to the soddie, in clear sight over the flat ground. From here I could make out which dresses were drying on the line. We were to be close neighbours indeed, only about two miles apart if he was to build where we stood now. Without a single tree to hide behind. He squinted as if measuring the distance, seeing if it was worth his time. "I'd be happy to."

Clappe took Rachel's basket of dried dung and I kept her in my sight as she skipped through the long grasses, her light brown dress giving her the look of a young deer. Clappe fell into easy step beside me and I found I could not resist asking the question that had been on my mind since he arrived.

"What brings you to Indian Territory?"

He shrugged lightly, "I left things in the city that I'd rather forget and for someone like me, this is the only life available. There'd be no way for me to make a living any other way."

"You could stake a claim in gold, or work at a lumber camp," I said evenly.

Something about that seemed to amuse him. "I doubt I'd last long in that kind of work. Men, other men, have never treated me equal."

"Still, farming's an awful hard row."

"There's many kinds of hard in the world. You seem to manage."

"I have William. The children help some too."

"I'll just have to learn, and work hard."

"You've brought half the store home with you. Things can't be so hard."

"Everything I have is on that schooner. I've almost no coins left."

We reached the soddie and I called for Thomas to bring out the jug of water and the no-cake I'd made that morning, plus plate for our guest. I saw my son's face brighten when he saw that it was Clappe with me.

"Thomas, why you've grown and inch since I last saw you."

"Sure have," Thomas set down the jug and the plate of no-cake. Rachel brought Beth out from the soddie and the two of them set to bending the tall, dry grass over to make little wagon covers for their corn husk families.

The sun was bright on us and made the grasses sing with chirping insects. Our drying clothes rippled under the breeze. Small birds flew high under the blue, cloudless flag of a sky, and Clappe's hair fairly glowed like a copper pan. All around smelt of sweet, dry grass.

I watched Clappe drink down the cool water, his throat working more delicately than William's. He had good manners with the no-cake and smiled open and easy without a drop of liquor in his body. Not that whisky had ever sweetened William's temper any. He reminded me a little of Jacob, only Clappe's easiness came from youth and innocence, not wealth and arrogance.

Lord, he was in for it. The winters on the prairie were as close to hell as I ever hoped to see; snow that fell like smoke until you couldn't see your own skirts, blown up and frozen into enormous drifts like iron.

Once we were done eating I went inside and threw into a gunny sack the promised jam and a few other things to repay him for the work he'd done bringing in the grain and hay.

Clappe looked into the sack and then back at me. "I can't take all this from you."

"You earned it, working the way you did. I'm only sorry we won't be able to help you get your soddie up before winter."

"I can do that just fine," he assured me, but there was something uncertain in his voice that made me worry for him.

"Thomas, why don't you go and take the girls inside, it's far too hot out here to play all day in the grass."

Once Thomas'd taken his sisters inside I laid a hand on Clappe's arm. "You've never built before, have you?"

"No Ma'am."

"Don't worry. The fact is, Will never built a thing before we came here, and if that's not saying a soddie's idiot proof, I don't know what is."

Again that smile, sweet and sudden, like June rain.

"Hardest part is the roof. All you got to do before that is pile up the sod nice and high, when you've got your walls, put up wood for the door and window frames, then put poles across the top, cover them with sticks and hay, and put more sod up on top of that to keep it all in place. The door's going to need leather hinges, but I can show you how to do those later."

His green eyes were focused, taking in my words. I liked that feeling of being listened to. Any fool could build a soddie, but building one to withstand the prairie wind in a howling storm was slightly more of an art.

He looked again at the bag in his lap. "I'm grateful for your help, if there's anything I can ever do for you..."

"You've worked plenty, if he'd paid you a fair wage you'd be able to buy everything in there twice over."

"But if there's anything you need," he stressed.

I'd almost forgotten that there were good men, man enough to never raise a hand to a woman. I had slipped into another world, where blood and blows were common as 'good morning'.

"I can stand for myself," I found myself saying, "but, I appreciate your offer."

His eyes were sad, deep as caves, hollow. "Husbands ought to treat their wives kindly. My sister had a husband that treated her awfully."

"You sister...the one with the baby?"

"She didn't keep him long. He died in his crib only three weeks after he was born. A tiny little thing, a fae child."

"And the mother?" I knew the anger a woman's grief could cause a man. William had raged at me for being homesick for the first few months of our journey.

"She died."

I laid my hand on his arm, the touch of his shirt surprising me, as I'd not meant to reach for him. "I'm sorry."

"I only hope she manages to find some peace in escaping him."

"And she will be with her child," I said, almost losing my own words in the crackle of the wind rushed grass.

"Maybe." He looked down, and for a moment allowed his hand to cover mine. It had roughened since our last meeting, travel and the loading of the schooner, never mind the driving of the mustangs, had raised blisters on his palm that had burst and scabbed.

"We'll be good neighbours," I said. "Life can be lonely out here for one. To hear people tell of it, winter on the prairie in one's own company is enough to break a man. Even with Will and children to talk to I feel the strain of being shut up inside, trying to keep the cold out. "

He released my hand and gathered up the sack. "I've known worse."

Chapter Ten
Cecelia

Laura had given me a great deal to think about in terms of the house's construction and of the kind of life I would be living under its roof. In the sack she'd pressed on me I'd found the promised jam, ruby red and thick, three bars of soap, two candles, and a pamphlet of simple recipes, much thumbed and stained. Aside from the pamphlet each item was clearly handmade. I'd never thought of making soap before, it had been bought when I'd lived in Ohio and the candles came boxed from a merchant.

That night I slept in my tent, or tried to. Sitting with her that day I'd seen the sinew in her brown arms and lithe neck. How could such a woman stand to be struck like a dog by a man so weak he had cheated me by fleeing, rather than by threatening me off? Why in God's name didn't she run? With strength like that in her arms, why didn't she knock him down?

She'd told me that she'd grown up and married in England, yet she was almost indistinguishable from the hard, American born women I'd seen in the towns I'd fled through. Was that what I would become? Grubbing in the soil for turnips as dirty as myself?

That first day of work on the soddie was the coolest I had so far experienced on the prairie, which spurred me to work as hard as I could. Fall would soon catch me up and I had no wish to sleep outside under the first heavy rain, let along the first snow. The grasses hissed under a steady wind and the ripping of the sod had me panting hard enough to hear my own blood pounding.

Manning my sod cutter and driving the mustangs occupied me for most of the morning. I hadn't thought it would be so hard to keep the blade of the thing in the earth. It bounced out of the hard soil and off of stones, cutting irregular chunks of sod. The mustangs too were wilful and sometimes wouldn't walk when I shouted at them. There was nothing in my book that told me how to get a straight line from the plough, it seemed to assume I would manage that much on my own.

When I quit work to sweat through my midday meal I noticed William himself watching me from the doorway of his soddie. Despite there being at least two miles of land between us, the prairie was so flat and bland that my eye caught on their house often as the only thing in a sea of grass. It was easy to pick out the figure of the man; his dark hair was like an ink blot against the parchment coloured grasses. I raised a hand in greeting and saw him unmistakably turn his back and go inside.

A charming man indeed.

I spent that afternoon cutting the crooked strips of sod that I'd ploughed up. I had to do it with a spade, which made my shoulders ache. I managed to tear off the end of a nail while working, exposing the raw skin underneath, and the tough grasses sliced my hands as I hauled the chunks of sod up onto others. The soil was heavy and dark, full of insects, earthworms and long crawling things with many legs. I squirmed to feel them run over my fingers.

As I piled the sod, I realised that one wall was coming up thicker than the others, and wasn't entirely straight. What could I do about that? With the spade I tried to cut down some of the stacked sod, but that only caused the wall to buckle. I struck the wall with the spade, which lodged in the earth and refused to budge.

"Oh you…you blasted thing!" I pulled hard on the handle, when it came free I was sent sprawling to the earth, covered in a shower of dirt and insects. I leapt up, clawing at my collar to get the wretched crawlers off of me, only just holding back a shriek. Part of the wall had collapsed and would need rebuilding.

"Oh God, if my Father could see me…if Franklyn…oh Lord, help me."

No divine aid came and soon I had to force myself to get up and continue my work.

I had the walls waist height by the time I started losing daylight. My hands were so ingrained with dirt that I looked like a miner. With no running water anywhere but the far off creek bottoms I went to the Deene well and drew myself up a bucket, which I slopped into my own and took back to my tent. I didn't ask because that would give the miser a chance to say no. If he wanted me away from his well he'd have to force me. Despite my brazen Clappe-ish strides my heart was in my throat while I drew the water, but the soddie was quiet. Deene must have been away in the fields, or else inside, eating his dinner. My stomach snarled. I would have to cook something.

Was there no end to it?

I made a fire on part of the prairie that I'd stripped of sod. Once I'd washed my hands I dug about in the schooner and found the pot and 'lug pole' I'd bought in town. Who had named that contraption and what a 'lug' was I did not know and frankly did not care to find out.

Though I'd hardly cooked for myself the whole way from Ohio, only really blackening meat or heating water, the pamphlet gave instructions for cornmeal mush. I boiled water, which took so long as to make me wonder if prairie water was somehow incapable of even that simple application, and sprinkled in cornmeal, stirring and watching it thicken. The resultant mass was edible, but not as good as Laura's had been. I realised I'd neglected to add salt.

That night I slept within the low walls of my new home, looking at them in the growing dark, marvelling what I had accomplished and dreading the work that was left to do.

*

The novelty of being on my own and working for my bread had been wearing thin even before I reached Indian Territory. Pride had kept me upright and desperation had kept me working on Deene's field, but building that soddie came close to breaking me. It was the loneliness as much as the work. I think I could have stood it if I'd had someone to laugh with, or to sing, as Laura had at harvest, then I wouldn't have felt so helpless. Being by myself was a constant reminder that the only person around to take care of me, was me.

I dwelt more and more on returning to Ohio, but doing so made me think of Charles and I could hardly bear that. I still checked the horizon for horses or a carriage, listened for them at night. The wellspring of my fear was bottomless and some nights I woke in a sweat, drowning in it. The thought of living in his house again, where he held every key and decided my every day for me, was a terrible one. I'd seen no one in those last months but him and our few, silent servants, felt nothing but helpless. Imagining my return to that place terrified me. I knew that if Charles ever had possession of me again he would lock me away and leave me without even a window to the outside world.

To keep myself sane I began to think of my brother, Franklyn, his memory kept my fears at bay. I could dream of him finding me and taking me back to his house, of him barring the door to Charles and promising to keep me safe. This daydream, though it was paper thin, helped me to face each fresh cut, bruise and aching muscle; it helped me to face the memories of Charles when they came, because in my mind at least, my brother listened to what I had to say about my husband.

I spoke out loud to him, told him what I suspected he already knew, that I married Charles out of duty. How despite that I'd made myself be a proper wife, managing social events and the house, making arrangements for gifts and cards of condolence and celebration.

Franklyn would pull faces at that and I told him that he was lucky to have his wife to remember such things for him. He could be so improper at times, arriving at the house unannounced, wearing good trousers with old work shirts and smoking indoors even in mother's rooms.

It was his lack of airs that made it easy to be frank with him. I could tell him how I'd hoped until the wedding night that I would grow to love Charles. How in the end I couldn't feel either love, or womanly affection for him. My only solace was the birth of my dear Charlie, whom I loved with all my heart. Even with my pregnancy over, the restrictions Charles had placed on me; that I was to avoid exerting myself with managing the house or tending to correspondence, were not lifted. I was not permitted to go to town or even to receive or write letters.

In my eyes at least, Charlie was perfect, whatever others said. Whatever his father said, or the endless parade of doctors that came to look at his motionless legs and tell us what we already knew – that he would never walk, or even crawl. Charles blamed me for that. He said again and again that is was the stress of my infrequent visits to my parents prior to my confinement that had 'deformed' our son. I was to be kept inside, to prepare for the next child. Charles was determined that another 'mistake' would not occur.

Franklyn didn't yet have children, but I knew I wouldn't have to explain to him that when Charlie died, there was no comfort for me in that house. Charles was indifferent to his death and said often that I was young and would have other, stronger children, if I followed instructions that he brought to me from the doctor, and didn't repeat my errors.

Charlie was the strongest child I'd ever seen. There was never a louder cry, a brighter grin. It still made me sick with grief to remember standing in the nursery looking down at Charlie in his cradle, pale and blue under the lamplight.

I'd denied Charles the possibility of more children, this I couldn't share with my brother, even on the wide, lonely prairie, but I would tell him how, one night after supper, Charles said he would have me put away in an asylum if I didn't control my grief. He'd taken the key to the nursery and locked it up. I'd started to flinch when he touched me, to stay in my room rather than share the dining room or parlour with him. He gave orders that no food was to be taken to me upstairs. So I did not eat until I felt I would faint, only then would I sit at table with him. I couldn't look him in the eye.

He began to bring the kitchen maid to his bed. I heard them in the hallway, talking. It insulted me, but I was almost relieved. I didn't want him near me.

The night I fled, Charles had wronged me beyond what I could endure. I spoke aloud while I worked on stacking the endless chunks of sod; told my brother how Charles had caught me passing a note to the boy that brought our groceries, to be delivered to my family. In it I had written what had happened to Charlie, what was happening to me, and begged them to visit me and not allow themselves to be turned away.

Charles had dismissed the boy, then thrown the note into the fire and taken away my writing things. He said he would summon the doctor that night, and come morning I would be on my way to the asylum, where I would stay until he believed my wildness was under control. Then he would have me returned to his house.

It was hard, recounting what happened after that, as my memory of it was so blurred and uneven. I must have been half out of my head, but I did remember taking jewellery from my dresser and a small amount of money. Charles had locked me in my rooms, but he had not considered the door to the servants' stairs, which was behind a curtain in my parlour.

I imagined that Franklyn would be the only one to not think me insane when I told of how, standing at the door to the kitchen garden, a voice in me cried out for the final time, 'What are you doing? Have you taken leave of your senses entirely? Charles was right about you, you are hysterical.' I swore to him that it was grief and fear for my own future safety, rather than sheer madness that forced me onwards.

Being alone on the prairie I had no one else and I spoke to my brother for hours on end, just to hear my own voice in the silence. I wasn't yet lonely enough to hear him answer, but I could see his face clearly and sometimes imagined what he would say to me. How he would have chided me if he'd known I'd boarded a stage early that morning not knowing where it was bound for, only that it was headed west.

I told him as I stamped down my dirt floor how I'd left the stage in a town I didn't know the name of. How I'd watched a man, a soldier, walk across the dirt road that separated one line of stores from another. How he walked with his head up, eyes taking a full look at the world ahead, looking at the other men before him as they looked back with indifference, or with nods of acknowledgement. How my focus on him was broken when a man tore open a door and threw a naked woman into the street.

He called her a whore, was shouting about being cheated. She was shouting back, in some language I couldn't understand. I saw, though I was fearful of staring, that she was an oriental.

It came to me then, what to do. I knew then that I would disguise myself, as a man. He would laugh at that, I knew. Tell me how only I could come up with a plan so childish, but he'd be all fondness and smiles.

Sometimes I missed him so much I could hardly see for tears.

Chapter Eleven
Cecelia

Building up the walls took three days of cutting and hefting sod. After that I journeyed to the creek bottoms with my mustangs and brought back a log to split into wood for window and door frames. It took a further two days to cut enough slabs that weren't crooked or splintered or faulted. I had trouble getting them even, never mind getting them to fit in the windows and door. In the end I hammered them in with the axe handle and none of them came out level. My hands were by then ingrained with black earth and covered in nicks, scrapes and splinters.

On the sixth day it rained, so I spent a miserable day in my tent, while all around the water rushed into the grass, turned the floor of my house to mud and began to drip through the canvas over my head. All the while a smug thread of smoke came from Laura's chimney, the light of her lamp glowed in her perfectly square windows.

While I whittled away at endless pieces of wood I spoke with my brother, anything to block out the sound of the rain. I told him how I'd decided to move on as soon as possible, get further from Charles, who I feared more than anything else. I had yet to put my plan into action and so when I approached a man loading a wagon, it was as a woman. I had no other choice, I'd not yet got up the nerve to make good on my scheme to cut my hair and don men's clothes. I told him that I needed to get further west to visit my mother, who was very sick. At the time I'd fretted that my telling the lie would somehow make the thing true.

He'd find it funny that I was worried about something as silly as that, once I told him about everything else I'd been through since leaving Ohio.

The man said he had a friend who'd be hauling buckets and tools out west in short order. He warned me that it wouldn't be a comfortable journey. I gave him mother's maiden name, Miss Clappe. I wanted Franklyn to know how clever I'd been, he was the only one who ever thought I was clever.

I asked if all the men that were around were going out west and found that most were, looking for gold or farmland.   Remembering Franklyn's laugh I could imagine it issuing form him at the ideas running through my head. After all he'd heard me complain over the rain outside the drawing room window, had tried to interest me in the goings on of the country, in walks, in riding. To him it would seem impossible that I ever thought I could do it; claim land and make a home for myself with my own two hands.

The journey was indeed, not comfortable. I spent several weeks sleeping in between stacks of buckets and other crude wooden goods. By day I rode on the plank wagon seat until my teeth felt they would shake loose and my bones seemed bruised all over from the rocking and the holes in the road. My traveling companion spoke little and seemed as wary of me as I was of him. In the towns we passed through he laid out his goods and I wandered the streets to stretch my legs and use my dwindling coins to buy food to share that evening. I grew dirty, thin and could not get the stink of horse and smoke out my dress, which by then had been stained all around the hem by mud and ordure.

One thing I didn't want was for my brother to think that I'd been alone in a world of terrible people and strange men. The tool merchant, a man named John was, I believe, a good man and there were others of his kind that I met along the way. Not many, granted, but enough. Looking back on it, I know that he probably didn't believe me when I told him my mother was sickly. I think he helped me anyway, because he could tell I needed him to.

*

The rain exhausted me. When it ended I spent days in wet boots, with wet socks and at night I could hardly sleep for discomfort. I continued to speak to Franklyn, out loud now, though I'd been alone for so long that my voice cracked when I tried to speak. I imagined him responding, telling me not to lose hope, but I couldn't make the words ring true.

I longed for the sound of another person in the tent, their breathing and movement, their life. For over a week I had felt no one's touch, not a handshake or a friendly embrace. More and more I found myself with my arms around my own body, seeking comfort.

The only good thing that came from the storm was drinking water and the knowledge that it would be the last rain I suffered out of doors. It spurred me to make myself the best home I could. When the rain cleared and the stifling heat returned, I started my work again.

I hammered scraps of wood around the frames to try and make them more level. I'd bought screens in town, and I took them and fitted them into the window frames, putting store-bought shutters on over them. They were all slightly crooked, but I made them fit as well as I could. With the aid of the schooner I was able to climb up high enough to lay poles, harvested from the creek beds, over the top of the house. Onto these I heaped freshly dried grass and covered it with sod. I wouldn't know if the roof was adequate until it rained again.

I wanted my brother to see it, to see me.

Inside, without a door, I lay down on my grass stuffed tick and closed my eyes. Not since I'd opened the kitchen door at Charles's house and looked out into the misty night had I felt such a sense of numbness and lightheaded fear. With the raising of the house I'd brought home to myself the knowledge that all my money was sunk into land that I couldn't farm, and a house that I was convinced would collapse in the next strong wind. My eyes stung under their lids, and I felt tears trail down my face. My heart beat in a panic.

Why, in Lord's name had I left that morning? Why had I not gone to my brother and at least tried to make him believe me when I told him how afraid I was? He would have seen it my eyes that it was no fancy on my part, and protected me. Even at that moment I could have been in his house with his wonderful wife, being cared for while Franklyn saw to it that I was provided for and free of Charles for good.

But instead I'd run away and was, for all the distance between us, still terrified of my husband.

Now I was lying in the middle of nowhere, in a building hardly fit for cows, with an aching back and dirty, torn nails, and a barn still to build, mustangs to feed, a wash to get on, food to cook, land to prepare. All life's work stretched out between me and the grave. I was so tired, all I could do was lay there and let the tears run.

A knock came, and I jerked upright, turning to the doorway, where Laura stood, her hand still raised to the empty doorframe.

"Sorry," as she stepped back into the light I saw the consternation on her face, "I only came to see how the inside looked and to help with the hinges."

I scrubbed the tears from my cheeks. How much more pride could I lose before I consigned myself to the gutter in sackcloth?

"I'm glad, I wanted to have a door up by tomorrow night." I stood up and bid my eyes to stop burning. "Would you show me how to go about making one?"

She stepped into the shadow of my shuttered hovel and looked around at the stove and the cupboards, and the walls, which I'd been so stupidly proud of only two weeks since, when I'd first raised them off the ground.

"I wouldn't mind a sit down, I can make a cup of tea, if you have some. Thomas has the girls, I'd appreciate a rest."

I noticed for the first time the sweat patches under her arms, the way wisps of her hair were caught on her damp throat.

"You've worked hard this morning," I went to the stove and started to pick chips from the bucket beside it. "Please, let me."

She sat on one of the boxes that I'd left on the floor to serve as chairs and I could feel her watching me as I struggled to set a fire, filled the kettle and set it to boil. "I take it William isn't at home."

"He's hunting, hopefully shooting some game since we're down a side of pork," she sighed, "I put it in brine but it already rotted through."

"Shame," I said, measuring tea and putting it in the little tin teapot I'd bought for myself.

"Well, means I can help you today."

"That's true."

While the water boiled she made me get out leather strips and a knife. There was a basket of scrap wood from the door and windows and she showed me the method of making holes in the wood, threading the leather in such as a way as to produce a hinge when the wood was secured to the doorframe.

I made the tea and strained it, pouring out two black cupfuls.

"You have to be the only man in Indian Territory with a teapot."

I flushed. "It was drilled into me that it makes the only tea worth drinking."

"That's true."

"I don't have milk I'm afraid, didn't think it would survive the trip."

"Oh, it's passable," she said dryly. "Sometimes I find myself dreaming of fresh milk, still warm, Or sweet butter, cream in my coffee...perhaps one summer William'll buy a cow. I'd settle for a goat."

"I confess, butter making would be beyond me, even with a bowl of cream set by."

She smiled a half-smile, "Then you should marry."

Her eyes wandered the walls of the soddie, the air around us was warm from the stove and it smelt of parched grass and earth and tea. "I imagine she'll be happy to have a house already built. Some days I wish William would've made the journey alone and been done with all this before we married."

"How do you do it?" I asked. "All the work, the unending work. I've fair killed myself setting up my house and it's still a board floor and a door away from habitability. Then there's wood to cut and the barn to build and hay to get in for my mustangs...how, how do you manage to keep on with it day after day?"

She gave me a strange look and for a moment I thought I'd pushed the bounds of my disguise too far. After a second's pause she set down her beaker of tea and laid a hand on my arm.

"When work is all there is between you and hunger, you find a way to get it done. Besides, sometimes you get a nice bit of butter on your bread, or a side of bacon, or a clean filled tick – and it reminds you why you work the way you do, to make them out of nothing."

I took her words seriously and after I'd seen her off on her way back to the house, through the waving grass that chirped with a full complement of insect life, I sat down and contemplated the hinge she'd made. When had I ever made something out of nothing? Only Charlie, and he had been taken away from me so quickly.

Fear surged in me as I thought of him, of his tiny, motionless body. It made my hands shake and I looked down at them, clenching the fingers tight. Once more I felt the dread of his approach, the rising of the hairs on my neck as if he stood behind me. Even thinking of the possibility had my heart beating out of my chest. Even death could not inspire such despair; Charles could do far worse things.

Chapter Twelve
Cecelia

At the end of my first month as a settler I had a home for myself and one for my mustangs, who I had named Edgar and Smythe, the last names of two girls I'd hated at school. My mood was crushed, for I'd seen in the building of things that my lot would be harder than just poking seeds into the ground and reaping succulent vegetables and ripe fruits. It was all very well to claim a piece of unsettled land from the savages, but keeping hold of it, farming it, looked a grave lot indeed. I began to understand why Deene was so prickly, he was on the knife edge of prosperity and going broke.

My home was a mess, there were dirty pans to wash, and laundry to do. For the first time I began to understand the sheer weight of Laura's work, and how Deene was a lucky man to have her to keep things neat at home.

It took me two days to set the place to rights and those two days were filled with failures. Firstly I burnt my hand heating washing water, then I chipped an enamel mug that I'd bought new. I gouged my dirt floor with the heavy wash tub and Laura came upon me as the soap I'd been mashing with water slipped out of my hands, bowl and all, to spill all down my trousers and onto the grass.

"For God's sake!" I kicked the wash tub. "How did she do it?" Our girl at home had been whipcord thin and as vacant as a darkened house, yet she had managed these tasks like the donkey going into Bethlehem, never faltering, always keeping on.

I heard Laura laugh and turned to catch her covering her mouth with her hand. I glared at her.

"I'm starting to think I was not made for this," I admitted.

"It'll come." She came over and picked up the bowl, "I was just coming across to see if you needed anything, with the house. But it looks good and finished."

"I wanted a puncheon floor," I admitted, thinking of those split logs underfoot, warm and solid and clean.

"Wants don't go far out here."

"Probably because they die of thirst."

Her smile was smaller, rueful. "While Will was hunting he met one of the men from town, heard some land on the other side of us has been claimed by a man from Texas. Jamison Neaps."

Another man to be wary of. It was the price I paid for not being able to move further west and cope with the solitude there. Outwardly I nodded my head in interest.

"Do they speak well of him?"

She considered. "They say he leaves a good farm behind him in Texas, managed by his brother, so he knows his business. He has a woman with him...a native woman."

"As a slave?"

She shook her head. "As his wife, common-law. A lot of men do it. I met a woman like that when we were coming from Ohio, wore dresses and cooked corncake the same as any white woman."

I was shocked, and in a moment I saw Laura take a small step back from me and smooth her sacking apron. She'd caught herself, I saw, because she realised she was gossiping with a man, and angry with herself for doing so.

"Better get back, Will's off getting wood for winter, but he'll be back soon."

"How are the children?"

She tipped her head a little to one side. "Well. Though Beth's gone sickly. Still, she's a tough thing."

I nodded. "Well, I hope she gets better soon."

Laura smiled, and we parted company. Just hearing another voice had lifted my spirits and to see a smile directed at me almost had me in tears. My talks with Franklyn had been less comforting since the building of the house. More often than not I ranted to him, asked him how he had missed my unhappiness, how could he have failed to see how much I hated and feared my husband? I knew, deep down, that he would side with Charles against me, a mere woman telling tales, and that made me feel lonelier than ever. I was glad Laura had come to call.

I did my washing with increased vigour, in a better mood for having seen a friendly face. Cutting wood was another job that I'd need to do before winter and there was no time like the present. I hitched up the mustangs, only making two mistakes with the harnesses, and drove them warily away from the soddie.

"To think Smythe, that I used to sit and read of an afternoon, under the arbour, with tea and warm scones." The horse twitched its ears but offered no comment.

Rocking on the hard seat of the schooner, dust trailing behind me, I rubbed a roughened hand over my sunburnt face. It was likely that I'd never wear a dress again, clean or otherwise. No woman would be allowed to own land and farm it herself. Besides, even in trousers I was afraid Charles would find me, I didn't have the courage to be myself again. The next person to see me as Cecelia would most likely be my undertaker.

It was a fair ride out to the creek bottoms, and once there I drove along beside the ravine until I found a broad ramp of earth that led down to the water. Having backed the mustangs down it gingerly, I took out my rifle and my new axe, and set about finding my first tree.

To call them trees was rather overstating them, they were more woody shrubs than full trees. I'd heard of the fires that gripped the prairie if but one fire or lantern was left unattended, eating up mile after mile of grass and homes and families. Perhaps those fires were the reason the trees were so small, if they'd grown to the top of the ravine, the fire would have taken them.

I'd envisioned myself felling a tree with a few hard blows. Evidently the muscle of my imagination was better developed than those of my body. It took me a hail of blows to get even halfway through a single trunk and once I'd caught my breath, begun again and finally felled the thing, there were branches to strip, and lengths to cut off, and then the whole lot had to be loaded into the schooner.

The horses whickered for their freedom but I ignored them. I'd had enough trouble getting them hitched to the schooner, I was not going to free them only to have a wolf come upon us. I wanted a chance of a swift escape.

I cut more wood, moving slower as my palms began to blister, and my back started to ache. Angry at my own weakness I put more energy into swinging the axe, and had a good pile of wood in the schooner by the time I had to admit defeat.

I sat down by the rear wheel, leaning my back against it, the rifle in my lap. What would it be like in the winter, I wondered, not speaking to anyone for months instead of days? I didn't want to think about it too much, the idea of it made me want to run straight back to town.

The scrub across the creek parted and before I could jump or make a sound, a deer had made its way to the creek. It was a large animal, not the first I'd seen, but the only one I'd been so close to. While Cecelia held her breath at its beauty, the part of James Clappe that resided in me said, 'shoot it you idiot, that's meat you'll need to survive'.

The rifle came up and I aimed. The deer glanced up, I fired.

It took me a while to drag the body through the creek and up into the schooner and by then the disgust I felt for its bleeding, warm corpse had faded a little through familiarity as it had fallen on me twice in the lifting. I knew nothing about skinning or gutting a deer or how to preserve its meat for winter without help. It would be wasted. Perhaps Laura would accept half of the meat in exchange for her help with the butchering.

As I drew the rocking schooner up by the Deene soddie, I saw that their wagon box was still absent; William hadn't yet returned from collecting his own wood. It was probable that he would have to chop a great number of trees, to cook and boil water for such a big family.

I climbed down from the seat just as Thomas came running from the house.

"Mr Clappe, Beth's sick."

"How bad is she?" I asked.

"It's the fever. She wasn't so bad this morning, but it's worse now." Thomas was pale and I guessed that he'd been sitting by his sister, feeling helpless and waiting for his father to return.

"Will?" Laura came to the door, her skirt wet on one side, with what I couldn't tell, "James! Beth's got the fever, she needs quinine but we never bought any."

Neither had I. It hadn't crossed my mind to bring back anything other than castor oil.

"I need to get her to town," Laura said, "Will has the wagon. He should've been back by now."

"Get her," I said, "Thomas, get the deer off the back of the schooner," I ran around and started flinging the wood onto the ground. "It's too heavy to go fast."

I couldn't see if Laura had gone for Beth, but Thomas was already dragging the deer away. I had most of the wood off when Laura returned, cradling Beth in her arms. I leapt from the back of the schooner and took Thomas by the arm.

"You take care of your sisters, make a start on that deer and your father will be home before you know it. You have a gun?"

He shook his head. "Just an axe."

Neither would be much use to him if danger came calling.

"I daren't leave the baby," Laura said and I saw for the first time how pale she was under her layer of dust.

"Go," I said and she ran back to the house to fetch Nora. I knew that if we were attacked by wolves or Indians I would hardly be able to protect myself, let alone Laura and her two children.

"Thomas, you're in charge until your father comes, understood?"

Laura came hurrying with the baby in a sling. She'd propped Beth on the seat in the schooner and now climbed up and put her arms around her, talking softly. I climbed up and took the reins.

90

As I turned the schooner and started in the direction of town, I dearly hoped that all four of us would return.

Chapter Thirteen

Laura

I should've been praying to God to spare my daughter, but all I could do was curse a bottle of whiskey that'd already been drunk up and pissed back into the ground. If it weren't for that whiskey or Rachel's damn gilded buttons, we could have afforded the quinine. I would've given up the cook stove and endured cooking in the lean-to and chilblains all through the winter if it would've spared my daughter.

James stopped the mustangs at his soddie and ran to get a bottle of castor oil, I dosed Beth with it as we started on our way to town. It would take hours to get there. I tried to remember what it'd been like for Will when he'd had the ague. There'd been the aches, the chills, and I cursed myself for not spotting it in Beth when she'd started crying from the cold. Her bowls were loose, purging the sickness.

Night was coming fast. James wasn't too good with horses, but he had his mustangs going as fast as he could. I wished we could have left the schooner behind and ridden, but I never would have been able to keep Beth stable, weak as she was.

That castor made her stomach worse but we couldn't stop. I made a napkin of my apron. The smell was enough to strip paint, but James didn't say a word.

"Shush now," I murmured to Nora as she wailed in hunger.

"You know," James said after long minutes of Nora's screaming, "it's so dark out here, I can hardly see you."

He was giving me a kind of promise that he wouldn't look and I took it gratefully, putting Nora to my breast and letting her suck. Beth was weak in my other arm, burning up with fever. Her lips were so very dry, like grasshopper wings.

Never had a journey taken so long. I swear we could have made it to Ohio twice in the time it took to reach town. No sooner had the schooner rolled to a stop outside the pharmacist's house than James leapt down to bang upon the door, shouting for the owner.

I carried Beth, Nora anchored to my chest. Beth was out like a drunk, her head resting on my shoulder, skin hot and dry as a bake stone. The door of the pharmacy opened, and a small man in a nightshirt appeared with a lamp. His face, angry at all the hubbub, changed when James told him about Beth. He motioned us inside.

"I've given her castor oil," I said, laying Beth on the table in a little room behind the shop. Around us were bottles and jars, a desk piled with books and papers.

"She'll need quinine, something to bring down the fever," the man shook his head, "I'll do what I can, but there's no doctor here you see."

The pharmacist, Greaves, roused his wife and together they gathered fresh rags to clean Beth and the medicines to administer. They made her a bed by the hearth in hopes of breaking her fever. It was all I could do to change her soiled napkin and hold her in my arms, my hand keeping a cool cloth on her face.

Mrs Greaves, her face pale and all her dark hair tangled with sleep, brought me bread and butter, but I couldn't eat it, couldn't do more than sip a cup of tea with my free hand. She sat beside me, her large thighs quaking beneath her nightgown as she lowed herself to the rug.

"Dear, it'll be alright, Arnold knows the fever, he nursed two of our own children through it when they were only small," she showed me pictures in a small brass locket, one of a stiff faced man, the other a small boy, with a halo of white-blond hair like cotton.

"But he…" I said, knowing from that old picture that the boy had never grown up, never sat for another photograph.

Mrs Greaves nodded sadly, "He's never lost a child to fever since Rupert. We were new to America then, he didn't know much about the medicine here, the herbs that grow. We were low on stocks, didn't have the supplies to treat our own sons. After Rupert died Arnold was desperate, rode to a trading post and begged some Indians for help. If they hadn't been the friendly sort Lord knows what might've happened. They helped him find what he needed to save John, my dear, and it's what'll save your little girl. Even now, my John's in New York State, apprenticed to a doctor."

I clasped her doughy hand in mine and for a moment, then Beth cried out at the pains in her legs and I went to rub them, trying to soothe her.

When William had suffered the ague and fever, he'd recovered from the worst of it soon enough, but the fever that had troubled him raged in Beth. Her whole body was dry and hot, wracked with shivers as the chills set in.

Mr Greaves kept her dosed with quinine, castor oil and a tea to help with the fever. His wife bathed her and helped cleaned up her mess. Through it all I couldn't leave her side.

At some point in that long night, James wrapped a blanket round my shoulders and sat with me. He didn't move save to freshen the rag which cooled Beth's head, or to bring me more tea, laced with brandy.

"Laura, perhaps you ought to get some sleep," Mrs Greaves said, laying a hand on my shoulder. She'd prepared a stack of clean rags and a basin of cool water to wash Beth with.

"I'm not so tired."

"I burnt myself out watching over my boys when there was nothing I could do. I know it's hard to turn your eyes from her for a minute, but I will take good care of her while you rest."

I shook my head. I had to watch her or who knew what would happen.

"Maybe just go outside for a moment," James suggested quietly, "get some air and wash your face, you'll feel better." He touched my hand. "It's something my mother used to say."

I needed to use the outhouse, still I hesitated.

"Mrs Greaves will come and get you if anything changes," James said firmly. "I need some air myself."

He stood and took my hand, helping me to my feet. My legs shook after sitting so long, crouched by the bed they'd made for Beth by the fire. I walked with him to the rear of the little room, through the door into the kitchen and out into the small garden beyond. I went straight to the little outhouse around back of the garden. When I came out, I went to the garden pump and washed my face with a handful of cold water. My eyes felt sandy and my dress was sticking to me.

James was sitting on a low stone wall by the pump.

"I'm so sorry this happened," he said. I could see the worry on his face. Too young to have whiskers grow over night. "I only wish I'd never gone to cut wood, that I might have been there when she was taken sick."

"It's not your job to be there," I said, my voice cracking from thirst. How long had it been since I'd had a cup of tea pressed on me? It felt like days.

"I feel as if it is," he said, "since I've been on the prairie...you've shown me such kindness, and your children...I feel as if I know them all. I would never have any harm come to them, if I could help it."

He was so earnest. I could see how young he was, thinking that what was happening to my little Beth was a rare thing. I'd lost children before, for no reason anyone could give me. I'd known other children bit by snakes and dead in a moment, or caught by all manner of illnesses. Travelling west we'd seen little graves as often as we saw motherless families.

I wished he'd never have to know. Never have to bury his own child, or his woman. Maybe that's why I reached for him, to hold back that sorrow. I put my arms around him, feeling the roughness of his coat under my hands, pressing my cheek to his smooth one.

For a moment he didn't move, but then, slowly, his arms lifted and went round me. I felt hot tears in my eyes, falling down my wet face as the weight of his arms made my heart hiccup. I couldn't remember the last time I'd been held.

For a moment I closed my eyes and let my chest squeeze with gratefulness. The sound of the kettle clanging onto the grate made us break apart, I hurried back to Beth's side without looking at him, feeling foolish.

Mrs Greaves had bathed Beth and laid her down again, with a fresh cloth on her forehead. Her fever was still high, her skin already dry again. I rubbed water on her lips and stroked her hair, sticky and dirty as it was. My poor little Beth, she could hardly open her eyes. Her little red mouth formed a word, and I had to lean closer to hear it.

"Pa," she whimpered, squeezed her eyes tightly shut, "want Pa."

"He's on his way Beth, well on his way by now," I soothed, rubbing her legs to dispel the cramps and aches that troubled her. If he did not arrive in the next hour, horses in a lather and dark circles beneath his eyes, I would never forgive him. Never.

Chapter Fourteen
Cecelia

Laura slept in the back of the schooner with my coat over her. Beth, curled up beside her, was still feverish, but Laura was determined not to wear out the Greaves's good will. As she'd made Beth comfortable in the schooner, I'd stood in the kitchen with Mrs Greaves, watching her put food and a full water skin into a sack.

"You're very kind," I said, knowing that the food would embarrass Laura, who was so set on a fair trade for everything and who didn't have any money with her to pay for the quinine and castor oil Beth had taken. I searched my pockets and found two dollars, it was luck that I had anything at all.

Mrs Greaves took the money with a silent nod and slipped a pouch of quinine into the sack along with the food.

"Do you think she'll recover soon?" I asked. I knew she'd given Laura her assurances, but if tragedy was coming for her, I wanted to do all I could to lessen its strength.

"There's no telling, but...I will pray for the child and she seems strong, though she will need good care, as will your wife."

Stymied, my hands accepted the sack she handed me. In the time it took me to find my tongue she left the room to see to her first customer of the day. Hot spots glowed on my cheeks and I found myself caught between laughter and horror.

After a long while of bumping over the ruts in the grass, I became aware of movement in the back of the schooner. Laura climbed up to sit beside me with Nora in the sling across her chest. Dark clouds had gathered on the horizon before us and the air was a cool breath that flattened the grasses and lifted the manes of my two mustangs.

"Looks like rain," Laura said, softly, so as not to wake the baby.

"Hopefully we'll be back before it hits."

We passed a moment in silence, and I sensed that she had something on her mind.

"I'm grateful to you, for getting Beth to town so quickly. I think they thought we were married, the way we all pitched up."

I made a noise at the back of my throat.

"I didn't mean to let her think that. She said it and I should've set her right. Though I didn't see the point." She twisted her rough hands up in her filthy apron and glared out towards the clouded horizon. "Felt almost nice, having a husband with me, rather than one doing all he can to stay away from home. I don't know why he hasn't come with Rachel and Thomas."

I didn't want to talk about the state of her marriage. Whether or not she was happy with William was no concern of mine. Tired and on edge from a night of keeping up my appearance as a man in front of strangers and worrying over the health of Laura's daughter, I was not inclined to be charitable. I wanted her out of my schooner and back in her own house.

"Are you angry at me?" she said sometime later, in a voice so soft and so unlike her own that I felt my temper waning.

"Just tired."

"I couldn't stand it if you were angry with me."

I glanced at her then and saw how tired she was, how bruised by the fear she had for her child and the disappointment in her husband. My heart of stone cracked a little and some kindness found a way to flow through. I thought of Charlie, of the sleepy weight of him in my arms. I wouldn't wish a loss like that on my worst enemy and there I was, blaming her for her husband's absence.

"I'm not angry," I said, "and I hope you don't think me forward when I say that I was glad to help out a neighbour, and a friend."

She moved across the wooden seat and after a moment rested her head on my shoulder. It was almost as if she were a lady in my parlour, and both of us, swathed in silk, were comforted by our closeness, our ability to rely on our friendship. With the reins in one hand, I put my arm around her, and smoothed her shoulder through the faded calico of her dress.

The feeling of familiarity lasted until we came to the soddie. The door to it opened and in its black maw I could see the faint spark of a lantern, and the shadow of William Deene's body against it. The sight of him pulled Laura from my side, and within that instant we were separated again by my deception.

I pulled the mustangs up and climbed down. By that time, Deene had come around the side of the schooner and was helping Laura from her seat. He went around to the back and lifted Beth from her bed, and she threw a feverish arm around his neck and whimpered. Deene's beetle black eyes met mine, and he gave me a nod, before spiriting his wife and daughters into the soddie.

Alone, I turned the schooner and headed back to my own house. Despite the difficulty of keeping my disguise around her, I hadn't wanted to see Laura go. I wished I could tell her, tell anyone, what it was that I'd left behind me, but the risk was just too great. Leaving her with Deene meant going back to my soddie alone, to the ringing silence. So absorbed was I in hating the quiet around me that I was almost at my door when I noticed that things were not as I had left them.

Firewood. The uneven lengths I'd cut myself down at the creek bed were stacked in a fairly well built pile against the side of the house. I stopped to examine it. My first thought was that Deene had brought it himself, but the pile was stunted, not the kind a grown man would build. With my hand on the rough surface of the pile, I remembered telling the children to stay inside the soddie until Laura or their father returned. Thomas had disobeyed her, perhaps Rachel too, though I doubted it. He must have carried the wood himself, making trip after trip to my home, to pile my wood against my house. I wondered what had happened to my deer, though if retrieving it meant speaking with Deene I'd prefer he kept it.

Not for the first time I wondered that Deene's son could be so much a gentleman, despite his father. I laid a hand on top of the rough pile and felt my heart break for Thomas' good soul and the waste of it under his father's disapproval. I ached so badly for my own little one that I could hardly see to close the door on the lonely night.

*

Mending my clothes gave me ample time to tell Franklyn of my journey west. I eased his mind by telling him how John was very proper about our arrangement. That while I slept in between his goods, he rested beneath the wagon and kept a watch. He even gave me a portion in his meals. The names of the places we passed meant nothing to me, so I seldom asked and didn't often remember when he told me where we were. Each town was much the same as the last, the same rough people and dusty buildings.

Fixing a hole in the knee of my trousers reminded me of the shameful day that I'd exchanged my dress for the rags I currently wore. I described the foulness of the woman I'd sold to and her wretched stall; the smell of old dust and slight damp, as though the clothes were piled into sacks in a shed when the customers went home of a night. Her clothes looked cobbled together from all the worst rags, more like a laundry pile than a garment anyone would wear.

Franklyn always had such trouble ordering dresses for me and Mother on our birthdays; I doubted he'd appreciate the fullness of the deception the seller had tried to play on me when she'd whistled through her brown teeth and offered me a simple trade, with no extra money from the sale of my dress and nightgown. However stained the hem, the dress was the height of fashion and well made from fine fabrics.

I didn't fall for her patter but though it was crushing at the time, I amused myself by impersonating her in my new home, imagining what Franklyn would make of her assessment of the very gown he'd bought for me that spring "I'm no fool Missus, cheap as chaff, that's what that is and as for the boots, they'll wear to nothing in a week, the leather's tanned uneven, sewn as if by a blind man. I'm giving you a very good deal even trading you, never mind you asking for more into the bargain."

She told me the men's castoffs were the last clothes I would need to buy. They were certainly the last ones I could afford.

After the harrowing trip to town with poor Laura and her youngest daughters, it was good to laugh with Franklyn about it all.

*

After a fairly restful night's sleep - I didn't think I'd ever sleep soundly on a grass filled tick - I found the work of ten men waiting for me. I thought that the wood stacked against the soddie could not possibly be enough for the winter, when I'd need a fire all day and extra fuel for washing and cooking. I'd have to go and cut more. There were no chips in the pail by the stove, so I had to make do with drinking cold water that had been in the jug since before my impromptu trip to town. The leftover cornbread I'd kept aside for breakfast had grown fur in my absence and something had chewed a hole in my sack of cornmeal, spilling it over the floor. I'd need to make a rack of some kind to hang my supplies on.

It was almost enough to drive me under my blanket and back into sleep. It was only the knowledge the no one would do the work for me that got me dressed and outside to tend to the mustangs.

There'd been rain during the night and the grasses all around were wet with it, bent and heavy. The air was full of the scent of wet straw and soaked dust, above, the sky seemed a thousand miles higher than before. Finally, a reprieve from the fierce heat.

The mustangs were not eager to be coaxed back into their harnesses and driven to the creek bed, but I urged them along. By the clear running stream, I left them to crop grass and took my axe from the schooner. Setting about a likely tree, I soon remembered why chopping wood had vexed me two days previously.

I had half a load and was soaking my hands in the stream to take the sting from my blisters, when I realised that I wasn't alone. The wet flick-flack of laundry being slapped against a rock downstream cut through the rush of water and grass. I went around a curve in the bank and found myself in the company of a stranger.

"Hello." I took in her wide, bare feet and calico dress as reassurance that she wasn't a threat, though she was clearly an Indian. She was older than Laura, engaged in beating a man's shirt against a rock, she paused to look at me from under dark brows.

"Morning," she said, voice heavy with a strange twang. "You're Mr Clappe?"

I nodded. "Are you - travelling - with Mr Neaps?"

She nodded her head. Her hair was down to her waist, loose and enviably dark. She was the first Indian I'd seen up close.

"I heard he was moving out here soon, has he come to build?"

She nodded. "Before it snows. We need a house, barn," she seemed unmoved, "many things."

"Your English is good, did he teach you?"

A head shake. "I taught me."

Remembering my manners was difficult, being by a creek with an Indian instead of seated in a parlour with ladies, but I tipped my hat. "James."

She made no similar gesture. "Martha."

"Did you choose that name?"

Again, her disinterest. "No."

There was nothing to say to that and I found her lack of warmth unsettling. "I'm sorry I interrupted you," I said, hating her a little for her blankness, which was almost hostile. She was the first woman I'd seen, other than Laura, for some time. I'd been hoping for other potential friends to help me through the winter and ease my loneliness. I'd not planned on the only other woman for miles to be a tight-lipped native in a hand-me-down dress. Perhaps Jamison was a friendly sort, like Franklyn, or the traders that had helped me reach the west.

"It's good to talk to someone new," she allowed, "I haven't spoken with anyone since he brought Mr Deene to our camp. Jamison likes me to stay in the wagon when we're in town."

Inwardly, I felt my hopes for my new neighbour dwindle. Another William Deene to contend with; possessive and suspicious.

"I haven't seen anyone for a while either," I said, "only the Deenes, my neighbours."

"I've only met the man. The night before last, he came back with Jamison. They were drinking, talking."

While Laura and I were struggling to get quinine and castor into his daughter.

"Well, I hope to make Mr Neaps' acquaintance soon."

She wrung out the shirt, her knuckles pale as she twisted it as hard as she could, the way I'd seen the kitchen girl wring a chicken's neck. I took it as my cue to return to my own business.

Once I had the schooner fairly filled with wood, I climbed up onto the seat and started the drive home, my hands so raw from the axe handle that I could scarce hold the reins. I was thinking about Martha, about what she thought of being 'wife' to Neaps, when I noticed a figure by my soddie. My first thought was of Charles and I felt my chest fill with dread, my heart pounding in a panic - but it was William Deene at my door, I recognised his coat. What could he want to see me about? Surely he wouldn't come in broad daylight to warn me away from his wife, he'd be too proud for that. I wondered if he'd been drinking.

I climbed down from the schooner, taking my rifle with me.

"Good afternoon Mr Deene."

"James," he nodded his head in greeting and as he'd used my first name, I allowed myself to relax a little.

"How's Beth fairing?"

"She's looking a mite better, still down with the fever though."

"I hope she gets better soon."

He nodded, stuck his hands in the pockets of his worn trousers and glanced at the soddie. I followed his sloe eyes and felt a small sliver of pride for what I'd accomplished in building my house all alone. No matter that one corner was already sporting a leak, which I thought could be fixed easily enough. I'd just have to find out how.

"It's a fine house," he said, as if following my thoughts, "better than I thought you'd build."

"You didn't think I'd be building here at all, once you'd seen me off."

"I did think perhaps I'd seen the last of you, no point denying that. You should know that when we made our deal, I had an honest intention of helping you build."

"You just decided later that it was more worth your while to squeeze a few days' work from me before leaving me to fend for myself." I was surprised by my anger, so long dormant, compressed by every hard task I had encountered on my own. As I'd piled sod on sod to build my shelter, I hadn't realised that I'd been building up a wall of resentment for him.

"My wife paid you off, in the end. I know that."

The jars of chokecherry jam and bars of strong brown soap she'd given me. "Your wife does more credit to you than your actions."

His mouth, so like his eldest daughter's, drew itself into a bloodless scar. "I've only come to tell you that the deer you left behind at my door is in the smoke shed, should be ready for you to come by and get it soon."

I looked on him without much trust, taking in as I did so his newly shaven face, trimmed up thatch of dark hair and the neatly mended elbow of his clean shirt. I could see Laura in each favourable addition to his appearance. This was her gesture, something she had forced him to do, whether intentionally or not.

"Let me know when it's ready and I'll come and fetch it."

He looked about ready to head back, but I stopped him out of a sense of duty. "I was about to put on some coffee, would you stay for a cup?"

He shook his head. "I've work to do."

I realised too late that the invitation was all wrong. When I'd practiced my mannerisms I'd modelled Mr Clappe on my brother for his strength and personable nature, but he was a higher class than Deene. A man like Deene would have proffered whiskey, tobacco, perhaps just a seat and a comment on the state of the harvest. As he walked away I wondered what Jamison had offered to get him to his fire side. Perhaps all three, and the lure of his exotic companion besides. The two were probably already allies and I would be the one left in the cold, save for Laura. How would I survive with only my imagination for company and nothing on the prairie to feed it?

Chapter Fifteen

Laura

Preparations for winter had me working from sun up 'til the very last part of the sky fell into blackness. William was in a frenzy hauling wood and shooting deer to smoke. Even at night he brought axe handles in to whittle. There wasn't a morning that didn't start with me sweeping a pile of wood curls up for the stove.

What with the days getting shorter and coming in colder, I was working on a pile of winter things for all of us. Sitting at the table with the kerosene lamp across from me I listened to the repeated scrape of Will's knife as he made a set of pegs to hold a shelf on the wall.

"Make sure you sew it on tightly now," I warned Rachel as she looped her thread through one of the gilt buttons Will had paid so dearly for. "You don't want it falling off and getting lost, we can use them on your new dress next year."

Her face was twisted up in concentration. "I'll make them the strongest buttons I've ever had. You won't even be able to cut them off with shears."

I smiled at her. For once, we were all at peace, Nora was sleeping peaceably, like a baby in a picture. Thomas was polishing a harness by the stove and Beth sat on her tick, practicing her stitches on a piece of rag. She'd recovered from her fever in the weeks since returning from town, but was still thin and weak.

It was at times like those that I missed music. Neither Will nor I owned or could play an instrument. It would have been lovely to hear a hymn or ditty played in the warmth of the soddie, to hearten us against the coming cold.

"Thomas, could you come here and try this shirt for me?" I asked, biting off a thread and checking the old shirt, one of Will's that I was making over.

He pulled off his own work shirt, buttoned the other on and moved his arms back and forth. "Plenty of room in it," he said.

"I wonder about the colour." It had been white, a good church shirt, but was now shades of grey all over, yellow under the arms. "Do you think we might dye it? Make it a nice plain brown? That'd be the thing."

Thomas took the shirt off and handed it back to me, "Thank you Ma."

I ruffled his hair and he ducked away, back to polishing the harness.

"Did you see Clappe's putting up a smoke house?" Will said, putting down his whittling to swig from a cup of coffee so full of molasses it was a wonder the spoon hadn't stuck fast in it.

"I did see him working at something the other day," I said, turning my eyes to the shirt I was folding. "A smoke house? Well, I suppose it's not too late yet to be thinking of some smoked venison later on. Maybe he got a taste for it after you put up that deer for him."

He took out his pipe and stuffed it with tobacco from his tin. "He's going about it wrong, going to have smoke coming right in that side window."

"I'm sure he'd take your say in the matter, you could go over there tomorrow and talk to him about it."

"He reckons he's too good for us, there's no way he'll take any advice of mine," Will muttered.

"I should think he'd welcome some advice. Seemed like he wanted to start fresh with us."

He glared from behind a screen of pipe smoke. "I didn't ask for your opinion on it."

I shut my mouth and pulled out a petticoat that wanted re-hemming. There was a point Will reached when he wouldn't take being pushed along anymore. He was like a mule, ready to bite. Having him take the news about the deer to James had been my idea, I'd hoped that they might bond better as neighbours, perhaps allow me to see more of my friend. But it looked as though I'd be spending the winter months sealed up in the soddie with Will.

"I've decided it's time we get a dog," William said after a while. Rachel was still sewing buttons, slowly and crookedly, but she looked up at this.

"Really Pa? Oh, can I name him?"

He ignored her, looked at me instead. "If you're going to bolt off and leave the children to fend for themselves, they'll need a good guard dog."

I bristled, but didn't jump at the bait. "It's a good idea. I've been meaning to ask for one since summer, what with you generally taking the rifle out with you."

With narrowed eyes he gestured for Rachel to come to him, lifted her to his knee when she abandoned her needlework and went.

"What kind of dog shall we get sweet pea?"

"Can he be a big, yellow dog, like Uncle Jacob's?"

I watched the playfulness harden on Will's face. He didn't like to be reminded of his brother, who had no need for a guard dog, but kept a few hounds for his own amusement.

"We'll have a real dog, not a plaything with fur," he chided her, "and he'll keep you all safe in the winter, when the wolves come howling." To me, over her shining hair he said, "Jamison's driving to town at the end of the week, he's intending to buy glass for his windows, said he'd take me in with him so I can find a good dog."

"You'll have to invite him back for dinner," I said, without much heart, I'd already figured that Jamison must be a man exactly like my husband to earn his ready respect.

"I might very well do that," he said. "He wanted you to have a go at teaching his girl to sew."

The thought of female company, even if it was with the squaw of a man I didn't much care for, filled me with excitement. "I could do a proper meal with dessert if we have the sugar to spare."

"I thought perhaps he'd agree to leave her with you while I'm in town," Will said, as I folded the edge of the petticoat into a new hem and started to sew. "Keep you from being worried while I'm gone."

"Maybe Mr Clappe would appreciate a trip to town with the two of you," I said, knowing he wanted me kept away from our neighbour and that he was using Jamison's woman to do just that. "You could ask him when you tell him his smoke house is going up in the wrong place."

He glared at me over Rachel's head, but said nothing else on the matter.

I mended the petticoat and he slid Rachel from his knee so as to finish his axe handle. I showed her which buttons would have to be unpicked and moved back into line. She didn't thank me for it.

It grew late. I bundled the needlework into my basket and settled the girls down to bed. In the darkness, with the lamp wick still aglow, I breathed in the scent of damp earth from the walls and hoped that I'd have another chance to see Clappe before winter came.

During the past few weeks I'd seen him from a distance as he hauled wood and stacked it around his house. I'd been guilty of remembering his arms around me. The moments I'd spent in his company were the best memories I had of the summer, save for the first time Nora offered me her gummy smile and the moment Beth's fever broke.

*

The next day William disappeared after breakfast, saying nothing, but heading in the direction of Clappe's soddie. I kept an ear open for gunshots.

Around midday I put out a meal of cold bean porridge and bread. Thomas had been mending the little fence around my garden and he was sitting by the door to the soddie, cutting a new post when Will came back.

"Thomas, finish that and go straight to Mr Clappe's. You're building his smoke house with him," William said, on his way to the food I'd laid out.

"You're sending Thomas to help him?"

"The man has less than a mule's understanding of building a good smoke house, Thomas can show him how it's done. I've neither the time, nor the patience," he scowled.

"It's very neighbourly of you," I said, wondering what had brought this on.

He started to heap a plate with beans. "Hardly matters now, there's nothing I need the boy for. Might as well have him do a good turn for a neighbour."

I knew Will, and there was precious little chance of him doing anything Christian out of the goodness of his heart. Somehow he was out to gain from Thomas's labour. I just couldn't see how.

"I'll be heading to town tomorrow," he said, watching Beth sleep on her tick, "does she need more quinine?"

"I believe we have enough for the moment."

He grunted. "At any rate, once that smoke house's built, I'll not owe him a thing for buying her medicine."

So that was it. He'd give James the free labour of his son, rather than part with the money he was no doubt saving for carousing with Neaps.

William spent the rest of the day putting up the new shelf in the soddie. It was almost dark by the time Thomas returned from Clappe's, he came through the door just as I was getting ready to send Will out for him.

"Thomas, you know better than to walk all this way in the dark."

He was taking off his boots. "Mr Clappe brought me back. He had his rifle."

I glanced at the door. "Did you ask him if he'd join us for dinner?"

"He said he had things to do at home, but that it was a kind offer."

William snorted.

I'd made venison stew and dished out bowls for everyone. The girls sat on their tick and Thomas rested on a crate brought up to the end of the table. It was too dark in the evenings now to eat outside.

"Did you get the smoke house finished?" Will asked.

"There's some things he needs to do for it, but he said thank you and that he wouldn't need to borrow me again," Thomas reported, turning to me he said, "Ma, he had me draw the smoke house in the back of a book, so he could look at it again. He has some old books he bought in town, and he can read all of them. He told me."

William scoffed. "He'll have plenty of time to read in winter when he's frozen to the floor of that trash heap he calls a house."

Thomas dampened his excitement and focused on his plate. I cast him a sympathetic look. "When it's too cold to get much done outside, I'll start teaching you your letters again," I promised, "you were doing well with it last winter."

His cheeks went pink with pride. I vowed that by the time spring came to the prairie, he'd be reading as well as me. Though Will could read some and work with figures like nothing else, he never understood my insistence that Rachel and Beth should also learn their letters, or even that Thomas should be able to read books unaided. Will's sisters hadn't learnt beyond studying the Bible, and mostly they'd spent their time in embroidery and chores, rather than in reading.

"I was thinking, next year, I should buy up a few hens and get us a cow. Fresh butter and cheese stored over winter would be a blessing," William said, scraping up the last of his stew.

"It would indeed," I said.

"Then again, odds are I'll be investing in some more land when the time comes around. Perhaps it'll have to wait another year."

I frowned. Rachel came to the table. "May I have some more?" she asked.

"There's a little left, be careful with the stove, and share with your sister," I returned my attention of Will, "what land?"

Will picked up a piece of bread and wiped off his bowl. "Well, the way I see it, Clappe can't keep that farm going on his own. Ploughing alone'll break him, he hasn't the strength for it. By late spring he'll be looking to be rid of his claim and sell everything on it so he can head off to town and get set up in some business or other."

I'd had the same kind of thoughts about James. He'd looked too green to survive, but I'd noticed a resolve under his cluelessness. He wouldn't take leaving the land lightly. I didn't appreciate William's words, the thought of losing my only friend made me waspish.

"He might surprise you," I said.

Will snorted. "You'll see. Come spring, he'll be long gone."

Chapter Sixteen

Cecelia

I was outside, attempting to whittle pegs for my newly built smoke house, when an unfamiliar wagon came rolling and jolting over the prairie. My first instinct was to rush into the house, to hide from what must surely be Charles or one of his men. Then I saw William Deene up on the wagon seat and realised that the bearded, stocky fellow beside him must be Jamison Neaps.

"Morning Clappe," Neaps called, "need a ride to town?"

Truthfully I did, as I'd had it in mind for a few days to get myself a guard dog; the wolf howls at night left me feeling nervous and vulnerable. Also, I felt a dog would at least bring life to the soddie, making me feel less alone and giving me something to talk to without fearing I was losing my mind. I could of course go to town alone, but the weather had started to turn and I was worried my mustangs would bolt in a storm, dragging the schooner with them.

"It's kind of you to offer and I graciously accept," I replied.

I could not mistake the way in which Neaps looked to Deene, who inclined his head as if to say, 'I told you, he talks like a man who doesn't know an acre from an acorn'. I ignored it and made quick work of shutting up my house, packing a few things and climbing up to the wagon seat beside Neaps.

"We'll be staying overnight, making camp on the edge of town, so's to start back tomorrow morning."

I nodded. I'd suspected that this would be the case, but as the wagon continued to jolt towards town I realised what an awkward thing it would be to pass a night with two men. I could only hope that they'd view my reluctance to relieve myself outside with them as some kind of eastern quirk.

Neaps drove carelessly, the wagon shook whenever it struck a hole under the grass. He had a bottle between his legs and took frequent nips from it, offering it to Deene and myself. I refused and again the two of them shared a look. I began to sweat, my body tense all over. They would soon become suspicious of me if I failed to convince them of my maleness. During my weeks alone I'd let the practice of walking, talking and eating like a man drop. I struggled to get back into the character of James Clappe, as if he were a coat I'd outgrown.

"I expect Martha's having a time of it, she's not been around many children," Jamison confided, "not since I met her anyway. I dare say she'll enjoy a bit of female company."

"I thought it'd do Laura some good, having a woman to talk to, I've no time to make sense of what she thinks the children ought to be doing. She's after teaching them all to read a whole book over winter."

Jamison hawked and spat between the rumps of the horses. "She'll be putting them in school next, there's your help in the fields gone."

"I'm lucky in that respect, no school around here. I'm hoping she'll be done with this foolishness by the time some do-gooder comes and sets one up."

I kept my mouth shut.

"Now, Martha," Jamison said, "she can speak English well enough even if she can't put pen to paper, but I shan't be bothering with the education if she gets herself a baby. T'would be a waste of time and effort."

The talk continued in this vein all the way to town, with brief intermissions, during which my travelling companions chomped pipe stems or got down to pass water unsteadily at the side of the wagon. It was the kind of talk I'd heard plenty of on my way west, in towns and from travellers encountered on the road. I kept my eyes on the grasses swaying in our path.

We arrived in town late in the afternoon. Jamison left the wagon by a sort of shed that offered chains for the safety of the horses. There were evidently thieves about everywhere.

"We ought to get something to eat and ask who's got dogs to sell," William said. Jamison nodded in agreement, "I can get my glass later on, store's not going anywhere."

"I'd appreciate some decent food," I said, trying to ape their enthusiasm.

Jamison nodded his agreement and the three of us set off for a little place that he'd been to on a previous visit; a timber building with clapboard and a few benches inside that offered food and beer. I had a plate of eggs with toasted bread and a cup of coffee, it was the first meal I hadn't had to cook for myself in months, my first eggs since leaving Ohio, and I enjoyed every mouthful.

We learnt that one of the store owners was selling off a litter of animals barely out of puppyhood. Jamison started his pipe off as we headed over to the store in question. I contributed nothing but nods to their conversation.

The dogs were mongrels. Four of them; brown and black creatures with hopeful faces and barks that cut the air as they circled their crude pen in excitement. We were around the back of the store and the owner, a stout man with a thick moustache and a clean apron over dirty clothes, was naming his price.

"They're hardly worth the trouble of drowning," William said.

"They're in demand, I had six more'n this only two days ago."

"I can't say I can see paying more than a dollar and for that I'll want the black fella in the back."

"He's the strongest of the litter," the storekeeper retorted, "he'll cost you double. The rest are hardly worth the dollar, but him, he's got the makings of a great guard dog."

"Then I'll take the pale one, for seventy-five," Deene said, triumphant.

The storekeeper narrowed his eyes. The palest dog, a light brown with a dark snout, was the smallest of the bunch, thin and short legged, but it was the one barking the loudest.

They shook on the deal and Deene handed over his money.

"And you, Sir?" the storekeeper tucked the coins into his apron pocket. His large, pink face was already showing signs of weariness, clearly he wanted to be rid of the three farmers with hardly a dollar to their names.

I cast my eye over the dogs. There was the black one and the thin fellow that Will was hauling out of the pen and inspecting. The two remaining animals were reddish brown and had curling hair on their throats. One had a white ear.

"That one," I pointed out the one with the white marking, "I'll take him. For seventy-five."

"That's a bitch," William said scornfully and Jamison laughed with him.

"It's no matter," I said, and offered my money to the storekeeper, "she'll do just fine."

*

Jamison bought his glass and we put it and the dogs into the wagon, using rope to keep the animals tethered.

Jamison leapt down from the wagon and hitched up his frayed trousers. "I think it's about time for a drink."

The saloon, a plank building with a dark interior and a sawdust covered floor, was just as appalling as it'd been when I first passed through. It smelt like spilled liquor, sweat and tobacco. It was early in the evening, hardly dark outside and there were only two other men in there with us.

"First round's on me," Jamison said, raising a hand for the barman, gesturing for three glasses. There were only a few bottles behind the bar and they were all identical. Choice was limited for the inhabitants of the town, but then, I knew that already.

William leant on the scarred table, watching the only women in the place, a pair of them holding up the bar. All the lamps were low, but I knew whores when I saw them, and their low, lace trimmed bodices spilling pale, liquid flesh were hardly a disguise.

The whiskey came in thick glasses, carried by the barman, his soot coloured moustaches dropping with sweat. It was warm in the saloon, a damp, corruptive heat. Jamison paid, and the barman went away without a word.

"To neighbours," Jamison said, downing his shot and exhaling in appreciation.

"To neighbours," I echoed, gulping my glass and coughing. It was like the stink of creosote, only in my mouth and burning my throat.

The two men laughed, and William clapped me on the back.

"Never had a proper drink," he took his whisky in one swallow, bared his teeth. "Did they not carry this vintage at your father's club?"

I glared at him, my eyes still wet. "Another."

He smiled nastily, waved for the barman.

The second shot was worse. As the glasses were refilled continuously, I gained a little control over my facial expression, keeping it blank as the awful liquor burnt a hole in my stomach.

"Oh she was ugly," William was saying, as I put my glass down for the tenth or twelfth time, "young though, and she had thighs like risen dough. She worked for my father, cleaned the fireplaces and polished all the brasses. I met her on the cinder path between the house and the river, she let me lay her in the grass and look under her skirts. After, I showed her mine - she said I might as well put it in."

Jamison laughed with him, laughter as dark and smutty as a lamp chimney.

"Mine was a friend of my sisters. I made her come into the cellar with me, in the dark. I put her hand on my prick and she petted it like she would any fine pony."

My head felt loose on my neck and my eyes were heavy. The heat of the whisky made my legs and stomach warm, but my hands cold. I wanted to sleep. I wanted to be sick.

"Clappe? Who was she, your first girl?" Jamison asked.

I blinked at him.

"He never has, look at him," William crowed, "he'd blush to see a woman's shoulder."

"Don't tease the lad," Jamison said, nudging William with a wink, "clearly he's one of those religious types."

"I'm no more religious than you," I found myself saying, my weightless head opening it's numb mouth and letting the words come. "I had a girl in Indiana."

"Oh really, and what did this fine woman look like?" Jamison asked.

My mouth moved without my consent, spilling words like wine from a cracked jug. "She was fair and good. Soft, though she was a hard worker with arms like thick rope. She came to my tent one night, crept in and begged me to take her with me. She lay with me and she would have come west too, only..." My mind, muddled with the picture of Laura crouched at the mouth of my tent, the stars bright behind her, stumbled. "Only she had a husband and child."

Jamison slapped me on the back. "It's a good story, even if it is a tall one."

William said nothing.

Fortunately, Jamison started looking to the whores in their corner and quickly forgot about his teasing of me.

"What would you say to some company tonight, eh Will?"

William followed his gaze and I watched him smirk. "Could be a cold night, wouldn't want to catch our deaths."

Jamison lifted a hand to the women and they came across, hips swishing, swirling their skirts. One was thin and pale haired, her exposed bosom topped with bones that stuck out like antlers under her skin. The other, fat and with threads of white in her dark hair, had fingers short and thick as the pipe she was sucking on.

"How much?" Jamison asked.

The women shared a look, and the thin one spoke. "Fifty cents, that's each go mind."

I was appalled. I'd heard on my way west that most saloon girls, though coarse and immodest in many cases, were not generally whores. They enticed men into the establishment and talked them into buying more drinks, as well as entertaining them with songs and dance. This saloon was clearly of the lowest sort. The whore had named a price lower than that of the bitch I'd bought as a second rate guard dog.

Jamison agreed to her terms, stood unsteadily and ushered them along with us as we left the saloon.

Our camp was to be on the grass not a hundred feet from where the wagon was secured. Jamison had the blonde and William took the pipe smoking woman. Not wanting to see what they were doing, I went to the wagon and sat on the backboard. Nearby, laid on the damp grass, I could just about see the moonlit shape of William Deene's buttocks, lifting and falling, luminous as toadstools. His grunts and the woman's piercing, 'hiheehiheehiheehi-hi-hi-hunh!' carried through the air.

I felt my dog nudge under my arm and patted it gently. I thought of Laura, and wondered if she knew what her husband did when he went to town alone. I wondered, did she care? Or was she just relieved to be left to her sewing and her children, where she could pretend she was a widow.

Chapter Seventeen
Laura

When Jamison brought his woman across to the soddie I felt a sinking in the stomach. She looked right through me when she climbed off the wagon. Will gave me a squeeze and told me to 'be good'. Then they were gone over to Clappe's, to take him off to town with them. I was glad Will had extended some neighbourly help to him, even if it was doubtless just to keep us from speaking while he was gone. I felt a little sorry for Clappe at the thought of Will and Jamison making sport of him and his manner.

Still, once they were gone I was stuck with silent Martha. For all the company she provided I could've put a bonnet on a stump.

Inside, I put Rachel to jarring the coffee I'd been parching. Thomas was fitting a blade to one of William's axe handles. Beth and Nora were sleeping, which only meant that I was given no excuse to put off teaching Martha to sew.

"How about some coffee?" I said.

She nodded and sat down at the table, looking about her with a tight, expressionless face. My heart was in my boots. I'd wanted some female company for as long as I cared to remember, some friendly talk and a smile. It seemed I wouldn't be getting it, but I determined to get the best of what was on offer. Silent suspicion was a change from silent anger.

I put on the pot and took out my work basket, fussing with the pieces of cloth I'd already cut for my new dress and the half knitted scarf I was working on. Once the coffee was ready I poured a cup for myself and one for Martha. Sitting opposite her, I saw that her hands were very clean, the nails short and scrubbed. She had the wrinkled fingers of a hard worker.

"I heard you need some help with sewing," I said.

She nodded, and took a bundle of cut out pieces from a sack she'd brought with her.

I puzzled through the pieces, saw she was in the process of making a shirt, using an old one as a pattern. Some pieces had been stitched, but clumsily, and the stitches were already coming apart.

"You want finer work on the thin cloth," I pointed to where it had ripped. "You can't pull the thread hard, you've got to keep it gentle and steady."

She was staring at the seam, not blinking. I wondered if she was offended by my 'lesson' or she just wished she'd been left by her own fireside in peace. I was quickly getting used to her silence and small expressions, I only hoped she'd get more at ease with me, else it would be a long stay for her.

"Why don't you try making a seam on another piece while I unpick this?"

I took the stitches out carefully, not wanting to cut the thread to pieces and waste it.

"Ma, can I have some scraps for Pudding?" Rachel asked. Pudding was a ragdoll she was making, in need of drawers and eyes, as well as some hair and an overall wash.

"Once you've put the last of the buttons on your new dress."

"But I've already sewn them on, you took them off."

"That's because they weren't put on straight, once they're sewn on right, you can have a scrap to make Pudding a matching dress."

With a huff that put the woes of the rest of the world to shame, Rachel went to fetch her little work box.

"Little girls, harder to corral than cats," I remarked.

Martha's mouth hitched up, like it wanted to smile but couldn't remember how. I watched her blunt, fingers as she struggled to sew straight lines of tiny stitches. Two of the fingers on her right hand were crooked, clearly broken once and poorly set. The off shape of her index and middle finger meant that she was forever catching herself with the needle.

I reached across and took it from her hand. "You can hold it like this," I showed her, holding the needle between my thumb and my ring finger, "with practice it won't even feel strange."

For the first time her eyes met mine, knowing.

"I've had my share of cuts and scrapes that made it hard to sew, but the work couldn't wait."

She took her hands from mine, holding the needle and making motions with it, practicing a stitch in the air.

"Was it your husband, giving you 'cuts and scrapes'?" she said. Her first words to me.

"No," I glanced at Rachel and Thomas, both of them lost in their work, still, I lowered my voice. "Did Jamison do that to your hand?"

She shook her head. "Someone else, a long time ago."

"I'm sorry."

She ducked her head as if it didn't matter.

"Is he...kind?" I asked, and even as the words left my mouth I knew I'd stepped over a line.

Her face didn't change. She only picked up the pieces of the shirt and tried a stitch with her new grip. "He doesn't hit me."

She sewed, I finished unravelling her earlier work and picked up my knitting. She had a whole sleeve done and I was casting off on the scarf I'd made for Thomas when she spoke again.

"You and Clappe are stepping out?"

She'd kept her voice barely a whisper, but I froze, my eyes darting to hers. I'd done nothing but I was already guilty. I knew that. Guilty of wanting.

"Your husband doesn't like him," she continued, "said to Jamison that he acts better than he is. Seemed as though he had reason to be acting jealous."

"I'm faithful," I said shortly.

She looked at me, into me. "Jamison told me he'd kill me if he caught me making a fool of him. He's like your husband."

My body was cold.

"I don't mean to frighten you," she said, "only, your husband is a suspicious man, and what with you being the only lady that's been decent to me since I came here, I wouldn't want you in trouble."

My throat was tight, I realised that her rudeness had been a kind of defence against any scorn from me.

"I'm not a lady," I said finally, "I'd say we're just about even."

"Barefoot prairie wives," she said hollowly.

I nodded.

"You lost a stitch," she said, pointing out the mistake I'd made in my distraction.

"I can fix it."

It was hard to be comfortable with her in the house. I knew she was just like me, tied to the fate of the man she was with, but there was a difference to her that made me sad. I knew little about the Indians, only the massacres and skirmishes that reached us as news; scalping, burnt farms, stolen horses, children sold to Mexicans down south. William said she was Osage, which meant nothing to me. Sitting in front of me, wearing a plain calico dress, white bonnet strings bright against her dark skin, was my first Indian. I tried to imagine her in skins, with beads sewn to her clothes and knotted in her hair. It was as hard as imagining a lamppost on the prairie. It seemed wrong to me that she was so far from her people and their ways.

"Do you miss your family?" I asked, after a while.

"I haven't seen them since I was very young." She bit the end from the thread and picked it from her straight, white teeth. "Do you miss yours?"

"Not often." It was true. Only sometimes, when I was half dead with tiredness, feeling my eyes grow wet, knowing there were a hundred things I'd get the sharp edge of Will's tongue for leaving undone, I felt myself wish for my girlhood. Wishes were hard to hold onto on the prairie, they took to the wind like feathers.

We worked until she'd pricked her fingers too many times to keep her patience. By then I'd laid aside my finished scarf and boiled up a bean porridge. I woke Beth and gave her a small bowl, which she almost manage to finish. After dinner, Martha made me a gift of a berry pie, which she'd baked specially. I could see in her face the shy pride she took in it, and knew that had I been rude or unkind to her, she would still have presented me with it. I was glad to have earned the kindness fairly.

While we ate the pie I decided that I liked her.

As the night began to draw in, my mind turned to what the men were getting up to in town. I dearly hoped that Will would remember to get us a dog before he went to the saloon to lighten his pockets.

I suppose there are some women who spend their lives wondering if their husband is unfaithful. They might lie awake, alone at night and picture their husbands in the arms of neighbour women, servants, whores. All their lives, wondering, until their husband passed away, or they did, and all that fretting died with them.

Will had been using whores since before I married him. I knew, because after we were married he used to come home drunk and talkative. He'd climb into bed, smelling of beer and tell me about the woman he'd fucked before coming to bed with me. Back then it had horrified me, I'd often left the bed to go and sit by the fire in the kitchen.

Gradually he wore away my sensibilities, that, or I'd simply became too tired to give up my bed.

Since we'd been in Indian Territory he'd had little chance to indulge his habit. I knew though that, when he went to town alone, he took more money with him than he needed and never came back with goods to account for the balance. As soon as he'd put the idea to me, of his going off to town with Jamison, I knew he'd be stopping at the saloon.

My thinking was - better some whore than me. Let her carry his next child. Let him spend himself elsewhere, even if he spent our money in the process.

It was Martha who spoke about it first, after Thomas had gone to feed and water the oxen with Rachel. Beth was sleeping and I had Nora at my breast. We hadn't lit the lamp, the fire from the stove provided some light. I was surprised to find myself smiling.

"I suppose they've got to drinking," she said, plaiting three lengths of rag with her quick fingers.

"It's likely."

She shook her head slowly, "Jamison's one for saloon girls, and for the whores. I wonder that he comes back from town with any money at all."

I was poking wicking into candle moulds, so they'd be ready to fill in the morning, my arms a careful circle around Nora. "I wonder that about William too. Though with what we earnt this year, I don't know what kind of woman would offer more than a handshake for it."

"I don't think I've met a man that wouldn't spend his last cent on a woman."

I tipped my head to one side, struggling with the sharp tin where the holes were punched into the mould. "My father wouldn't. I never knew him to be away from the house overnight unaccompanied. For business he would take Mother along and leave us with his sister."

"Perhaps it's only the men out here," Martha allowed. She paused, as if considering, and I believe she read my mind, for she said, "Mr Clappe, he doesn't seem the sort for whores. Is he a drinker?"

"Not that I've seen."

"And he has no woman?"

"No. Though he's been to town, and he spoke of leaving things in Ohio that he could not replace. Perhaps he had a girl there but couldn't marry her." The thought made me ache, the way I'd ached for separated lovers in the stories my aunt had shared with me on the nights she took care of us.

"He looks like someone who would marry well," Martha said, "not a working man."

"I expect his family were rich, maybe it was a scandal that stopped him."

Her eyes were shrewd. "You've thought about it."

"There's little enough to think about out here. Good gossip is hard to come by." I could feel a flush creeping up my neck.

"I imagine I'm the source of most of it at the moment."

I nodded without thinking, putting aside the mould.

Martha said nothing else about it. Once the fire'd burnt too low to see by she went behind the screen to change for bed. I settled the children and undressed to my shift. We shared mine and Will's tick. She smelt like smoke and sweat, gave off a soft heat that warmed the bed.

"What kind of scandal?" she said, after a while.

"He has a sister, he said she had a bad husband. Maybe she got into trouble, shamed his family. Maybe he got a girl in trouble himself, though I doubt it, he seems...innocent. Of women at least."

She sniffed, thinking. "I suppose he'll be married before we're into winter. A long courtship out here is barely ten days."

She was right. The shortage of women meant that there was fierce competition for any daughters or widows. I thought of Rachel, sleeping only a few yards away. Would she marry a good man, or would she marry someone like Jamison; a man four times her age with land to work and no patience for her disobedient nature? I thought of her, all grown, marrying James, and tasted jealousy as bitter as a nettle leaf.

We slept, and I slept very soundly. Martha was good company, quiet and still. For the first time in a long time I let my guard down enough to rest and didn't wake until the sun was well up. Opening my eyes to the far side of dawn, with the smell of coffee rising from the stove, was the nicest thing I'd woken to in quite some time.

After breakfast I fed Nora and Martha took Rachel and Beth's interest by showing them how to turn a long braid of rags into a mat. Thomas and I went outside to feed the oxen.

I was scattering hay into their feed box when I turned my head and caught him looking at me. It was just a look, in the shadow of the murky barn, but it cut through me. I straightened, dropping the last of the hay.

"Ma..." he stopped there.

"Mmm?"

"Why were you talking about Mr Clappe last night?"

"Women's gossip."

He scraped a little straw up with his fork and shook it to get the clean bedding off of the shit, which he dropped into a bucket.

"Pa said you were sweet on him."

I would gladly have taken a thorough beating if it would have kept the secret of me and Jacob safe from my son. The shame of it made my face burn, and my hands shook as I tried to appear unmoved.

"Your father was drunk, and when men drink they sometimes say horrible things that they don't mean," I said, smoothing my skirt and clenching my fists to keep my hands still. "He was very sorry later, for what he'd said."

Thomas wasn't looking at me anymore, and I was glad, because the confusion and worry on his face made me feel like I'd been dropped into the well.

"I don't ever want to drink then," he said.

"That's very wise of you," I said, feeling my chest getting all bound up. He was so sweet, and kind, my little boy. I wanted to keep him with me always, to remind me that there was good in the world, even in Indian Territory, where it seemed only the bad ever stuck around, braving the wind.

Outside, I rested against the wall of the barn and closed my eyes to the sun, letting the chill morning wind scour my face. I would not let my son turn into his father. I had to save Rachel from my fate, and make sure that Thomas became a good husband, a good father. Though I'd lost all my tenderness, all my rosy youth, I would tend theirs closely. They would not grow up twisted and dried out in our sod shack. They would have timber homes and warm clothes and money enough that they could buy whatever they needed. Beth and Nora too.

I opened my eyes and looked out to the horizon, many, many miles away. The air was thick with the scent of ox and shit, the grass singing in the wind, a song edged with the hysteria of a coming storm.

It was fine to dream, though I barely remembered how, but what could I do for my children? Rachel would marry who William approved of, Thomas would help him on the farm until he found a local girl and began to farm himself.

All I could do was love them, and, if I was honest with myself, there were times when I couldn't even do that.

Chapter Eighteen

Laura

The men arrived that evening, just after Martha and I collected the freshly washed and dried clothes from outside. The wagon appeared on the horizon like a ship and Rachel went outside to watch it rock and ramble closer. It stopped at Clappe's soddie and I saw him jump down and make his way to the door.

Martha piled her work into her sewing sack and tucked the clean pie plate on top.

"It was good to have company," she said, as we watched the wagon draw nearer.

"You should come again. Both of you," I said, knowing that Jamison, if he was anything like Will, looked down on visiting as a waste of valuable time.

"Maybe we will."

When the wagon stopped at the house, William leapt down and a pale brown dog followed him. Rachel made a beeline for it and chased the poor thing around until it lay down flat in the grass and growled.

"Rachel," William said, a growl of his own. She came and hugged him around the middle.

"What's his name Pa?"

"You'll have to think of one," he said.

"Martha," Jamison said, "time to get home, horses need a rest."

Martha climbed up onto the wagon and soon Jamison had the horses turned and they were on their way back to their camp.

"I said I'd be over to help him get that soddie up before it starts to get cold," William said, heading into the house, "Lord, what a mess."

I felt my shoulders tense up. William's idea of mess was a few tangled blankets on the beds and used cups on the table. Perhaps it was because it was me who did all the tidying and cleaning, but it was a mess I could live with. Now he was back what he said went.

"So you're going to help him build?" I asked, taking the cups to one side and stooping to bundle up the bedding.

He caught my tone. "Don't go making it like that. I owe Jamison, he paid for some drinks in town and gave me the ride, of course I'm going to help him."

I knew it wouldn't have been a few drinks, but chose not to mention Clappe and the bargain Will had made and broken with him. You don't taunt a sore headed bear.

"Get some coffee on," he said, sitting down at the table and using the bootjack to tackle his dusty boots.

I put the pot on and glanced out the door to where Beth, Rachel and Thomas were all sitting around the dog.

"Be careful you don't get nipped," I called.

"Don't worry Ma," Rachel answered, "he's not going to bite us, are you, Stick?"

Rachel and her knack for naming things sometimes put me in mind of my unfortunate grandchildren. What horrors of baptism would she visit on the heads of her children? At least 'Pudding' and 'Stick' were taken.

I sat down at the table opposite William.

"Any news from town?"

He shook his head. "Nothing much. Indians still giving trouble, some Catholics've started work on a farm about twenty miles from town and there's a worry more'll join them." He leant on the table, making it tip his way, observing me. "It was quite a busy night, at the saloon. Lots of people passing through town."

"I'm glad you had plenty of men to talk to."

"Oh, weren't short on company," he said, rubbing a hand over his unshaven face, "Clappe in particular. I'll say I was wrong about him. I thought he might be a little, you know, light footed, but he's got a way with the girls. Didn't seem shy about bringing one back to camp either."

I kept my face blank. I'd had a lot of practice. He wanted me to be offended, to feel, what? Betrayed? Disappointed? I was annoyed that I did feel something, a twisted, horrible knot in my gut. I felt everything he'd wanted me to feel and something else; envy.

"How was entertaining the Indian?" he asked, still watching me closely.

"Fine." I went to the stove to pour the coffee. "We had a good talk, got on with some of her sewing. She's not half bad at it, considering."

"Considering?"

"Her fingers. Two were broken and set wrong, or not at all. She said it was before she came to Jamison."

He grunted. "Doesn't surprise me. He told me she was on her own when he found her, she probably got caught stealing."

I said nothing to that.

*

That night, once the children were sleeping and Stick was curled up in front of the door, William rolled over and pushed up my nightgown. As he climbed on top of me, I surprised myself by putting my hands on his shoulders.

There was a moment of silence. I looked into his black, gleaming eyes and he looked into mine. I don't know what he saw there, I didn't know myself what I was feeling.

"Did you go with a woman?" I said.

He looked down on me without saying a word.

After a moment I let my arms drop and he pushed my legs apart. While he worked I thought about Jacob, about the moment of pure, bodily bliss he'd given me against the wall. For months before that I'd felt like more of a farmhand than a woman. I'd been packing and carrying baggage on our journey, taking orders from Will from before dawn to nightfall. All I had in front of me were more years of being a worker, a wife, a mother – not a woman. Being with Jacob was crude; the stickiness, the sweat, his breath, the slow drip of escaping liquid between my legs. I could hardly remember the feeling itself, what people called pleasure.

Clappe entered my mind, I couldn't find the will to make him leave. Would he be different? Kinder, loving? I thought of him on top of me, how he'd touch me, as though I was something expensive and sweet, to be savoured. His skin looked so soft. I knew that's how his hands would feel on my arms, my chest, brushing against my thighs. I knew he'd whisper things that would kindle a fire in my tired heart. He would hold me, afterwards. His red hair on my bosom, damp and curling. Under the sheets though, wouldn't he feel the same as Will, as Jacob? Wouldn't it always feel like this?

I told myself I didn't believe Will and what he'd said about the girl in town, but what if it was true? What if he was the same as Will, only younger? Less bitter?

William reached his peak, clutched at me, one hand gripping my breast, movements growing ever shallower, until he let out a breath and rolled away.

A silence stretched between us, then the thing that had brought my hands to his shoulders, crawled into my throat and said; "Do they like it, the town girls?"

Whether he was really asleep or not, I don't know. He didn't hit me when he was sober, though there was a first time for everything, God knows what I said was almost a blasphemy against him, against our marriage.

But he did nothing and after a few minutes, I forgot to be afraid.

Lying there, I wondered what Clappe was doing in his soddie. That small home where there was no one to hurt him and, God forgive me, no children. No smell of shit that clung to the walls no matter how fresh the napkin on Nora was. No sound of snoring or coughing. Nothing but his bed and his leisure.

I wondered if he'd wanted a girl. Will'd said he had one but Clappe seemed too bashful to me to even talk to a saloon woman. He had a sweetness to him, like he wouldn't think to pay for it. I wondered if he'd ever known a woman. Surely he must have? How long had it been since he'd known the touch of a girl or shared her bed? I couldn't picture Will going without for long, for him it was like his tobacco or throwing back his whiskey, a reward for working the land and putting up with me and children.

Just on the edge of sleep, in the space where it was possible to forget how plain I was, I wondered what he would do if he opened his door and saw me in my nightgown, under the moonlight? With him, would I like it? And after, would it be like sleeping beside Martha, so calm and restful that I'd wake up and not curse the sun for rising?

Chapter Nineteen
Cecelia

The day of our return from town I had such a headache that I hardly spoke. The liquor, the lack of sleep and the early start had sheared away my layers of previously gained strength. I was a young woman again, clinging to the rocking wagon, trying to hold myself together.

I vowed to myself that I would never again touch alcohol.

The dog, when I lifted her from the wagon and took her inside, proved to be disobedient and excitable. She sniffed every corner of the soddie, then jumped onto my tick and sat down.

"You needn't think you're sleeping there, Missy."

From then on, she had her name.

The trip into town had a lasting effect on me. I'd seen the private world of men and it had surprised and worried me. The image of Deene with his whore kept creeping into my thoughts when I least expected it. At night it slipped into my thoughts more often than the images of Charlie; though it brought me no less pain. It was rarely the face of the saloon girl that I saw under Deene's heaving body. It was almost always Laura.

I don't know why it brought me so much horror, to see her held under his large body, to see hands with dark hair growing on them paw at her bosom. Even in my mind the image appalled me. Sometimes she was calling for help. Sometimes she made the noises of delight that had carried from the whore's mouth to my drunken ears.

Sitting outside one morning, a week after returning from town, I saw Deene setting off for Jamison's camp. I watched him going into the distance, disappearing into the waving, crisp grasses. Their hiss and whistle washed over me as I looked to the shape of the Deene house and sipped my morning coffee, watching Laura's laundry wave like a string of handkerchiefs.

Whether it was a longing for female company following the visit to town, or a little worry over how she was getting on, I couldn't help myself wishing for an excuse to call on her, but I didn't know how I would look her in the eye after those dreams. There was also the threat of Deene returning to consider. Better to leave her alone.

At around noon though, I gave up on trying to distract myself. I'd been watching the soddie all morning, and I knew I would keep watching until he returned, then curse myself for not visiting when I could have.

"Missy," I called and after a few long moments she left the grass by the side of the woodpile and came to me.

I took my rifle and we headed across the grass. I'd already realised, after our few brief days together, that Missy would never be a guard dog. She was to be a pet; a source of company for the lonely winter. Perhaps I'd known that even as I'd handed over the money for her. Did that make me nothing more than the silly city dweller Deene knew me to be? I suppose so, but she gladdened me on the two mile walk all the same.

The little girl, Rachel, was outside when I reached the soddie. She was peeling potatoes, dropping neat curls of skin, like snakes, into the bucket at her feet.

"Morning," I said, as Missy snuffled forwards and tried eating a stray potato peeling from the ground, "is your mother about?"

She nodded. "In the barn."

"Everyone else inside?"

"Pa's with Mr Jamison, helping him to build his house." She gave me a look with her dark eyes, so like those of her father that I felt his dislike coming through them.

"And your brother?"

"He's cleaning the stove."

"Ahh," I tried to remember the kinds of things I'd said to the sweet little girls that belonged to the wives of Charles' business associates. "You know, your new dog is the brother of mine. This is Missy."

Again, that sloe eyed glare. If I'd been raised on the prairie, I might have lost my interest in manners too. "I'll go see your mother then."

The little sod barn looked more like a hill every time I saw it. On top the grass was about a foot tall, and the recent rain had bent it over and rounded out the edges of the roof. I pushed open the door and baulked at the smell of ox and dung.

"Laura?"

My eyes adjusted to the shadows and I saw her, sitting on a pile of straw in the corner. She looked up at me as if I'd caught her thieving, when she moved the pale tracks of tears on her face caught the light.

I let the door swing shut and shuffled over the straw scattered floor, then knelt and took her hand.

"What is it? What's happened?"

She shook her head, mute with tears. Without thinking I put my arms around her and pulled her against my chest so her head rested in the hollow of my shoulder. I felt the dampness spreading on my shirt and her thin back shuddered under my patting hands. I made the shushing sounds I'd made for Charlie, as my mother had once made for me. After a few moments she became calmer and I rocked slightly, listening to her gulp in breaths and let out dry sobs.

She lifted herself from my arms and I reluctantly let her go.

Laura wiped her face on her sleeve.

"Lord, what a stupid mess," she said, voice cracking, "you'd best go help yourself to something inside while I clean up."

"I will do no such thing, tell me what brought this on."

She shook her head. "Nothing. Nothing at all, just a woman being foolish."

"Laura," I laid my hands on her elbows, rubbed the coarse fabric of her dress. "You can tell me."

She looked me in the eye, finally. "It's nothing."

I fixed her with a firm look. "I will not be leaving this barn until you tell me what has brought you so low. I'll not leave you to cry in the dark by yourself. Is it Beth, is she sickly again?"

She looked away, shook her head slightly.

"Will?"

She didn't move.

"Has he done something, hurt you?"

"He only," she said, and stopped, as if surprised that she'd said anything.

"Tell me, it's alright."

"He only slapped me. He's done worse. Just…he was sober as a judge and he's never done that before without a drink or two in him. I thought not having the whisky would be enough to stop him doing worse than yelling."

I didn't know what to say. I'd offered to protect her once, when I'd seen that first bruise on her face, but now I knew more and wasn't fool enough to believe I could save her from her marriage. I'd barely escaped mine, and I still had nightmares of Charles shaking me awake and dragging me out to a carriage with bars on the windows.

"Winter's coming now," she said. "All those months of snow and the wind howling and less and less to eat, to talk about. I counted on being cut off to keep him from drinking, but now he doesn't need the drink to get mean. What if he starts on them next? The children?"

She seemed to recover herself, enough that a splinter of anger worked its way into her voice. "You were in town with them, you know what he did there. He spent every last cent he took with him and now he blames me for the loss. He's angry all the time."

"You deserve better than him," I said. Or maybe it was the spectre of James Clappe, the figment I'd invented finally taking voice.

"I don't think anyone gets what they deserve," she shook her head, "unless I did something so bad...God, listen to me. You know I helped build this place? Helped rake it out of the dirt? I am not some little girl with a hope chest and frilly skirts. I just...I've gotten so tired. It's like I see all the days ahead, just one long life, no joy, no hope."

I thought of all the times I'd watched her working, cooking, or just walking in the long grasses. How she'd looked like a woman born from the earth itself, rather than chained to it, covered in it. Buried alive under the grass and sod and the wide, dry, sky.

I put my arms around her. She wasn't alone, I knew the fear of loneliness, of being trapped in someone else's life, tied to them. She turned her face against my throat and I squeezed her gently. It was the first time I'd had the comfort of touch in months.

When she lifted her head and kissed me, I gasped against her mouth. I was overflowing with loneliness, all the pain I thought I'd left scattered across the country was born again in my chest. I clung to her and she to me.

My mouth moved with hers, soft and warm, for only a moment, before she pulled away and covered her lips with her hand.

"Oh God," she squeezed her eyes closed.

It was over so suddenly that it might have been all in my mind, only the tingling in my lips, the heat in my face, assured me that it had been real. She had kissed me. I had kissed her back.

"It's nothing," I said, moving back and getting to my feet. I had to get away. "Don't trouble yourself over it."

Laura stood, straw clinging to her dress. My arms remembered the softness of her, and the comforting smell of skin and cotton, dough and smoke, still lingered in my nose. My admiration and interest in her mixed up with something else. Something I'd felt once before, in the garden behind the pharmacist's small house.

"James, I'm sorry. I just want..."

"You're married," I interrupted her, as she came forward. "Married and a mother."

She looked down, cowed.

"You deserve better than him, but you are his wife, and you shouldn't cheapen yourself by indulging in adultery. I won't help you. This was a mistake and one I hope we can put behind us." The worlds tumbled out in a rush and I turned for the door, opening it to let the light flow in. "Goodbye Laura."

"You're wrong," she said suddenly, taking a few steps towards me and catching the door with her own hand. "I made all my mistakes years ago, and this, this was no mistake. I've seen you look at me," she said, almost gently, "since you arrived, all you've done is look at me. And the way you talk to me, the way you held me while Beth..." she took a breath, and I saw her strength returning. "It is your mistake if you walk away from me, because you want me as much as I want you."

I let go of the door and fairly stumbled into the light. Missy, who'd been snuffling in the grass, came to me, then trailed off in the direction of home. I followed, my feet hardly feeling the ground, certain that the burn on the back of my neck was the product of Laura's eyes, watching my every step.

Back in my soddie I sat on the packing box I'd left in one corner as a chair. I wanted to scrub the feel of her lips from mine, but no matter how many times I rubbed my sleeve over them, her touch remained. The imprint of her body was on mine.

I had let her get too close. I had forgotten the point of my presence in Indian Territory; I was there to hide and live out my life away from Charles. To do that I had to keep up the pretence of James Clappe, which meant I would never again have female friends. I had been a fool to think that Laura could fill that gap in my life. She saw me as the man I pretended to be, and unknowingly I'd tempted her into a desperate advance. No, I could not let that happen again.

For the rest of the day I forced myself to concentrate on sewing myself a new shirt. Soon, God willing, winter would lock up the land and provide the perfect barrier to Laura's company. By spring, she would have lost the impulse to betray her marriage, I was sure.

Still, as I undressed and laid down to sleep, I remembered the desperation on her tear-streaked face. My heart shivered for her, but I couldn't do anything about it. I had my own life to protect, I could not take responsibility for hers. If she wanted to run from William, she would have to do it herself. I squashed the part of me that knew it wasn't that easy. Not for her, with her children.

Still, I did not sleep.

Chapter Twenty
Laura

William got Jamison's soddie up only a day before the first winter storm arrived. The screaming wind threw rain against the shutters and down the stove pipe to sizzle on the coals. It soaked the walls until damp oozed in. Besides going outside to feed the animals twice a day, William sat by the stove, smoking, working on a bench for beside the table, and playing Patience.

I had a pan of dough in the oven and Rachel was working with me on a rag rug like the one Martha'd made. Rachel cut strips from our old clothes, Beth plaited them, and I pinned them into a round, ready for sewing. William was watching us over his card game.

"I swear there's at least a dozen other things that need doing," he said, after we'd been going for a while.

"I don't doubt it," I said.

"I mean, the whole house is in need of a good clean, it's like some animal's den in here."

I looked up at him, raising my eyebrows. "Well, you built a dirt house, you should expect a little of it to rub off."

He glared at me, but for once I felt no more than a twinge of fear. If I didn't want him to touch me, he wouldn't. If he raised his voice or his hand to me, I would give him as good in return. No one else was going to save me. I didn't know if I was brave or just too worn out to feel afraid.

"Thomas, how's that work coming?" I asked.

He was sitting on his tick, our Bible laid out on his knees.

"I've almost got it," he said, for I'd set him to commit a psalm to memory. "Only, this part I don't understand. What does this word mean?" he spelt it out for me.

"Iniquity? It means, sin," I said, "all the sins that keep us apart from God."

"Oh," he found the word on the page and read the lines around it, "Have mercy on me, O Lord, for I am in trouble, my eye wastes away with grief, yes, my soul and my body. For my life is spent with grief, and my years with sighing. My strength fails because of my in-iniquity, and my bones waste away...does that mean that sin makes us ill?"

"I suppose, in a way," I pricked myself with the needle and shook my hand. "Sin makes us sick at heart, even if we don't know it. That's what I would think it means."

"Do you think they're sad because of the sin?"

I honestly didn't know, my own Bible studies had ended years before, I could no longer remember the part he was studying. I'd begun to think of the Bible as a collection of stories anyhow, stories that had as much to do with me as the Indian's fables. They didn't comfort me anymore.

"I think anyone who has sinned and lost sight of God would be sad," I said at last, accidentally catching William's eye as I looked up. He was watching me. What was he thinking of, his sin, or mine?

Thomas nodded, though still seemed confused. He went back to his studies and I was glad that the matter was settled.

When I next glanced up, William had stopped watching me and was puffing on his pipe.

Winter already seemed so long. William hadn't spoken of inviting Jamison and Martha for a meal, so I didn't even have that to think of. No letters had arrived from home for months, and now, with the weather worsening, I would have to wait for spring.

Worse than the weather, or even Will's temper - my monthly flow was four days late.

I could not imagine surviving another child coming into the world with Nora still feeding from the breast and the six of us already overflowing the soddie. If I was pregnant again I would be heavy with the baby by the time spring planting rolled around. That was an experience I didn't wish to repeat, trying to pick roots and stones with my belly weighing me down.

"What are you looking so down for?" William asked.

"Oh just...wishing we could take the children to church, have them taught the Bible properly," I said.

He sniffed. "They get enough of that here. And it never helped us any did it? Never taught us how to plant a row or skin a deer, that's the thing to be teaching them."

"But perhaps for Christmas, it might be the thing to go to church and see the people from town."

He'd come back with word that they'd finished building one. It seemed the only thing to get us away from the house, just for a while. He seemed to consider it.

"Jamison mentioned going over for Christmas, that there would be celebrations and a church dinner."

Food, his other vice, and one I shared. By the end of December we would be some way though our provisions, getting tired of the items we had in bulk, namely cornmeal and beans. I imagined a dinner set out for all the church goers, with platters of roasted meat, jugs of rich gravy and a pudding full of fruit.

"It might be nice to tag along with him," I said, "catch up with the news in town."

William drew the last coil of smoke from his pipe and set it aside. "Maybe."

I left it at that, and rescued my bread.

*

The weather continued to worsen, soon the baked earth of the prairie had become a wallow beneath the rotting grass. The wind had teeth and claws and the new mufflers I'd knitted were put to a harsh test as Will, Thomas and I took to the fields. Slogging through mud, I picked turnips and cut the greens off with a long knife, separating them to be used as winter feed. At times I couldn't feel my hands and at others my fingers felt as if they were on fire.

I watched William, two rows ahead, attacking the ground and the vegetables as if they had wronged him. Thomas trailed in his wake, collecting the turnips in the wash tub.

I wiped the mud from my hands onto my skirts, or at least, on to the gunny sack apron I'd put on over them. I couldn't help myself, the need to get clean had my skin twitching. My nails were filthy, broken.

"Gee yourself up," William shouted at me, "need twenty rows done before night."

Thomas coughed. I heard the rattle of phlegm.

"We should stop soon, for a meal," I called, worried for Thomas' chest and needing to check on Nora.

William didn't answer.

I hacked at turnips until I felt the urge to hack at my husband's throat. Finally, he dropped his knife on top of the tub of vegetables, waved Thomas around to the other side and left me to follow on with my own basket. By the time we reached the soddie it was raining and I was soaked down to my skin. The thick braided sticks of the basket handle had cut into my already numb hands, my face was stiff from the cold.

William and Thomas had already taken their load to the barn, to get it out of the rain and I took mine there before dragging myself to the soddie door. Inside, I noticed that the stove was burning low. I'd expected to find my dough on its second rise but it sat where I'd left it.

I didn't have the energy to get angry, didn't even take off my boots, just walked over the sacks we'd laid on the floor to sop up rain and sat down on a chair. William was already seated and Thomas was taking his boots off.

"Nora's been crying Ma," Rachel said.

"Time for her feed I expect," I looked over to Beth, sitting on her tick, a blanket around her. She'd been feeling the cold more than any of us. "Are you feeling better today sweet pea?"

"A bit," Beth said. She had her doll tucked under her arm.

"That's good, soon you'll be able to come outside and get some air." Though God knew enough of a cold wind was slipping under the door.

"Rachel, make up some coffee," William said.

Rachel was sitting on the end of the tick, sewing dresses for her doll. She sighed as she put the work aside, but I ignored it. Next year she'd be out in the field, which would put an end to her high-strung ways.

I was surprised by my own bile; she was my daughter, if she was warm and pretty inside, stitching on her doll, I should be glad and grateful. I found that I wasn't. I wanted to slap her for leaving my dough to over-prove while I slogged in the mud for fistfuls of frigid damn turnips.

I looked at Will. Already he'd started to let his moustaches grow in; shaving in cold weather was a chore for him. There was a tightness in his face and I knew the work was telling on him too. A harvest in high summer was exhausting, but in the cold and wet it was a miserable task.

"Days like this I wish we were down in Texas," he said, a small smile tracing his mouth. "There's those that're down in a pit of debt, have to let their slaves go to auction for hardly more than I paid for Stick."

Stick pricked his ears at the mention of his name, but soon settled back down under the table.

I'd thought of owning a slave before, for the housework and to help in the fields. My family had never been able to afford one, and neither had William's, even before '34, when such a thing was possible. Now of course, there were no slaves in England, and though the option would have been open to us south of Indian Territory, we couldn't afford the land there.

There were of course, concerns that abolition would take hold here. I'd heard talk in Ohio and knew that New York State had freed its slaves some years ago, even before England, though some were still indentured. Myself I didn't think the idea would catch on, it was different here than in England; they needed the slaves too much, especially down south.

Rachel poured coffee and brought it over, along with a basin of warm water and a piece of soap. William and I washed our hands and I got up to fetch the bread I'd made the previous day, now a little dry, along with a dish of chokecherry jam.

"Rachel, would you punch down that dough before you sit down to lunch?" I said. "It's already had far too long to rise."

"Damn your lazy ass, child," William exclaimed, startling me. "You've hardly a thing to lift your finger to sitting in here all day and still you don't have the sense to do one chore?"

Rachel's cheeks burnt, and I avoided her gaze. I couldn't offer her my support because I wanted to shout at her too.

"By the time we get back tonight, I expect this place to be clean and tidy, and for you to have set things out for dinner. And if I come in that door and see you with a doll, or a trinket in your hands, I'll spank you 'till you can't sit about all day. Understood?"

"Yes, Pa," Rachel said, and took herself over to the bowl in which the dough had risen like a large mushroom.

"You should chide her more," William said, "I know she doesn't pull her weight."

I lifted my hands helplessly. "She'll learn."

"Not if you don't make her."

"I'll keep more of an eye on her in future," I said, then got up and went to where Nora was dozing in her cradle box. I had to wake her, there'd be no time to get a feed done otherwise. She was growing well; her belly rounded and her little arms and legs putting on fat. I stroked her fine hair and held her close. I still feared the cold and the wet would snatch her from me before spring came. Leaving her while I worked outside was getting harder to bear.

My clothes were still damp when William stood and headed back out into the cold. Thomas stuffed his feet into his boots and followed me. It was still raining lightly and we had to unload the basket and tub before taking them out to the field to fill them again.

"We'll soon have them all in," William said, walking along side me with Thomas trailing behind, "then it'll be time to bring up the potatoes."

I looked back at my son, held out a hand, as if he was a small child in need of my touch to comfort him. Our eyes met, his a mirror of my own, then he looked away. I turned back to the muddy field and the cold rain, neither of which could dampen my spirits as much as Thomas had.

Chapter Twenty-One
Cecelia

From the soddie I could see Laura and her husband in the far distance on a square of brown earth hemmed in by rolling, wet grasses. Their tiny figures like dolls, bending and rising and dragging miniature baskets with them.

I'd made myself a little two sided shelter that rested against the back wall of the soddie. It provided a place for me to hang the second deer I'd ever killed. The thin timber of the roof kept most of the light rain off of me, but some still managed to blow in around me, my hair was pasted to my scalp with hot sweat and cold drizzle.

Carving up a deer was the hardest and foulest chore I'd yet encountered on the prairie; Thomas had described it to me, but actually performing the process was much worse than he'd made it sound. The rain kept most of the insects away, but a few flies remained yet and buzzed around me as I started quartering the deer, a task that soon had cold-hot needles of pain shooting through my shoulders, what with the reaching up and the sawing back and forth.

When I cut up the middle of the hanging body, the wound dripped blackish blood onto the ground, and the smell of part-digested grass made me gag. I didn't want to reach inside and touch the bluish purple organs that hung on cords of fat and thick veins. My eyes watered and I stifled a sob as I put my hand in. It was still warm inside.

Cutting up the deer had already taken the best part of the day and left me so sore in the back and arms that I couldn't do any more. There was nothing for it but to move the rest of the carcass inside and work on it again in the morning. It would not fit in the smoke house as it was. I spread sacks on my makeshift table and laid what remained of the deer on it. The bucket of offal I left on the bench outside; maybe Laura and her family could eat those things, but I couldn't. I saved only a small portion, for Missy's supper.

I washed my hands and arms in a bucket of water and used it to sluice down the bench. I still didn't feel clean. Since the bath I'd taken in the creek on my way to town, I'd had only poor, quick washes, standing in my tub with an inch or two of hot water around my ankles, washing myself down with a rag.

Inside, I dispensed with my breast band and put on the cleanest of my shirts. Soon I'd have a smoke house full of meat, my work had accomplished that much. A good evening's rest was my reward.

Unfortunately 'rest' was something my mind had great trouble with. At least, it had done, since Laura had kissed me. I could still hardly believe that it had happened, my skin went cold whenever the memory resurfaced, but with it came the worry that Deene was hurting her. I was afraid for her, but also afraid of her. I couldn't separate my disgust from my concern. It all seemed to mix together in my head until I hardly knew what I felt.

God, I didn't want to think about it, to think at all.

It was too late, of course. Lying under my blankets, feeling the lumps of cornhusks in my tick, I thought of her lips against mine. The warm shadow of her body again echoed through me. I imagined the comfort of that, of her touch and... I was half wanting it and half wanting to tear myself away and run into the darkness outside.

"Why am I such a fool?" I covered my face with my raw, scrubbed hands.

Missy ate her supper, oblivious. I longed for real company, for Franklyn, to remind me who I really was and what I was meant to feel. Laura said that I watched her – but that was only natural curiosity, seeing a woman so different from myself. I had maybe wanted to care for her, to help her with Beth and to ease the pinched look of fear and tiredness from her face, but that wasn't wanting, not like she meant. It only meant that I cared.

"Goddamn that woman," I said, then cupped my hand to my mouth. What was becoming of me? With the thought of Laura, and the taste of the curse on my tongue, I was more Clappe than Cecelia. I shivered. Was I losing myself?

"Don't be stupid," I said tartly.

Missy looked up from her clean bowl and looked at me as if she was worried for my sanity. It was true that I had started to talk to myself more and more, but that simply showed that I was lonely, not mad.

"I should really start to feed you outside," I told her. We both knew that I would do no such thing, she was company after all.

Missy came and arranged herself over my feet. In the pocket of darkness that was the inside of the soddie, I felt a similar darkness aching in my chest. The loneliness was a terrible thing, only growing stronger with every hour; it had the smell of old smoke and the sound of the grass whispering unkindly, it left the taste of burnt coffee on my tongue. In the warm darkness of my bed, I clung to an armful of blanket and longed for the soft, brown, goodness of Laura Deene. Telling myself that I only wanted a friend to cling to in the dark, someone who cared for me.

I was woken by the low growl of the dog.

Sitting up in the dark, my sleepy, comfortable state was cut with ice when I heard an answering growl from beyond the soddie door.

Missy was sitting in the middle of the room, I could make out her dark bulk against the glow of the fading embers. Frozen to the bed, I couldn't blink, could hardly breathe.

Then, from outside, from all around, came the unmistakeable howl of a wolf pack. I'd only heard it from far, far away before. Up close, through only about a foot of sod, it was like hearing a cry from beyond the grave.

For a moment I couldn't trace the choking sound that followed the awful howling, then I realised that it was me and I clapped my hand over my mouth.

I believe that in that moment it was James Clappe who rose to my defence.

Tripping out of bed, I groped for the lantern. Found it. Lit it. In the pale glow I saw Missy with her hair standing up, her teeth bared. I found myself thinking orders as if speaking to another; find the rifle. Check it. Loaded. Open the patch box. Stop those fingers shaking. Get the powder horn. The bullets.

The howl came again and I dropped the box of bullets. They rolled on the floor, escaping my shaking hands as if on purpose. My eyes blurred with terrified tears. I took the rifle in my hands, eyes fixed on the door.

Please God, let it hold. Let it hold, be merciful.

The door rattled and I let out a small scream. Missy leapt at the door, snarled, lowered her nose to the floor and sniffed. I knew then what had drawn them; the blood, the innards in their bucket outside. They could smell the deer inside the soddie. Oh God. How had I been so stupid? No matter how tired I'd been, I should have put it in the smoke house, well away from me. I'd as good as laid my table for them.

Something struck the easterly shutter with a heavy thump. The leather strip that held one side to the frame snapped, the shutter swung on its bottom hinge. Then came the sound of claws on wood. The dog almost knocked me down as she leapt across the soddie. I raised the gun and fired. The shot took a chunk out of the remaining shutter. Splinters fell amongst the spilled bullets. Something hit the ground outside. I could hear my blood drumming.

The patches of greasy material fell from my hands, I rammed the patch, powder and bullet. I looked through the wedge of space between the shutter and the frame. The outside air was clean and charged with night. Six pairs of yellow-green eyes reflected the faint light from the window. There came sounds of scrabbling, of sloppy flesh ripping between teeth.

The Deene place was out of running distance, invisible in the dark. I was alone.

The howl came again, cutting through me.

Clutching the rifle in my hands, I opened my mouth and screamed back.

Silence rang through the air, then the wolves cried again. My voice dried in my throat.

Scratching came from the door, I turned to it, only to hear a thud as a wolf leapt at the window. Missy tucked her tail down and kept low to the floor. We were both out of courage.

I dropped the rifle, made a grab for the packing crates that made up the bulk of my furniture. There weren't very heavy, but I stacked them against the door. Stepping on bullets and stumbling. Nothing I could do for the broken shutter. I took the rifle to the furthest corner of the soddie, dragged my tick across and tipped it up onto its side, sealing me into the corner with the gun. Missy nosed her way around the edge just as I was wedging it against the wall. I rested the barrel of the gun on the sackcloth tick. The discarded sheet lay on the dirt floor like spilled milk.

Outside, death howled for me.

*

The sound of the packing crates scraping across the floor woke me from my stupor. I couldn't call it sleep. I opened my eyes to find that I'd been passed out against the wall. Sunlight came in through the gap in the broken shutter and the gaps around the door. Grabbing the rifle from the floor I aimed at the sound.

"James?" The boxes scraped inwards, the door began to open.

My tired eyes found the tangle of my clothes on the floor, the breast band just peeking out in the gloom. I shoved the tick away from me and made a leap for the clothes. Just as my hands closed on the bundle and I stood up, Laura opened the door fully.

There was a rifle in her hands. Her face was blank to me, washed into shadow by the sunlight spilling in all around her.

"We heard you shooting at the wolves last night," she took a step into the room and her features became clear. She looked me over, and all my relief turned to fear as her expression became unsure.

I crossed my arms quickly over my breasts, too late to keep her from seeing them through the thin material of the shirt.

"Laura..." I didn't disguise my voice, there was no point. I knew how thin and delicate my body looked without Clappe's thick shirts and trousers to hide in, and how my small breasts poked out like pears.

"I..." she said, the word stuck like a splinter in her throat "You...you're not..."

"Please don't tell your husband," I took a step towards her, feeling the coolness of a bullet as my toe struck it and rolled it across the dirt.

"I kissed you." Her soft brown eyes had become as scared and betrayed as those of the deer that I'd butchered the day before.

"I'm sorry, Laura," I started, but she was shaking her head, bidding me away with her hand.

"Don't speak to me," she said, "don't you dare speak to me."

She left me, flinging the door shut and blocking out the light. I took a step after her, but my foot sank down on a splinter several inches long and I stumbled, falling to the floor with a cry of pain. Clutching the ball of my bleeding foot, I hunched over. Dirty, tired and afraid; I almost wished the wolves would return.

Chapter Twenty-Two
Laura

I struggled back to the soddie, my heart pounding and my face burning with shock and shame. I couldn't keep my hands from going to my belly, as though I was trying to shield the baby from my shame.

"What in the hell were you thinking, leaving the children alone?" Will shouted. He was standing in the doorway glaring at me. "I only went to see Jamison and I come back to find you left no sooner than I set out."

He was right in front of me but all I could see was her. I was too shaken up to think what to say at first. "I went to see if…to see that Clappe was alright."

"Why'd you sound so guilty then?"

"I don't sound guilty. I don't sound like anything," I said, guilt thickening like old milk in my belly. All the past weeks of secret thoughts, letting myself remember Clappe's touches, thinking of him in bed with me. The notion of what I'd done hit me like a falling tree.

"I suppose you found him fine as a June day and drinking tea out of his mother's best cups," Will sneered as I passed him.

"He wasn't dead, if that's what you mean," I avoided his eyes, fetched my apron and shook my hands behind my back so I could tie the strings without them shaking.

"Well we've lost enough time to social calls today, get the baskets out and find that lazy-ass son of yours, we've got potatoes to dig."

William only got angrier as the day wore on, seeing him curse Thomas up and down the muddy rows of potato plants only made me angrier. At him, at her and at myself.

"I better not see you crying," he snapped at Thomas. "You want to stay inside and take care of the house? I'll have your mother sew up a dress for you."

I turned and saw Thomas struggling to pull up a stubborn plant. The wet stalk slipped through his hands and he fell backwards into the mud.

"For the love of God, can't you pull up a fucking plant properly?" Will jerked it out of the soil, held it up so the roots showered Thomas with thick lumps of mud. "Your sister could pull these with no trouble, get your goddamn ass out of the mud and work like a man." He swung the plant back like a whip, ready to strike Thomas about the head with it.

"William!" My voice carried across the prairie like the report of a rifle. I winced inside, wondering if she could hear me. "If you strike him I swear to God I will lay you out and bury you to your neck in this slop."

"If he worked as he was supposed to, we'd be done with the field by now."

"If you think that, you're more of an idiot than I thought you were."

"And if you did your share, instead of flapping your jaw like the empty headed bitch you are, perhaps the boy'd learn to stand on his own two feet!"

"Come with me, Thomas," I said.

"No, the boy stays with me."

I held my arm out to Thomas and gritted my teeth. Before I had believed I hated Will, now I knew what hate was. He'd slapped the children to discipline them, as I had, but this was a threat of a beating, unwarranted. I could see that he had no love for Thomas, for any of our children. For that I hated him, deeply.

"I said, he stays by me. Get back to your own row," I said.

Will let his arm swing and caught me across the face with his hand. A slap, open hand. A warning. Still, I stumbled in the mud and almost fell.

"Shut up and get back to work."

Through watering eyes I watched as Thomas stooped and started picking the potatoes from the plant Will'd uprooted.

The sudden heat of my anger had finally done what Will hadn't managed. The iron in me was cracked, weakened. Clappe, whoever she was, had done this to me, made me hope then snatched that hope away. I trudged and picked, hating them both, hating myself most of all.

*

By the time the light failed, I was sick of the sight of potatoes and thorny inside with the need to be alone. Thomas was quiet as we dragged the baskets of vegetables back to the house but I couldn't reach out to him.

Rachel was stirring a pot on the stove when we got back. I knew I should offer some encouragement, tell her the leftover stew smelt good, but I couldn't open my mouth. My head felt heavy.

Will washed up and then lit his pipe, waiting for the stew to come to him at the table.

"Rachel'll have to join us out in the field tomorrow," he said.

"There'll be no one to watch Beth and Nora," I said.

"Pa, you said I was to stay here and cook like Ma," Rachel said, "it's cold outside, and I hate all the worms out in the mud."

He banged the table to silence her. "There's only one of us doing a decent day's work, and that's me. The two of you," he gestured to me and Thomas, who had wilted on his tick, trying to make himself small, "can barely make up one man's labour. Rachel will have to join, or it'll take too long to get the potatoes out and stored. First snow can't be more'n a week or two away."

"But Nora-" I began.

"I've decided. Beth'll be with Nora, Rachel can run to and from the field to check on 'em every once in a while. That's the last I'll hear of it. Put on some coffee."

I was too tired to fight, to tell him Beth couldn't look after herself, let alone a baby. I went to the stove to put a pot on.

"I'll tell you something else," he said to my hunched back, "today's the last time you'll be going off on your own to see Clappe. I've put up with it long enough. From now on, you're to have nothing to do with him - that clear?"

My mouth tightened in anger and I felt for the first time the loss of my only friend, who'd never been.

"I won't be going up there again."

Chapter Twenty-Three
Laura

It snowed not a week after the last potato was put into storage. The endless hard flurries meant the narrowing of our small world down to the inside of the house. For once panic didn't rise in my throat at the thought of being trapped with my family. Every inch of frozen crust was another barrier against the stranger I'd thought my friend.

It'd been a hard few days. The work, the cold, the exhausted meals, the worry for Beth and Nora, the coughs and sniffs that forced me out of sleep all through the night. I saw Thomas and Rachel grow tired and pale, their small hands chapped by the wind. William soon lost his patience with Rachel and there wasn't a day when the backs of her legs weren't spanked red. Her quivering lip and wet cheeks made me ache for her even as my fingers froze. Though often I found Thomas's quiet despair was even harder to stand.

The baby I'd thought was taking shape in me turned out to be nothing at all. During the harvest my monthlies arrived with unexpected force. So that was a blessing, though it was hard to feel anything close to relief.

Through it all, the small dreams I'd entertained of Clappe's hands on my skin, or his settling a quilt around me against the winter cold, brought me none of the comfort I'd come to depend on. I hated her more for that than the lies and humiliation. She stole him from me when I needed him most.

Being indoors after the harvest with access to hot coffee and blankets should have cheered me, but it did little to soothe my hurts. Again and again I thought of James and how I would have used this freedom to visit him – only to remember that I had no friend to talk to now. Even Martha's company was gone, as Jamison didn't bring her by on his few visits.

Often I took myself behind the barn and sobbed into the crook of my elbow. Every time I thought of how she must see me, a plain old country woman pining for her imagined young buck, I shuddered with humiliation and clenched my fists in pain and anger.

As the snow continued to fall, day after day, we were trapped within the walls of the soddie. Our work slacked off and though it had been a poor distraction, to do without it was unbearable.

The first time I took out the Bible to begin a writing lesson, William snapped at me.

"No more of that foolishness. They're schooled as well as they ought to be, and Beth's too young to learn anyway. It's a waste of your time."

I was sitting on the edge of our tick with Rachel and Thomas on either side of me. Beth tucked under Rachel's arm, trying to see the Bible pages.

"There's nothing needs tending to right now," I said, keeping my voice even, mindful of his temper, "it's hardly a bad thing, them learning a little more."

"We were taught all we needed to know. When they're grown and farming for themselves they'll be thankful they know acreage and yield, no more. So put that book away."

Every time I tried to sleep, or when I let myself be idle for a moment, he was waiting. Clappe in his trousers, crouching by me in the barn, his worn shirt soft against my hands as I kissed his uncommonly smooth mouth. Clappe, her mouth wide with shock and her nightshirt hanging around her, clinging to a pair of breasts as high and pert as those on a pretty statue I'd seen once in the garden of Jacob's fine house. I couldn't settle it in my mind, them being the same person. What the hell was a woman alone doing out on the prairie, parading around in trousers?

I got angry with myself. What did it matter to me? I wanted nothing to do with her. I'd fallen for her act and made a fool of myself. I didn't want *her*, just the fairy tale she'd come up with, James Clappe, kind and generous, a man unlike any other. Well! It was true. He wasn't real, he'd never been the same as Will or Jamison because he was a fiction.

But God, I'd *kissed* her. My face twisted and I shivered, remembering her thin, vulnerable body. The bare shoulder and the nightshirt flapping around her slim, pale thighs. My heart filled up with care that so surprised me I felt my eyes well.

"What's got you so vexed?" William said, while the snow fell like goose down outside.

"I'm just pent up, being inside all the time," I was sitting in the chair opposite him, turning a heel on a new stocking, or I had been, until my fingers went idle and my mind started conjuring up Clappe's face. "There's only so much work to do without having to teach the children-"

He sighed so hard that it was practically a snarl. Stick pricked up her ears and Rachel stopped playing with Beth and her dolls.

"There's plenty of work to do without you starting that argument up again." He turned to Thomas, who was polishing his and Will's boots. "See, even the boy's making himself useful."

"I can be useful," Rachel said, "Ma, what is there for me to do?" I knew she wanted to be in Will's good books again.

"You could help me make a new set of candles, we're running low now." This was because Will was avoiding the use of the lamp, in favour of the slightly cheaper candles that I made myself. It also meant that once the darkness set in, earlier and earlier each night, we had little to no light in the soddie.

"Will, are we going into town this year, for Christmas at the church?" I asked, as I watched Rachel grate old wax into the little pan I kept for melting it down.

"Well I suppose now that they've gone and built one we have to go."

"What's church like?" Beth wanted to know.

"You just sit still and then sing some songs," Rachel said.

"But for Christmas they put up decorations and you sing special songs and hear the story of Jesus and sometimes there are presents," Thomas said, in that moment a boy again, rather than a tired servant polishing his master's boots.

I set the paraffin to melt on the stove and dusted off my skirts. "And you'll get to see the other children, if there are any in town."

William snorted. "I suppose they'll be taking a collection for the children, so that they can have candies and mittens."

Rachel and Beth lit up at the mention of candy.

"If so, we'll give what we can," I said, "I only hope we can get there, the snow's coming in so thick."

"Jamison said he's putting runners on his wagon box, making a kind of sled. Told me he'd be glad to take us with him when I went to check on him after the wolves were here."

"Will he have room?" I asked.

"Well, he ain't taking Martha, that's for damn sure," William said, "now they've got a church and a pastor, folks in town are starting to get a lot more vocal on the sin of cohabiting, and with a savage no less."

I thought of poor Martha, left behind in the soddie while everyone around her went to church to celebrate and be together.

"Clappe won't be going with us," William said.

"I didn't ask if he was," I said.

He frowned, like he wasn't expecting me to be so snappish, but thankfully the paraffin had melted, giving me reason to turn my back.

*

In England, Christmas had been a time for preparing mincemeat stuffed pies and boiled puddings loaded with raisins, sultanas and spices. We'd decorate with holly and go off to church to sing and hear stories while expensive candles burnt and the whole church was filled with the smell of pine and beeswax. Then there would be the turkey, fattened on good corn through the autumn and winter months, potatoes and candied parsnips. The children, Thomas and Rachel, still no more than babies, were given gifts, a rag doll with soft dark woollen hair for her, and a cup and ball for Thomas, painted green and red.

Of course I knew we were the poorest in our family, had been since we came to America. I was reminded of it each time I mended my old calico dress, or boiled old, tasteless bones for soup stock, but at Christmas it was impossible to ignore the fact that as far as our families were concerned, we were poor as the Indians.

I was peering into our stores when Rachel came to watch me. We were only a week or so from Christmas by then, and the snow outside was several feet deep where it had drifted across the wide prairie. Preparing for the trip was the distraction I sorely needed.

"Ma, what are you doing?"

"Trying to decide what to make for Christmas."

She brightened. "Can we make molasses cookies?"

"I'm afraid not sweet pea, that molasses has to last us now until the end of spring. I ought'nt to have made you the last batch of cookies, but after working so hard you and Thomas deserved them."

I had a few apples wrapped in torn gunny sacks and put away in a box, as well as a small paper bag of raisins that I'd kept folded up in an old tobacco tin especially for Christmas.

"We don't have any brandy though, that's the trouble," I said to myself.

"What will we make?"

"Well, that's up to you dear, you're going to help me. You and Beth." Thomas and Will were both absent, cutting roots for the oxen. "Shall we make a pudding?"

Rachel and Beth had got themselves into a state rubbing flour on the wet muslin when William came back into the house.

"What the devil is all this mess?" he demanded. "You think flour's so cheap you can afford to waste it on the floor?"

"We're just making a Christmas pudding," I said, the two girls having been scared into silence.

"Well for God's sake don't let them at the stores, they're even more wasteful than you," he snapped.

Thomas was taking off his boots, "It smells nice in here."

William cuffed him around the head.

"Don't you dare," I ordered.

Thomas ducked his head and came over to me, followed by William's glare.

Across the room, Nora woke from her nap and began to cry shrilly.

"Is there any child of yours that does what it ought?" William thundered, going for his pipe and dropping into his chair.

I went to see to Nora and the girls crept to their tick where they were supposed to be sewing up a new set of undergarments for their brother. I'd cut out the pieces of welsh flannel myself and Rachel was showing Beth the stitches. In my work box were the mittens I'd been knitting for Clappe – brown wool taken from an old muffler of mine. I couldn't yet bring myself to work on them, though I thought of her long pale fingers growing chapped with cold every time I saw the needles poking from the bag.

As I watched the pudding bob in the pan, sealed up in the floury muslin, I thought of Clappe. How would she be passing Christmas day? Alone and cold without the skill to prepare even one festive dish? I tried to ignore the pity I felt.

Chapter Twenty-Four
Laura

On Christmas Eve Jamison came by in a wagon box with waxed poles nailed to the axels. It ran across the snow well enough, save for where the ends of the poles gouged the icy crust and the thing had to be dug out of the snow. Jamison explained this while knocking snow from a shovel and stowing it in the back of the box.

"Miss Deene, you look a picture," he said, tipping his hat to Rachel, who was in her new dress and shoes.

"Come on girls, let's get you up into the warm, shall we?" I said, trying to steer Rachel to the side of the sleigh and away from Jamison. There was something in his eyes when he looked at her, like a man eying a sleek colt that would one day haul loads in the fields.

Jamison stepped around me and lifted Rachel, then Beth into the sleigh, where they soon had a big old buffalo robe around them. I climbed up with baby Nora, Thomas sat next to me. William had a seat next to Jamison and he lit his pipe up as the horses started to pull us through the snow.

The sun on the snow made it look like piles and piles of white sugar, but I knew that under it lurked holes and burrows that could fell a horse, or a man. Still, the snow sparkled, and it was lovely to see. The girls were wide-eyed with wonder. It was quiet, no insects, no waving grass, all quiet and still except for the 'schick' the poles under the wagon box made as they cut through the icy top of the snow.

As the sleigh passed Clappe's soddie I looked away, out over the wide, white prairie. I didn't want to chance catching a glimpse of her, not now that I was managing to keep from thinking of her for longer stretches. I didn't want to see the lonely house and wonder about the life of the woman inside.

"Is Mr Clappe not going to church?" Rachel asked.

"Hmm? No, Mr Clappe isn't going to church, at least, not with us."

"Why?" Beth said.

"Mr Clappe is a grown man and he was work to do. He can make his own plans," I said. "Now girls, what are you hoping for this Christmas?"

"Ribbons!" Rachel said and Beth echoed it, thought really she wasn't old enough to care for ribbons yet.

Jamison laughed, "I should think every little girl in the state is after some pretty ribbons for her hair."

"Did you get some for Martha?" Rachel said.

That made him laugh harder. "I'd sooner buy a bonnet for a hog than waste pretty ribbons on an Indian woman."

"What did you buy for her?" Rachel asked.

"Those glass windows for the house," he said. "She'll have light without a draft all winter."

Will hadn't bought me a gift since we were first married. Then it had been a second hand shawl. It wasn't even that I minded, what use had I for hair ribbons and silk handkerchiefs? When had I last cared about what covered my skin, so long as it was warm and dry?

At the edge of town Jamison left the wagon and put the horses into a small shelter there, where they were tied up with a few other pairs of horses and oxen. Many people must have made the journey for the Christmas service.

The church was a wooden building like the store. I made the children knock the snow off of their shoes outside the door on a little strip of porch. Rachel complained that it made her cold toes hurt.

When we went inside we were at the back of five lines of people. There weren't any benches. The only things in there were a stove and a table at the front with a wooden cross and two candles on it. It seemed no meal or gift giving had been planned after all. The floor was marked with wet footprints, at the far end of the room ladies and men were steaming in the heat from the little stove. We lined up at the rear, in the chilly air near the door. Everything smelt like new wood, wet wool and onions.

Throughout the sermon I couldn't shake a feeling of uneasiness. I felt as though I didn't belong in the small church, listening to story of Jesus' birth. I thought of Clappe too often, worried about her cold fingers, how thin she'd looked last time I saw her. I felt a chill that had nothing to do with the weather outside, even as my face burned.

At last we said the final 'amen' and the circuit rider rushed off to slap a hat on his bald head and travel on to the next town, where he'd be giving the same sermon. Jamison kept us waiting for him at the door for a long time. He was talking to a woman, one of the most obvious whores I'd ever seen, with yellow hair in crisp sugar-water and hot iron curls, wearing a frowsy dress with a crooked lace trim sewn on the bosom.

"Ma, look at the lady," Rachel said, "isn't she pretty?"

"William, perhaps we ought to take the children to the sleigh and get them settled."

"It's Jamison's wagon box and his horses," Will said. "Mind your own, Laura."

After a while Jamison came over, sharing a look with Will, winking and smiling greasily. Ignored him and we walked back to the wagon box. Rachel's shoes were pinching and she complained the whole way. Out in the cold air Beth's nose had started to run.

Crowded into the back of the wagon, I kept the girls close to keep them warm. We'd been expecting a meal in town, so I'd bought nothing but a bit of no-cake to keep the children quiet. We hadn't even been offered a hot drink. I could tell from Will's silence that he was dwelling on my failure to see him fed.

It was even quieter then than it had been during the day. The sky was completely black, only the lanterns on the front of the wagon allowed us to see a little way ahead. It was snowjng again. Nora started to whimper and I pulled a blanket up to my neck, reached under to give her a feed.

"I'll make us some hot tea and a bite when we reach home," I said to the children, "then you have to go to bed, or Father Christmas shan't come to give you presents."

The darkness hid the endless prairie and I could only tell we were close to home because there was a light in Clappe's window. I didn't want to think of Clappe, sitting alone on Christmas Eve. I wished the soddie had been dark, invisible. I was ashamed to find that I wanted her to be thinking of me.

"Thank for the Lord for that," Jamison muttered, "I was starting to think we'd never make it."

The whole sleigh jolted and Beth cried out as Will yelled and Jamison cursed. There was a lot of snow thrown up, the sharp whinny of the horse as it fell, taking the other with it. The wagon box pitched, but righted and then everything was still again, but for the horse thrashing in the snow.

Jamison jumped down with Will.

"It's her fucking foreleg," I heard Jamison say.

"And the other?"

"She's fine, but this'n, she's fucked. Get my rifle."

I pulled Rachel and Beth back from the edge of the wagon box. Beth cried noisily, leaving snot on my cloak. Thomas was up on the front seat, holding the reins as Jamison got the uninjured horse to its feet and undid the straps that held it and the other horse together.

Will brought the rifle and I turned my face away, heard the crack of the shot, the startled scream of the other horse. There was a long wait while the men moved the horse out of the way and finally hitched up the remaining beast. I watched the dark shape in the snow as we drove slowly away from it. From in front I could see the hole it had fallen into.

We went even slower after that, because Jamison and Will had to walk ahead, making sure there were no other holes under the snow. I took the reins and occasionally looked around us, into the dark.

"What are you looking for, Ma?"

"I'm just looking at the snow, isn't it lovely?" I said, looking for the approaching glint of wolf eyes. I knew Will and Jamison were doing the same.

At last we reached home and I helped the girls down.

"Take Beth inside now Rachel, I'll go and fetch Stick from the barn," I said.

The men were already turning the sleigh to go back for the horse. With the dog released and by my side I went into the soddie, found a candle and lit it so I could see to build up a fire in the cold stove. The light showed up the pale faces of my frightened girls. I had left the water bucket by the woodpile and I saw that it was full of ice. Rachel broke it with the dipping ladle.

"Why don't you put some water on for tea?" I said.

"He shot the horse, didn't he?"

"He did. The poor thing had a broken leg, it would have suffered a lot and been no use to Mr Neaps either." Except perhaps in a stew, if he, Will and Thomas could find it in the snow.

"Will he get another one?"

"Perhaps, in spring."

She put water on to boil and I put Nora in her cradle before changing Beth into a nightdress. While Rachel measured tea into the pot, I took the pudding from its coverings and cut pieces for us to eat when Will and Jamison came in.

"You can sit up with me until they come back, if you like," I said to Rachel, pouring us both cups of black tea. "You're a big girl now, after all."

"Shall I put the stockings up Ma?" she asked.

For a moment I'd forgotten the purpose of the day. "Of course sweet pea."

The soddie began to warm and the smell of the pudding, sweet and good, filled the air. It was what I had imagined my life would be like; there would be hard work, yes, but also this. The soft light and warmth of a Christmas Eve with my family. I only need a pair of arms around my waist and a cheek against mine to complete the moment. Someone to love me as they loved in songs.

When Will came through the door I felt a sting of disappointment and realised who I'd been dreaming of, coming in from the cold.

Chapter Twenty-Five
Cecelia

Since the night that the wolves had come, I'd hardly dared go outside. There was nothing to see but her house, besides which, the cold was unbearable, it crept in through the walls, froze the contents of my chamber pot and frosted my breath. I stayed wrapped up inside, afraid and lonely.

I couldn't speak to Franklyn anymore and felt stupid when I tried. Missy slept a lot, curled up against the cold and I was left by myself. The silence was as painful as the blinding whiteness outside. I kept imagining I heard Deene's footsteps outside in the snow, the thought of him began to scare me almost as much as the thought of Charles.

Every day I faced the same decision; stay, or go. Every day I came to the same conclusion; the only things of value I had were tools, and there would be no one around to buy those until spring. I had no way of surviving if I left it all behind. I was trapped. I knew all that, but my desire to run away and never see Laura again had me prepared to pack up all I could and walk off into the snow.

On the morning of Christmas Eve I was sewing the seam on a new shirt sleeve under the window when Missy started barking. That was how I came to see the sleigh full of my neighbours riding off to town, without me. The knowledge that I was alone, without a single person for miles to come to my aid, chilled me worse than the cold light from the window. It was like being locked up back in Ohio, helpless.

Letting the shirt drop to my lap, I looked out through the screen and wished for the Christmas services I'd become used to with my family, for the company of ladies draped in fur and thick, good wool.

God, was I longing for the wool and furs, or for the women underneath?

I covered my eyes and bit my lip sharply. What if I lost my mind before spring came? Alone and shut up with only a dog for company, April might find me raving, hair a dirty mess, frost bitten toes scrabbling at the bare dirt.

Perhaps I did belong in an asylum.

I took to the bed with my sewing and while Missy lay across my feet, I stitched, trying to ignore the pain of the chilblains that had swollen on my knuckles. I'd long since lost the light when the knock came at my door, making Missy bark. I stopped my work mid-stitch, hardly daring to breathe.

All the windows were shuttered, but where else could I be if not in my house? There was no pretending. The knocking came again, more urgently. I got to my feet, picked up my candle and unlatched the door. In the rectangle of black night and white snow stood Martha, muffled against the cold.

"Let me in."

Stepping back, too shocked to speak, I allowed her to enter the soddie. She took off her snow caked boots and took the candle from my frozen hand, using it to light a stand of three tapers on the table. All the while Missy was circling her, sniffing at her skirt.

"You've no fire," she said, looking in disbelief at the embers in the stove.

"It went out."

There was some wood split into stove lengths, I went to make a fire, conscious that she was watching me. Even though no one came to my home, I was still keeping up with my disguise. I had nothing else to wear and somehow it was easier to bear being dirty, cold and musty smelling if I could pretend that I really was James Clappe. To be Cecelia and feel the grease gathering in my hair, see the dirt caked under my nails, did not bear thinking about.

With the fire starting to catch, I turned and looked at my visitor. I should have guess she would not be allowed to go to town. She was wearing a pair of what must have been Jamison's trousers, with her own dark wool skirt kilted up over them for warmth. The shapes of her feet were almost indistinguishable in their lumpy brown stockings and she had a blanket wrapped about her, under her shawl. Her coat was also Jamison's, and I could see that it had been worn to holes at the elbows. All around her strong face hung the curtain of her long, black hair.

171

"Jamison went to town with Deene and his family," she said, after a silence filled only by the crackling of the fire.

"And you decided to walk ten or so miles in the snow?" Though I'd kept on with my disguise, I'd allowed myself to lose the rhythm of Clappe's coarser voice and had to work to regain it.

She was looking about her at the clutter of the soddie. "I knew you'd be here. Is there coffee?"

I'd never met someone so forward and honestly I didn't know her from a snow drift, but she had walked through the freezing wind to get to me, so the least I could manage was a pot of coffee. I put it on and sat down opposite her on a packing crate.

"It's hard, being out here alone," she said.

I nodded. Missy had settled by Martha's feet and was looking up at her without a trace of suspicion.

"Jamison doesn't want me in town. Since they built the church there, he says people've been talking."

I could imagine. "Towns a fair distance, all of it frozen over, I'm surprised he went himself."

"He's looking to marry," she said, a frown creasing her heavy hewn brow. "Marry a woman from town and start having children. Children to inherit when he dies."

I felt a flash of pity for whichever woman was unlucky enough to end up with Jamison, remembering the whore from town. Would having a whore for a wife be any less sinful than keeping company with a native woman? Well, of course, but only by the narrowest of margins. "Are there any women in town looking for husbands?"

Martha made a helpless gesture. "How would I know? I haven't been since we passed through to get here. Maybe someone's lost a husband, maybe there's a daughter been orphaned, looking for a man to take care of her. Could be one of the whores he was with when he last went there."

172

I felt myself start and flush. Martha shook her head. "Of course I know. She knows too, Laura, what her husband is like. Jamison and him, they're cut from the same cloth. Bad, mean stuff."

I was saved by the coffee pot, which was rattling on the stove top. When I had my back to her, pouring coffee and spooning in molasses, Martha spoke again.

"I think mostly Jamison hates women, thinks they only please him because they want his money - which is true." Her beetle black eyes found mine. "If I had anywhere else to go, I wouldn't be with him. He talks to me like I'm one of the black women he knew back in Texas. One of the ones he got with child. Like I'm no better than a slave to him. Which is also true."

"Why don't you leave? There has to be somewhere you can-"

She shook her head. "There's nowhere. What's left of my family had to leave here. They're living on a reservation in the south-east and there's talk of cutting the land back further. There wasn't enough food. Then we started to get sick. I was begging for food and coins when a white man knocked me down and stamped on my hand. You see, there are worse men than Jamison."

"And better ones."

She laughed. "For other women, probably. For me? White men who think I'm dirt, and most of the young men I knew are dead. The ones left drink and sit around because there's no point in making anything of the poor land that they're going to take from us anyway, or they rage and want to take us all on the move, on to a war we won't win. Even you don't want to be around me."

I couldn't deny that it was so, but I wanted to offer her solace, the kind of empathy that I wanted for in Charles's house. We were not so different in that respect, we both wanted to be understood, to have our pain acknowledged.

"I'm sorry things are so hard for you," I said and meant it.

She shrugged. "They're hard for everyone here, different, harder for some, but, hard all the same." Again she shrewdly eyed the chaos of my larder shelf, the heap of soiled clothes. "I knew you'd struggle come winter, alone, shut up with no one to put things to rights."

"I'm sure I'll learn to manage." Even as I said it, I knew my heart wasn't in it. "Truthfully I've been wanting to leave ever since the snow came down."

"But you won't get far in it. It was foolish of Jamison to take the horses out and I've no doubt he has more experience than you." She pulled her blanket and shawl closer around her, looked about at the walls and my tangled bed. "I would have thought you'd want to stay, for Laura."

My hand jolted the coffee cup. Martha smiled. It was the first time I'd seen her smile fully and the way her face transformed was almost unnatural; her eyes shone and her teeth, white as china, gleamed.

"I don't-"

"You care for her. And she cares for you, I could see it in the way she spoke about you. She thinks you are a rare kind of man, better than her husband. Kinder. Maybe because you've never had a woman, or maybe because you come from a better family. Maybe you were just born to be kind."

"She doesn't think well of me, not anymore."

"What did you do?" Her frown was like weathered wood.

"I told a lie. She believed it and then she found out the truth."

"Why did you lie to her?"

"Because I'm...I was in danger. I think I still am. The only way to protect myself was to tell a lie. When she became my friend I should have told her, but I didn't, and now it's too late."

"She might forgive you."

"I don't expect she will. She'd certainly be right not to."

"The lie you told her, is it the same one you're telling me?"

I blinked, fear souring my stomach. "What do you -"

"I watched you, chopping wood that day at the creek. You didn't move like any man I've met. Didn't talk to me like any man either. You have the thin hands of a woman, barely a whisker under that scarf you wrap over your face."

"Does anyone else know? Jamison?"

She laughed like a tin plate spinning on the floor. "Jamison's a fool and a pig. People like him, they never look too closely at a man once they know they could beat him. And Laura, I think she wanted James Clappe to be real, so badly, she didn't want to see what was plain to me."

I couldn't find the words to defend myself, to lie my way out of it. Even if I could have spoken, I knew it was useless. She was right, and she knew it.

"I won't tell Jamison, or anyone else."

"Why did you tell me, why let me know at all?"

"Because one day soon, Jamison will force me to leave here, when he has his new wife. I'll need your help then. And, because if you care about Laura at all, you will stay, and be here for her, because she is a good woman who has no one."

I had nothing to say to that, and with her bargain made Martha finished her coffee and bid me goodnight. I bolted and latched the door behind her, wrapping my blanket about myself against a cold that was not entirely due to the snow outside. I did not like the dark, and it was only partly because of the threat of wolves. At night it was always easier to recall the night that had marked the start of my total imprisonment. The night I'd come upon Charles as he smothered Charlie in his cradle.

Remembering how I'd slapped at him, uselessly trying to pull him away from Charlie made me angry; at myself and him. I should have done something, gone to Franklyn or the police. I should have been stronger. I hated myself and wished I'd had Martha's courage to escape with my son before it was too late. I'd told myself Charles was only upset that Charlie was different, that he would learn to accept him and relent in his treatment of me. That I would be allowed outside again once he saw that nothing I had done could have made Charlie the way he was. I hadn't let myself believe that it was getting worse, hadn't seen the stubborn hatred in my husband until it was too late.

The fear I'd felt in his house had paralysed me. That night I'd seen something so terrible I knew no one would believe it. Charles said that if I breathed a word it would be the asylum for me. Never for one moment did I believe he was not capable of it. I tried to be careful, to do as he told me, but my desperation grew and in the end he made good on his threat and summoned his doctor. Had I not fled I would've been locked away like a lunatic, with everyone around me believing Charles instead of me.

Perhaps Franklyn might have taken my part in it before I'd run away, but now who would trust my word? I'd proven myself flighty and hysterical, given to fancy. I had let my fear take me hundreds of miles and months away from Charles, but it had been too late for my son. Far too late.

Chapter Twenty-Six
Laura

Christmas day dawned, with it came the birdlike twitters of my girls as they searched their stockings. Thomas had a new axe head, flannel underwear and a pair of woollen stockings that I'd made especially thick and warm for him. The girls each had a pair, even Nora. I'd made her little woollen booties.

Clappe's mittens were still unfinished. Perhaps I could make something of them for Thomas.

"Ma, put my hair up!" Rachel launched herself into my lap, brandishing her new ribbons, a gift I'd had put away since last harvest, in case we hadn't the money for them later on.

"Ma!" Beth patted my hand, trailing her own ribbons from her little fist.

"Alright, alright, be patient now, Beth, come here."

"That's not fair," Rachel whined.

"I'll do your hair straight after, it won't take a moment."

While Rachel sat at my feet in a sulk, I brushed Beth's fine, flaxen hair and curled it around my fingers as best I could. Like me she suffered from poker straight locks. I managed to coax a small bunch of ringlets into existence and tied them neatly with the blue ribbon.

"Now you." I waved Rachel to my lap.

Thomas was by the stove, fixing his axe head to a handle while Will stood over him, telling him to whittle a little more on either side, to make it fit. On the stove I had a venison stew bubbling and afterwards there was to be more Christmas pudding.

"There," I said, releasing Rachel so that she could shake her curls out.

"It's too tight."

"It'll stay on then, won't it," I said.

"Go sit, you can't do anything right," Will sighed, taking the axe head and handle from Thomas's unresisting fingers. Thomas came to the table and sat down, looking at the fringe of brown paper decorations that hung all along the table's edge.

I touched his shoulder lightly. "Why don't you come play a hand of Patience? You can have the first go."

Will glowered from the stove corner as I took out the yellowed playing cards and dealt them into small piles on the table, setting up the game. Rachel and Beth wanted to watch, so I lifted Beth onto a chair and left them to the game while I picked up Nora and held her.

"Your first Christmas," I said, watching her eyes, which had turned a darker and darker brown ever since she was born. They looked about constantly, her little mouth pouting and making 'pop' sounds in wonder. "You've put on a fair bit, I swear you gain a pound every time I pick you up."

Looking at her, on the most peaceful day I'd had since Christmas the previous year, I felt my heart, bitter clod of dirt that it was, soften. My eyes blurred as I looked at my beautiful baby girl. Hadn't I thought she might not make it? Yet here she was, big and bonny and alive.

I tickled her and she cawed with laughter.

The touch of William's hands on my waist startled me. I jumped a little, and half turned to look at him.

"Getting big now, ain't she?"

I nodded, pulling away from him. "We'll have to add to the house before long."

He huffed. "We'll not be here next year. I'm going to put up a frame house come summer, give it a tile roof and proper puncheon under foot."

I doubted it. That floor would get drunk up along with the windows and the shingles and even the sticks of candy he'd promise to the children.

"You don't think I can?" he said, and all the eased-openness of my heart clenched shut again. "I can afford that house and I'll get it for us."

"I know you will."

"And that Clappe bastard'll be gone, ruined. I'll claim that land too, seeing as it's already worked, and hire me some men to farm it. Maybe get some Indians or, who knows, maybe we'll be getting slaves up here like Jamison had down in Texas. Get them living in this place and there's us, on up by the top field with a proper porch and a brass bed in a room with just the two of us."

I nodded, but if I were to speak God's truth, I was praying for him to drink and whore the money away. Spare me a room alone with William Deene. What if he was right? Would Clappe, or whoever she was, be gone by spring? Wouldn't that make me happy, to have the lying, troubled girl as far from me as possible?

I found myself wondering how she was coping, alone in that little soddie. In my head I saw the room Will wanted, with painted wood walls and the big brass bed with a down quilt. I felt the ghost of her hand on mine, thought of us tucked away like two spoons in the warm.

"I need a smoke," Will said turning from me and fetching his pipe from the pocket of his coat. My heart jumped and my face burned. What was I doing?

"Ma, come and play with us," Rachel called.

"What's the game?" I shook off my thoughts of Clappe and her little chilblained feet tucked up with mine.

"Old maid," Thomas said, shuffling the cards.

*

As much as I wanted to forget her, Clappe wouldn't leave me alone. While we ate our stew and pudding, her face, the startled, scared little face I'd seen that day in the soddie, came back to me. The smudges of sleeplessness under her eyes, her dirty hands marked with blood from splinters. She'd fought off a wolf attack but she'd looked at me in complete terror. Was she still afraid, hiding in her soddie for fear of what I might do, who I might tell?

Did she think about me as much as I thought about her?

I wasn't one to put pity about blindly but just as I felt for Martha, being stuck with Jamison, I felt for her, being alone. After all, there were only our three small homes as far as anyone could see and we had to rely on each other. Hadn't Will helped Jamison to build his home? And hadn't Jamison taken Will to town? I wondered, lying in my bed, feeling the cold try and get its fingers under the blankets, if she needed help.

I didn't want to think about those other things, of us in a comfortable bed, or sitting inside with a lamp against the darkness, sipping coffee and wrapping presents for the children. Just seeing those pictures of us in my head I suppose anyone would have thought us friends, but it didn't feel like that inside. Though I'd been without a friend for so long, maybe that's what it was supposed to feel like, like a marriage. A marriage without fists and being pawed at or feeling alone even next to somebody.

The next morning, once I'd built up the fire and put cornmeal mush on the table, I wiped my hands on my apron and sat down beside my husband. I knew what I had to do.

"Will, I was thinking we should maybe offer Jamison something for taking us to town, as he lost his horse."

William grunted.

"Besides, you're going stir-crazy stuck in here. A little male company would be good for you and for Thomas if you take him along."

I knew I'd raised his suspicions, so I let the idea sit and acted like it was nothing to me at all, thought all the time my heart was fluttering. Busying myself with dressing the girls, it wasn't until I had the last button done up and the last curl tied neatly that he put down his coffee cup.

"I'll be going over to Jamison's then. You want to bring the girls along?"

"Beth's still too delicate to go tramping through the snow, that trip to church knocked the wind out of her." It was an easy excuse for him to swallow, mostly because he didn't want the girls along and we both knew it.

"You'll be staying here then?" he said.

180

"I've mending to do and anyway I wouldn't want to leave Beth the whole day."

He nodded, and soon he was making preparations to leave. In his thick coat he wrapped his muffler around his neck, slung his rifle over his shoulder and took up the tin lantern to light his way if he returned after nightfall. I could tell Thomas wasn't keen on going away with his Father, as I slipped a piece of corn cake into his pocket I kissed him on the top of his brown, ruffled head. I kept thinking I could tell them both to wait, that I would go with them, or that they should stay to do some job or other. I almost said it a dozen times, but each time I squeezed my jaw shut.

"Be sure to tell Martha hello from me," I said, as William pushed the door open, letting in a dagger of cold air.

"Keep that fire up."

"I'll be sure to."

The door slammed shut against the wind and I heard their footsteps crumping away in the snow.

My stomach was a snake pit. I could make my excuses to the girls, leave Nora with Rachel and Beth and go across to see Clappe, but I was afraid to. Me, afraid of seeing a woman who wore men's clothes! Wolves were to be feared, Will's wrath, wild Indians and even the toothsome cold, but a woman? I pulled myself together. If she'd ever been a friend to me, I owed her this much.

I gave Will enough time to be focusing on his walking and not on looking over his shoulder at us, then started to put my boots on. "I'm going to walk over to Mr Clappe's soddie and see that he's faring all right, I'm expecting you to be a good girl while I'm gone."

Rachel took up a bonnet and started picking through my needle box. "I will."

"And you too Beth."

She was playing with Nora on the tick and waved her doll at me.

"I'll be back soon. Watch your sisters, Rachel."

Even with my thick shawl on under my wool coat and two pairs of stockings under my boots, it wasn't long before I felt the cold. My toes became numb, my fingers in their mittens started to burn and my breath froze on the inside of my muffler. When Clappe's soddie was within shouting distance, my nerves almost failed me, but it was the cold that pushed me forwards.

As I reached the door a dog began to bark inside and I heard the rise and fall of her voice within, shushing the animal. I knocked on the frosty planks of the door. The dog refused to be quiet and as the door opened its brown face pushed into the widening gap, sniffing and barking at me.

Clappe appeared in the slice of shadow, her eyes went wide when she saw me.

"Laura?"

"I'd appreciate you calling off your dog."

She seemed not to know what she was about. "Missy," she hissed, tugging the dog back by the loose skin of its neck. She opened the door wider and I took this as permission to enter.

Inside, the soddie was much as it had been the last time I'd seen it. I was surprised to see a shaving kit and scissors on the table, the rectangle of polished tin that served as a mirror propped up against a basin.

"Shaving, Mr Clappe?"

She brushed past me and put the mirror flat on the table, sweeping up locks of damp red hair as she did so. She was dressed as a man, I could see her hair was freshly trimmed. So, she was sticking with her disguise. That meant she wasn't leaving.

"Laura, I'm so sorry about what's happened. I never meant to hurt anyone by lying."

"What were you trying to do?"

"Stay safe."

I'd seen a trick once, at a fair. It was a circle of paper with a string on either side. On one side of the paper was a picture of a red bird, on the other, a picture of a cage. When the string was twisted, the paper flipped, over and over, the bird appeared to be caught within the cage. That was what she looked like to me, by turns the woman who had tricked me and the man who'd comforted me, blurred together through trickery.

"What do I call you?"

She bit her lip, causing a little of the illusion to fall away; she looked more like a girl when she was unsure.

"Come on, you have a name don't you? Let's hear it."

"It's Cecelia."

I snorted. "So you are from some hoity-toity Ohio family."

She lowered her eyes and nodded.

"You ran away from them?" I was curious, despite myself. Gossip was at an all time low, that was all it was, I certainly wasn't itching to find out more about her because I cared.

"I ran away from my husband. Charles."

Those words made my heart shudder. "He beat you?"

She shook her head.

"You spoke of your 'sister's' child." I felt my blood heat up. "Did you mean yours? That you left behind?"

"He died," she said, and I saw her hands twist up the cuffs of her shirt. "Afterwards Charles told me my moping was pathetic, shut me out of my baby's room and had all his things taken away."

I kept my face as blank as I could. It was a horrible story to hear, yet I couldn't help but think of my own stillborn babies and the little one, before Beth, who had lasted but a week before passing on. The hard crossing from England to America, months of jolting travel by wagon, hauling our possessions with us as one-by-one things had to be abandoned, or were traded, or simply broken beyond repair. Carving a home out of the sod, raising my screaming brood as we tried to sow seeds into the wild earth and protect ourselves in a land made of more dangers than boons. William there beside me all the while, always on at me, striking me, getting me with child, beating the daylights out of me whenever the whisky flowed.

She seemed to see all of this flickering in my eyes, because she slumped onto a packing crate and put her shorn head in her hands.

"You think I was too flighty."

"I think you cut off your hair and came across the country without hardly anything. You wouldn't've lasted out here if you had anywhere else to go." I said. "He'd have to do something a damn sight worse than lock up a room to scare you this bad."

She let out a breath. I saw her try and fail to collect herself.

"The night Charlie died, I was with him. I woke up and wanted to see him, but when I reached the nursery Charles was there. He didn't notice me come in. He had a pillow over Charlie's face…" Her mouth moved but only a choking sound came out. She waved her hands like she was trying to catch the words. I took hold of one and squeezed, scared to hold her properly.

"I tried to pull him away," she whispered. "I tried but…I couldn't. Then he left Charlie and shook me. He said if I told anyone he'd have me put away, tell my family I was mad. He didn't even see that he'd done something wrong. He made it seem like it was a kindness, because Charlie's legs were crippled and he'd never walk. I was so afraid after that. I couldn't sleep, could hardly eat. Charles wouldn't let me out of the house. He wouldn't let the servants up to my rooms in case I said anything. When he caught me trying to send a note to my family he locked me in my room."

I wanted to snatch her up and out of the shadow she was under. Part of me couldn't see how she could run away, not without first throwing kerosene over his sleeping body and striking a match.

"Did you have to marry him?" I said, "I mean…did your family force him on you? Would they not understand if you told them?"

184

"I didn't love him, but he's respected, wealthy and he's pleasant enough to everyone else. He seemed it to me too."

"I think they all do. Before the marriage licence's signed."

"He wanted everything his way," she said softly. "He decided where went, who I saw. When I had Charlie it only got worse."

"Seems he ought to be the one locked up," I said.

"It'd be the only way I'd feel safe I think."

"He'll never find you here."

"I feel as though he might. It scares me. Every sound outside at night might be him." She looked down at her hands. "Besides, I...I don't think I can stay now that, now that this has happened."

"Then why'd you kiss me?" I said, forcing the words out like coughing up stones.

"You kissed me."

"I kissed James Clappe. Why did you kiss me?"

Her thin shoulders wriggled under the worn shirt. "I kissed you back. I was surprised."

Something urged me forwards, nipping at my heels. "Would you kiss anyone if they kissed you first?"

"No, I-"

"Then why kiss me?"

She ran a shaking hand through her hair, small pieces from her trimming came loose and fell like sparks in the light from the window. I wanted to touch her hair, to slide my fingers into the short, curling locks.

"I...wanted to."

I hadn't known what I was pushing her towards until I got her there. Having her there, I didn't know what to do with her. My hand crept out without my say, touched the warm softness of her hair. Her eyes were on mine. What I'd felt for

Clappe hadn't faded with the distance between us. It hadn't faded now I knew what was under those trousers and shirt.

"Laura," her voice was like a breath.

I leant closer to her. It was so different to the first time, I was more afraid, more aware of how she was different to Will, to any man I'd seen or known. I felt still the protective, murderous rage against her husband, but she was soft, nervous, kind. It changed what I felt, somehow, knowing that she cared, that she was here where I could care for her, and where she could feel that care in the gentle press of my lips to hers.

The unfamiliar feel of a woman's mouth made me close my eyes and hold my breath, scared of what I'd see and who I'd be myself when I opened them again. I was no fainting lady, but what I was doing made my head spin.

We barely touched, but there was a boiling pot in my chest, overflowing. My blood ran hot and I could see, when I pulled back from her, the hectic flush in her cheeks and the sheen to her eyes that wasn't down to tears. Fear and want fought in me like snakes.

We moved together, I opened my mouth a little against hers, felt her warm, wet breath against my tongue. I touched it with my own and our lips came together, damp and sliding. My skin was hot and prickling all over. She shook and I tightened my fingers in her hair until she gasped against my lips.

"Laura!"

The dog leapt up and started to bark, I jumped. It was William, shoving the door open as fast as Cecelia could leap away from me, tugging her shirt straight.

William seemed larger than ever in his winter wrappings, like a bear. His face was red with the cold and rage.

"Get your things on, now," he demanded, pointing at my coat and muffler. With a heavy gloved hand he pointed at Cecelia, his finger like the wrath of God. "Keep your fucking hands off my wife, or I'll cut 'em off and leave 'em out for the wolves."

I stood up, fumbling for the coat, wrapping the muffler. I didn't dare say a word. I think Cecelia was too shocked to speak and William had me by the arm, pushing me out into the white bareness of the prairie before I had a chance to look at her properly.

He slapped me across the face, once, twice, a third time. My ears rang and the sudden cold on my flaming cheeks made my head ache.

"Whore!" he shouted, the word flying out over the snow. He hit me and I fell back into the snow. The icy layer cracked under me, scraping my hands. Hot blood ran from my nose, getting into my gasping mouth, running over my chin and staining my muffler. I couldn't get my breath, couldn't get my trembling limbs to push me out of the snow. Any other day I'd have mustered the strength to put myself right, but this time I knew I deserved it. I'd kissed her, felt the powerful feeling that men must feel all the time. A feeling that wasn't for me.

Above me I heard the click of a rifle.

He was going to kill me.

"Leave her alone!"

Looking up, I saw Cecelia, holding up her gun, stockinged feet buried in the snow. The earth tilted and she seemed to flow across the sky like smoke.

"Don't you point your fucking gun at me," William growled.

"You lay another hand on her, I'll do more than point it."

I coughed and spat into the snow, feeling weak. I knew I was going to be sick. To my shame I started to cry.

A shower of snow hit my face, it took me a moment to realise that Will had kicked it over me.

"Stupid bitch," he said, "get up."

"Leave her alone."

"Shut your mouth," Will snapped, "Laura, get your ass out of the snow and come with me."

"She isn't going anywhere with you."

187

Oh, if only that were true. I wanted to stay with her, more than anything. Going with Will meant more slaps, kicks, meant showing my battered face to the children and waiting for night when Will would hurt me all over again, just like when Jacob told him what we'd done. Only this was worse, far worse.

I wanted her to wrap me up in her bed and put snow on my bruises, to put her arms around me and hold me the way no one had ever done, the way I'd always wanted to be held. I wanted her to disappear, taking what we'd done with her.

But what else could I do? I couldn't leave my children at home with him. There was no telling what he might do in a rage if he didn't have me to blunt his anger on.

I let him drag me to my feet and stumbled as he forced me to march along with him.

I didn't dare look back.

Chapter Twenty-Seven
Laura

It was Rachel who'd told him where I was. Will and Thomas had turned back before they ever reached Jamison's, Will's suspicious nature being what it was. William found me missing and demanded of Rachel where I'd gone, though of course he knew. When she refused to answer he'd cuffed her around the head and left her with a large sloe coloured bruise. She told him where I was. I couldn't blame her for it. It was my fault she'd gotten hurt.

I suppose everything looked the same. I cooked, I cleaned, I talked to the children and got them to do their daily tasks around the house. I fed Nora and combed Beth's hair and put my girls to sleep each night. But over it all hung the threat of William's boiling temper.

Two days after he dragged me back from Cecelia's he cornered me in the barn where I was strewing fresh hay. The door was closed to the frosty air, the barn dark and filled with the steamy breath of the oxen, the ripe smell of their shit and the heat from their skins. He hadn't laid a hand on me since we'd been back.

"Will-"

He came towards me, pushed me into the corner and turned me round so my face was to the wall, the hay in its hanging net scratching my face.

"Don't, Will!"

He pushed my skirt up and shoved me further forward, one hand planted on my back to keep me still, the other around my throat. I wanted to turn and fight him, to kick him and bite his hands and scratch his eyes out of his head, but I knew he'd kill me. My fury held my tears inside me until he was done heaving and pushing, half choking me. Without putting my skirts down he threw me to the dirty floor and went out into the snow.

On the ground, surrounded by straw and shit and feeling like a dog trampled under a wagon, I felt a greater fear than I'd ever known. William had hurt me before, even forced himself on me, but now I knew there would be no end to it, not this time. I had gone too far and there would be no sobering light of dawn or a day good enough to make him forget. I rubbed my throat, knowing it would bruise.

What made it worse was that Cecelia was only a mile or so away. Her house was the only thing I could see across all the snow. It looked like one of the grass houses Rachel built for her dolls. The urge to go to her was stronger than it had been as I'd lain in the snow. I thought of the gentle touch of her lips to mine, the way she'd clung to me – wanting her but afraid of what we'd done. Perhaps we could forget it, she could be my friend. I needed her, either way.

But I wanted her.

"Ma?"

It was Rachel, carrying a bucket of fresh water. She stood in the doorway, looking down at me. "Are you hurt?"

"No, sweet pea," I dragged myself to my feet, tears at my own shame coming too easily to be held back.

"Is Pa still angry at me?"

I couldn't talk, my throat was too thick.

"I'm sorry I told him you went out."

I put my arms around her, smoothing her back, biting my lip to keep my sobs inside. She squeezed my waist tightly, hurting the bruises that coloured my skin under my dress. I didn't care, I didn't want to let her go.

"You're a good girl Rachel," I managed, "Pa loves you very much, he was angry at me, that's all, I promise."

"Why did you go to Mr Clappe's house?"

I stroked the softness of her braid, so like mine. I'd tied it only that morning, but it was already coming undone.

"He's our neighbour, Rachel. You know how important our neighbours are to us."

She pulled away from me slightly, looked up at me with her dark eyes. Since Christmas I'd seen warmth in them when she looked at me. I'd hoped that she was beginning to love me, that it would be easier for me to love her, as I had when she was small.

"Why don't we go back inside and start sewing up your quilt pieces?"

Taking her little hand in mine I led her out into the cold, walking back towards the soddie. In the distance, Clappe's house stood out like a small hill against the flat, frozen land. Further west, patches of tawny brown were showing through the white.

Spring was coming.

*

As the weeks passed, the snow began to melt. The weather became mild and clear. Every time I went outside to haul water or clean out the pot I saw more and more mud and grass peeking through the snow banks.

Every morning, once the chores were done with, Beth and Rachel took to the outside world like thirsty men to a pail of water. Running between the barn and the house, Rachel pretended to gallop like a pony, tossing her hair and whinnying. Beth followed after her, kicking at the ground and stamping on slush.

The fear that had stuck like a fist in my throat for weeks gradually loosened, as William had more and more to do away from the house, though there was never a moment when I didn't want to go to Cecelia and be comforted.

Fingerlings of our new crops were raising themselves out of the wet earth, corn and wheat furred the land in a haze of green. There was ploughing and harrowing to be done so that the crops of root vegetables could be put in for harvesting that winter. Once more turnips took up our every waking moment and William, no longer at my side for every hour of the day, became a bearable jailer, plodding in the distance with the oxen.

On the third day of our work in the fields, Jamison came riding towards us over the prairie. William stopped his work and turned to watch Jamison come closer.

He hauled the dun coloured horse to a stop and reached up to brace his hat, a faded thing with a narrow, upturned brim.

"What's Mr Neaps doing here?" Thomas said.

I didn't answer, but I picked up my skirts and led the children with their seed baskets over to where Jamison sat, talking down to Will.

"...in the barn," Jamison was saying, "I'm hoping to get there for early evening. Tomorrow morning there's a circuit rider coming through, lucky as hell. Want it done before I've got to get down to ploughing."

Will noticed us first. "Jamison's off to town, getting himself a wife."

"Who is she?" I asked.

"Hattie Bakewell, you met her at church, Christmastime."

I remembered the whore, wearing a dress of soiled lace and pink ruffles.

"Snow's clearing, ground's not so wet now, figured it was time to get the thing done. She doesn't have much, no point taking the wagon out for a valise of frocks and shoes."

As if he could pull his wagon with the one horse. As it was he'd be pushing it to bring Hattie back along with her one valise. I eyed the horse's legs and wondered what Jamison would do if one of those went down in a hole. He'd be done for, with nothing to pull his plough. How desperate was he to get himself a white woman to be his wife and have his babies? My guess was he'd had a rough time of it from the gossip mongers and was looking to trade up to a more acceptable woman before it came time to deal with the store holders again.

"Where's Martha?" I asked, realising that if he was off to get himself a wife, he must be looking to get rid of her. "Did she leave already?"

"Leave?" Jamison shared a look with Will, as if I was simple minded, "I've got a turnip crop to put in same as you, gonna need hands for that. No, Martha's not leaving. I'm gonna build up a little line shack for her by the barn. When the baby comes she'll be less of a use, but it doesn't look like that'll be 'til after harvest time. Towards the end anyway."

"She's pregnant?"

Jamison shrugged, "Neaps men, we're all virile as they come. 'Course it's not going to be a problem, there's schools run by good folks who take those type of bastards and give 'em work on farms and such."

William nodded, easing his hands from where the reins had bitten into them. "Know any that take white girls?"

"Got any you don't need?" he cast his eyes to Rachel and I fought the urge to drag him from his horse and push his face into the mud. He could marry his whore and I wouldn't bat an eye, but if he looked at my daughter like she was some sweet meat again I'd skin him and salt him.

I looked up and found William's eyes on me, he was prodding me, waiting to see if I'd rise to the bait. I didn't.

"Sorry we can't come, but stop by for a drink or two on your way back," William said, "you and Hattie'll be welcome."

Jamison grinned, his red mouth splitting his tangled beard. "It'll be a welcome rest. I'll be seeing you in a day or so then."

He turned his horse and set off for town. I watched him go, wondering if Miss Bakewell knew what she was letting herself in for. Whoring, from what little I knew of it, seemed a terrible occupation, but it came with its comforts, like scent and leisure and plush clothes. How would she get along with washing, ironing, sewing, planting, cooking, cleaning and whelping by day, while still whoring herself at night?

"Get back to it then," William said sharply, "got a whole field to plant up, or there'll be no supper for you."

You'd think that doing the cooking would give me the right to decide who ate and who didn't. It wasn't the first time I'd wanted to kill him with a hoe, or an axe, but the sudden image of his neck under my foot made me feel sick. I forced myself to turn around and walk back to where we'd been before Jamison rode up.

"Did he leave Martha on her own?" Thomas wondered aloud, flinging out a handful of seed. "She'd be best taking what she can get and leaving before the fucker comes home."

"Thomas!" I cuffed his head, lightly, looked up to see if Will was watching, but for once he wasn't.

"Don't you use such language, and in front of your sister! Shame on you."

Rachel elbowed her brother, the three of us carried on our sowing, walking in a line, throwing the seed and treading down the earth.

What had become of Martha? Thomas was right, Jamison had to know that Martha wouldn't stay put to be little more than a slave. What had he done to keep her from fleeing?

I remembered what he'd said to Will as the children and I came upon them. 'In the barn'. I knew then that he must have locked her up to keep her from stealing from him and running away. Not that there was anything to steal if he was riding his only horse, carrying his only gun. What was he worried she'd take? The very glass from his windows?

What was worse, there was nothing I could do. There was no way William would let me out alone and he wasn't going to come with me to set Martha free. What's more I could think of nowhere safer for her. There would be no place for her in town, or with Will and me. The only other choice was a reservation, or further west, alone.

I wished for the hundredth time that I had Cecelia to talk to, she'd listen and find a way to help. She'd gotten herself out of Ohio well enough. I couldn't talk to her though, might not have been able to speak if she was in front of me. What we'd done was something I couldn't look straight at. It was too much. It hardly mattered though, it wasn't as though Will would ever let me out of his sight again anyway.

How could I help Martha when I couldn't even help myself?

Chapter Twenty-Eight
Laura

Jamison was gone the rest of that day and didn't return the next. I tended my garden and watched the horizon. When would he return and how much food and water had he left for poor Martha, shut up like a cow in the barn?

My worry for her lessened my fear for myself. William was distracted with work, so I was no longer as fearful of being struck or taken back to the barn and forced. The worst thing was not being able to see her, to lay my troubles out for her and find a place in her arms. I ached for her kind voice, for the touch of her hand on my cheek. I felt often that I was going crazy, lit inside with the need for her kiss, her touch, my chest aching just to hear her voice.

Rachel, poking seeds into the plots I'd already dug, reached over and pushed Beth's dirty hands down towards the drills I'd raked.

"Like this, stupid."

"Rachel, watch how you speak to your sister."

She pushed her braid over her shoulder and squinted up at me, against the rays of the spring sun. "Is Mr Neaps not back?"

"No, he's not."

"But where's Martha?"

"Hush," I looked about, but William was nowhere to be seen, he and Thomas had taken the oxen out of the barn to graze on some of the new grass. "That's Mr Neaps' business and we shan't meddle in it."

Wishing that I could just take a shovel and go break Martha out, I put Beth on my lap and showed her how to poke the seeds into the ground. From the soddie came Nora's thin cry.

Stepping quickly through the garden, I reached the soddie just as Nora was giving herself over to wailing like an animal in a trap.

"Hush now," I picked her up, checked her napkin and found it dry. "Hungry, sweet pea?" Her red, scrunched up face gave no answer, but I sat myself down and held her with one arm while I undid the front of my dress. I was out of salve for my teat and had been making do with cooking grease. Of course Cecelia had known better than any man why I needed it. She must have used the same thing when nursing her poor baby son. I couldn't imagine the fear she'd felt, knowing what that man had done.

Once Nora had taken enough milk I put her to my shoulder and patted her back. She really was getting big, her little legs kicking and her arms clutching at me as I put her back in her cradle box. She picked up the ragdoll I'd made for her Christmas stocking, the head of it already wet with drool and started to gum it again, smiling up at me. I smiled down at her.

Lying awake that night, Cecelia and her husband entered my thoughts again. Although he had many, many faults, Will had made the little wood boxes for the children I lost, held my hand as we stood by their tiny hillocks in the ground. I didn't believe he was capable of doing away with a new-born. Whatever kind of man Cecelia's husband was, I shuddered to think what he might have done to her had she stayed with him.

How lonely was she, shut up in her soddie, facing the awful thing her husband had done? I wanted to comfort her, to make her smile again and forget her fear for a moment.

I wondered if she was lying as I was, wishing she was with me. My heart beat heavily in my chest. I thought of the soft, pointed breasts I'd seen under her night shirt, of her lip, lips that should have told me the truth the moment they touched mine, for no man's lips had the right to be that soft.

Seized by unnatural thoughts, by lust, I forced my eyes open and looked up to the dark sod ceiling. I asked the Lord for a great many things during the day, though mostly it was a word I threw into my begging without thinking He was actually listening. It had been a long time since I'd expected God to help with anything, but it was a habit I had and would never unlearn. I asked Him then, trying to believe, to protect me and my children from William and to protect my family from my own weakness. Finally, not daring to take too long over it, I asked that he keep Cecelia from her husband.

Chapter Twenty-Nine
Cecelia

Not knowing what he was doing to her was torture. Over and over I berated myself for not having the courage to pull the trigger of my rifle when I had the chance. The rage I felt towards him was strong, but not entirely new. I'd buried my anger against Charles, but now that I remembered what he'd done I felt it again, stronger than before.

My anger fed on my fear; fear of Charles, fear for Laura but also of her. The loneliness of winter gave me endless hours in which to think about our kiss, for I couldn't bring myself to talk to Franklyn as doing so only reminded me of how much I'd changed and how appalled he'd be at me. Wrong as it was, I had grown to wish for another kiss, and another. At first I'd blamed my total isolation for my lust, my desire to just be near her, to hear her voice. Gradually I'd realised that it had nothing to do with my situation and everything to do with her. Just her.

From afar, as a distant, doll-like figure, I saw Laura around the soddie, always with William, even if she was only throwing out the contents of their pot, or drawing water. My glimpses of her were brief, but enough to power my frustration, rage and guilt. I was sick with the knowledge that she was trapped with that man. Her and her poor children.

I wanted to take the rifle and go to the soddie, free them from William and his constant watchfulness, but my courage failed me as soon as the smooth stock of the gun touched my hands. I wasn't a killer. I didn't even know if she wanted me. That kiss, with her knowing who and what I was, it could have been an aberration, one she was now deeply regretting.

The weather turned warmer and the snow began to recede, revealing brown grass half rotted, with a haze of green pushing through. I saw more of Laura and two of her children, dark haired Rachel and Thomas, a tiny version of his father, as they worked part of their land.

My mind flew over and over again to the kiss we had shared in my soddie. She'd known who I was then and it hadn't stopped her. It hadn't stopped me. What did it mean? What did it make us? I'd never heard of such a thing as ladies kissing each other, not even amongst the lower classes. It had felt like something new and free, something that we two had created between us. I had never thought having someone's mouth against mine could make me feel so good, so happy.

What if she didn't feel that way? I could waste away the whole planting season and starve come winter, wanting and waiting for a woman who I couldn't speak to, or even see up close. I'd gambled recklessly when I'd left Charles for the world beyond his door and I was not about to find myself spending another winter hungry and alone. For better or worse, I had to plant.

The ploughing was hard work, but driving the mustangs and forcing rows into the stubborn soil helped me to exhaust myself, to the point where the knot in my stomach no longer kept me awake, though fear was still an ever present weight on me.

When I was woken after midnight on one particularly frigid night by a scratching, I thought it was Charles trying to get in, or perhaps the wolves, back to kill me. Missy was sitting by the door, cocking her head at the sound, and it was then that I heard it for what it was; a frightened hand scratching the wood, while through the door came a woman's voice, murmuring to the dog.

I pulled myself out of bed, grabbed my rifle and opened the door a chink.

"It's me, Martha."

I stepped back and let her in, putting the rifle against the wall as I closed the door.

She didn't light the lamp on the table, but put a candle on a saucer right on the floor and lit it.

"So he doesn't see the light." As she stood up I saw how ragged she looked; her dark hair was wild and tangled with small bits of hay, her calico dress was creased and the hem ripped so it hung limply to her ankles. Her feet were bare.

"What's happened? Did Jamison...?"

"Jamison brought his new wife home. Hattie, a whore from town."

Her long brown fingers circled her wrists lightly, and I saw that they were bloody and scabbed from being bound, with what? Rope? Chains? What had he done to her?

"Did he force you to go, now, at night?"

She shook her head.

"He wants me for a field hand, but she, she wants me gone, before this -" She put her hand on her stomach. "- Before it grows any more." She looked up and showed me a slice of white smile like a bone, "She said she didn't like me looking at her, 'that brown bitch's all eyes, she'll kill us both in our sleep if you let her roam around at night'. So he kept me tied in the barn last night while she was squealing on the tick that I made, that I stuffed and beat clean. Well, that's her job now."

"You're pregnant?"

She nodded. "And I'm running. You said you'd help me."

"Where are you going to go?"

She waved a hand as though she was batting away a gnat. "I need some food, something warm, whatever you can spare. I have to leave now."

"But you don't have anywhere to go, you said-"

"You don't know me," she said, sharply, "you don't know how I lived before Jamison. Or what it's like on one of our reservations and you don't have to. You said you'd help me, so help me, or I'll go with nothing."

I hadn't forgotten that she was an Indian, that she was, at heart, a savage. But I knew the feeling she had painted over her face; it was the same one that had made me run from Charles and that hadn't let me stop running until I reached the Deene's farm.

"Give me a moment to get some things together," I turned from her and went to the supply chest by the stove. There was a gunny sack bundled around the sheet of canvas I'd made my tent with.

"I'm sorry," she muttered.

"He's a no good lout," I said, "you're right to run, it's only...God, he should run. You should take my gun and shoot him right in the head."

She laughed, a surprised, cold little laugh, like a buzzard cry. "They'd hang me."

"They should hang him."

I stuffed a bar of soap, a candle and a jar of preserve into the sack with the canvas. I had no spare shoes, but there was my wool scarf and the hat I'd worn on my arrival. I had four cents hidden under the chest in a fold of cloth, and I took them out and put them on the table in front of her.

"If he comes here, you can shoot him," she said.

"If he comes here, he'll shoot me first."

She looked away. "He won't know I came here, or that you helped me...neither will Deene."

I put the sack on the table. "I'm afraid of him. Of both of them. Do you think I should run?"

"You'll stay," she said. "You'll stay for her."

I felt all my worries come flying from the shadows. "I think he's hurting her."

"He is. Jamison was talking about her. He stopped off with his new bride and came home telling stories about how William wasn't a 'hen pecked son-of-a-bitch' anymore. He said she had bruises, that she was scared every time he raised his hand to take a drink."

To have it confirmed to me was worse than imagining what he was doing to her.

Martha opened the sack and looked through the contents.

"I have an axe handle you can take too," I took it from the small bundle I'd carved over the winter. "You should be able to get a head for it in town."

She opened out the fold of cloth and touched the coins. "I can't take money."

"I'll be alright without it."

She sighed. "They'll never believe it's mine, they might put me in jail while they work out who I took it from."

I hadn't considered that. At least I'd had the luxury of trust while I'd been travelling as a woman.

Martha looked away, picked up the sack and the axe handle. "I should go, I have to find somewhere out of sight before day comes and Jamison goes out looking."

"He'll look for you by the creek, in the ravine."

"He won't find me." She tied the sack to her belt with a loop of twine, tucked the handle into it at the small of her back. I went to my small pile of linen and handed her a thin blanket made of dark wool, Martha put it around her shoulders. She wrapped the scarf around her face and put the battered hat on her head.

"You won't see me again," she said.

I believed her. Her flight would make mine look like the clumsy stampede of a hundred cattle. She was as practical as I'd been foolish. No one would see her go and no one would remember her as she passed through town after town. I knew that by the time her baby came, she would be in another state, with other people, with a different name.

"I wish I could be like you," I said, "as strong as you are, and free."

Her steady hands fastened the blanket across her chest, like a cloak. "There's no freedom, not anymore. I'm going where he chases me, where men like him will always chase us. And when there's nowhere left to go...well, by then I might not be alive to see what happens."

I wanted to say something about the towns growing and prospering on what had once been empty prairie. It wasn't Indians who built those things, who'd made the country rich and strong as it was. But I held my tongue, because I knew that to her it was all different, that to her it meant losing her home. I wanted us to part as peacefully as we could, under the circumstances.

We didn't touch; I didn't feel able to step forwards and embrace her. We didn't say goodbye. Martha only turned to the door and opened it. The light from the candle barely reached outside, and as soon as she left she was swallowed up by the darkness.

Missy whined and I closed the door, sitting back down by the table, looking at the candle on its saucer. There was no way I could go back to sleep, not with the wind whispering outside, carrying Martha away into the night.

Chapter Thirty

Laura

"Gone! The bitch slipped out while I was sleeping and ran off."

Jamison thumped his cup down on the table and made me jump. He'd been red faced and furious when he arrived just after dawn. He wanted to take Will out to search for Martha by the creek as soon as we were done with breakfast.

"How'd she get loose?"

Jamison scrubbed a hand through his beard. "Must've cut through the ropes with one of the tools, she made a goddamn hole under the door. Now I've got to fix the barn and get the planting done without her, the selfish bitch. After I kept her fed and clothed through the winter."

I glanced over to where Rachel was combing out Beth's hair. "Can you keep your voice down?" I asked him.

Jamison looked to Will, and Will glared at me. "Get more coffee on, for a flask," he said.

I went to the stove, wishing I was brave enough to fling the pot at his head.

Hattie was sitting on the supplies chest, hands folded in her lap. I wasn't expecting her to help. She'd done nothing but sit on her ass the night Jamison came back with her. There was me, sweating over a pot of venison stew and a loaf of bread baked with soft, white, store flour, and she, dressed in that same beribboned dress she'd worn at Christmas, laughing and leaning on Jamison's arm. Will had hardly been able to keep his eyes off of her low cut front. She was like one of those exotic birds in a cage at a fair – all song and puffed up feathers.

"You got any whisky?" she asked over her shoulder.

"None."

She sighed, one hand straying to a faint set of bruises on her wrist.

"Think she had help?" William was asking Jamison.

"You mean, do I think there's savages waiting nearby to come burn down my house? No. No, she's brown on the outside, white as a lily underneath, her own people'll have nothing to do with her. She talks about 'em like they're dogs."

Hattie tipped her catlike face up and glared at him. "What'd you need that slut for?"

"Are you gonna plant all those fields? Are you gonna mend the barn and plant brush fences?"

She looked down, cowed.

"That's what I thought."

"We'll all come across and help you out," William said.

"Thanks...think Clappe'd help for a couple've decent meals?"

Will snorted. "You think he'd be any help at all? I've been looking over at his fields the last few days, not a straight line anywhere. My guess is he's never even ploughed before."

"Could you spare your boy?"

Thomas was watering the oxen. William scratched his cheek as he thought about it.

"Can't say he'd be much help to you, best wait 'til we can all come across."

William stood up and motioned impatiently for the flask of coffee. I filled the watchman's bottle and wrapped it in a piece of sacking.

"Hattie'll be keeping you company," Will said, already turning his back and sliding his boots on.

When the men'd departed in the wagon I picked up the dirty plates and started stacking them. Hattie stayed where she was, looking at the far wall with bored, unsatisfied eyes.

"He's making a big fuss over that whore," she said finally, crossing her bare legs beneath her dirty skirt. "He don't need her for planting anything, her or her bastard. I think he's just mad as hell she left him, 'stead of him leaving her some place."

Her husband's coarse mouth had already set my teeth on edge and hers was no better. "Kindly keep your language civil in front of my children, Mrs Neaps."

"'Mrs Neaps'," she simpered, mimicking me, "how come you've still got those fancy English airs about you when you live in this barn?"

I looked up from the bucket and found Rachel's eyes wide, dislike rolled off her like stink from a skunk.

"You know what they say, manners don't cost a thing."

She snorted. "Men like your husband didn't come to me for manners."

I put down my cloth and leant on the sides of the bucket, "And men like Jamison don't take too kindly to lazy sluts who can't wash a dish."

Her jaw, full of crooked, brownish teeth, went tight, I went back to my washing.

Once everything was dry and my anger had banked down a little, I took the girls outside and found Thomas just coming out of the stable.

"Thomas, would you cut some stove lengths, I've a lot of laundry to do while it's clear."

"Sure," he glanced to where the wagon had been, "Pa and Mr Neaps out looking for Martha?"

"For all the good it'll do them. Two idiots hunting an Indian, she could be sitting between them and they wouldn't know it."

He laughed and I allowed myself to smile.

As he went to fetch his axe, I turned and looked out towards where the ravine ran through the prairie. In the far distance I could see the wagon, like a toy. A movement caught my eye and I saw Cecelia standing by her soddie, a tiny figure in the distance. She was waving.

I frowned, held my hands up to shield my eyes from the pale sunlight.

She waved a few more times, then, seemingly sure of my attention, she pointed across the prairie, slightly east of where I stood, to where Jamison's house was. After pointing for a few seconds, she turned and pointed away, not towards the ravine, but still further east.

I whipped off my bonnet and waved it over my head. Martha had run to Cecelia, that had to be it. From there she'd gone east, and that meant Jamison could search the ravine all he wanted, he wouldn't find her.

She waved back at me, then went still and just watched me. I looked back and, for a few moments I felt my fear towards her, for what we'd done, grow lighter in my chest. Though I'd prayed and suffered, the wanting would not go away. For the first time I looked right at what we'd done, like staring at the sun 'til you could see it even when you looked away. I knew I'd never stop seeing it then, that I would always think of her. I was still afraid, deep inside myself, but not of her, of what it was that pulled me to her. Like the world was suddenly backwards I was afraid of everything that might come between us, or would keep me from her.

*

Jamison's search was useless, two days after Martha disappeared he was forced to admit defeat. Martha had gotten away. She was free and Jamison had only bitter little Hattie to work for him. I was more than pleased.

When we were finished with our own work, planting the fields up, readying the garden and fixing the damage that the winter winds had done to the house and barn, William drove us over to Jamison's farm in the wagon. We were all going to have to pitch in to get Jamison's field's ploughed and planted in time. I treated the extra work as the price for Martha's freedom and I was happy pay it.

The soddie Will had helped build in the fall was still standing, smaller than ours but sturdy, with a barn beyond it. A yard of trodden dirt was strewn with splinters of wood and bone from where he'd chopped stove lengths and divided up deer. A smoke house sat off to the right and tacked on to the end of the soddie was a tarpaper line shack - Martha's new living quarters. I thanked God she'd never spend the night in there, it looked like a kennel.

"Mornin'" Jamison was coming back from watering his one remaining horse, "Hattie's got coffee on inside, you want to leave the children with her?"

"She's not coming out?"

Jamison grunted. "She's got work to do inside, place looks like a pack of dogs've been through it."

I picked up Nora, Rachel took Beth by the hand. Inside Jamison's soddie I found Hattie, her hair dirty and hanging loose, hard at work trying to make dough, working a sloppy mess in a bowl with her hands. I recognised the calico dress she was wearing, it'd been Martha's.

She looked up as I set Nora's cradle box down on the plank table by the mixing bowl.

"If she starts squalling don't think I'm gonna change her, I've got enough to be doing."

"I see that."

There was only a tick, shelves, the stove and a pair of chairs in the room. I guessed that the chest at the end of the tick held clothes. Everything was dusty, with soiled dresses and shirts hanging on the chairs unwashed dishes stacked in a bucket by the door.

"You can stop it with that look as well," she pointed a dough clagged finger at me, "I don't have any brats to pick up after me."

Ignoring her, I put my hand on Rachel's shoulder. "We'd best get out to the field. There's work to do. Why don't you fill up the flask and I'll fill one for Mr Neaps."

I took the coffee from the stove, filled the flasks and didn't offer another word to Hattie.   I hated to leave Beth and Nora under Hattie's beady eyed glare, but there was no time to waste and William would never let Rachel stay behind when all hands were needed.

We'd brought both yoke of oxen with us, one team pulled our plough while the other pulled Jamison's. We worked at it hard until just gone noon, by then a pile of stones had built up at the end of the field where the children and I had been dumping them.

"Laura, go fetch out the food will you?" Jamison said, as if I were his servant. William waved me off to do his bidding and I went to the house with a scowl so deep that I could feel it stiffening on my face.

Inside the soddie Nora was awake and whimpering hungrily, so I took her up and set her to feeding. Beth was wiping dishes as Hattie washed them, but aside from that the house looked no cleaner.

"They sent me in to get the dinner."

"On the table, are you blind?"

Hattie had managed to bake her wet dough into a gummy loaf that hadn't risen more than a hair's breadth. It sat in a cloth lined basket with a jar of molasses.

"Beth, sweet pea, do you want to come have dinner with me and your sister?"

She nodded, dropped her rag and climbed down from the chair.

Hattie pursed her lips, but said nothing as I took my daughters outside.

We ate hungrily. No one dared mention that the bread was unrisen and over salted. I wasn't pleased with the meal, if only because I'd always laid on a good spread for Jamison when he came by. I remembered the pie Martha had baked for her visit with us. Had she been a white woman she would have been a good wife to Jamison, better than he deserved. I hoped one day she'd make a pie for a man of her own, who loved her. At the very least she deserved to raise her baby in peace.

We were spending the night at Jamison's, so that we could start out early as possible on the rest of the ploughing. We'd brought our ticks on the wagon and a basket of food, cornbread, bean stew and chokecherry jam tarts. I could almost hear Jamison's stomach sigh in relief. I knew he had to be missing Martha's cooking.

Hattie ate little and spoke less, while Jamison got out a bottle of whisky and poured Will drink after drink. When he started telling stories about the slaves he'd owned in Texas, I decided it was time to put the girls to bed, before he got to unsavoury talk. Thomas put his tick down on a free bit of floor and lay down to sleep, curled under his blanket.

I stayed up, refusing to make the first move towards the dirty dishes. Hattie had done some work towards cleaning the place up, but the soiled clothes were still there, piled in a corner now and the floor was scattered with crumbs and dark spots where coffee or grease had been spilt.

The fire died down and the men grew drunker. Even Hattie was spark eyed from drinking a few cups of whisky. Uneasiness began to slide up my spine. I didn't want to go to bed, no matter how tired I was. I didn't trust either of the men, or Hattie, come to that.

"See, if she'd been a slave, like I've been saying they should be, I could have her found and brought back," Jamison said. "Sooner the government gets its head straight on the matter, the better. I could triple the size of my land and have niggers farm the lot for nothing. Grow corn as far as you can see."

William was nodding, ruddy firelight reflecting in his eyes.

Hattie rubbed a hand on the back of Jamison's neck. "Soon as they pass that bill, settle this place officially, we'll have our own house, two storeys, won't we?"

"Three storeys, four! Get ourselves a porch, grow tobacco and make whisky. Build a bigger farm than my daddy ever dreamed of."

He grabbed Hattie and hauled her into his lap, devouring her mouth while she wriggled against him. I looked away but from the corner of my eye saw that he was pulling up her faded dress. She wasn't wearing drawers. I got up, but William grabbed me and tried to pull me to his lap. I pulled away. Jamison laughed and Hattie's shrill giggle made William curse after me. Tripping on my skirts, I went to our tick at the back of the room, beside Rachel and Beth. They were sleeping. I picked Nora up and cradled her in my arms. The three of them around the table looked like demons in the fire's glow.

While Jamison embraced his wife, Will stepped around Thomas's bed and came towards me, kneeling on the tick and breathing whisky breath on my face.

"Don't be so cold to me."

I calmed Nora but kept her against me. "Lay a hand on me and I'll shoot you while you sleep."

He laughed. "You wouldn't dare. You've got nothing without me."

I just glared at him, praying that the hate in me would show in my eyes, wiping out the fear. He took my wrist in his hand and squeezed until the bones ground together. I clenched my jaw to keep silent. He huffed a laugh, struggled to his feet and went back for more whisky.

I laid Nora back in her cradle box and curled up on the tick, facing the drunkards, watching over my children.

*

We left for home the next morning. After a night of barely sleeping, listening to Jamison's coarse talk and his panting efforts on his new wife, coupled with the work of preparing and sowing the fields had me dead on my feet by the time we loaded our ticks into the wagon and set off. I would have expected a gift of some sort, as thanks for the work we'd done. As it was, Hattie's lack of generosity wasn't the greatest ill I was suffering.

Two nights of having Will's hands paw me in the dark while Jamison and Hattie coupled blatantly not three feet from us had me wishing for a bottle of strychnine to lace his coffee with. The anger didn't dissipate, even on the long ride back to our soddie. I didn't say a word to Will, though I doubt he noticed, being as sick with drink as he was.

Rachel and Thomas were both filthy, as there'd been no chance to wash anything more than our hands and faces. I was dusty, my nails rimed with earth. Both Beth and Nora had become fretful with being away from their home and their dolls, though Beth soon perked up when Will let Stick out of the barn.

While the girls stroked and petted Stick, I went to check on the garden and found green sprouts already coming up through the soil. Further out, the corn and wheat were almost two inches high, beyond that the grass waved, as bright and new as the down on a chick.

It was a busy day, but by the time the sun started to sink, I had everyone washed, and our clothes clean and dried. It was a relief to have control over the cooking again, to celebrate an end to Hattie's efforts I made a thick stew and a pan of cornbread sweetened with some of our precious 'company' sugar to have after.

Tired from helping me with the cleaning, Rachel started to yawn as I served the meal, and soon afterwards I put her and Beth to bed. Thomas, sore from a hard day of tending to the oxen and the garden for me, soon followed, then it was just me and William at the table. That night at least, it was a relief.

Chapter Thirty-One
Laura

The weather got hotter. It hadn't rained for weeks and the dirt was dryer than ashes. Every evening I hauled water and poured it over the onions, beans and roots that I was growing, but nothing could be done for the corn and wheat. We just had to hope for rain. Will wasn't speaking to me more than he had to, but if anything that made me worry more.

I looked towards Cecelia's place last thing each evening as I watered the garden and every morning when I emptied our pot. I looked for her at least a dozen times a day. I never saw more than a distant figure in the fields. I no longer cared if what I felt was wrong, was dangerous. All I needed was to speak to her, just once. I needed to know what she thought of it.

I was looking for her when the cloud came over the horizon.

Shielding my eyes from the sun, I looked up and saw the strange, shimmering cloud as it grew on the edge of the prairie. Around me the grass waved and hissed in the wind.

"Ma," Thomas ran up behind me. "What is it?"

"I don't know." I squinted. It was like nothing I'd ever seen before, but it was coming closer, making a huge shadow on the waving grass of the prairie. "Where's your father?"

"In the barn."

"Your sisters still in the house?"

"Yes."

"Get inside and give a shout to Pa, tell him to come out here."

After a few minutes I heard Will coming over and turned to look at him. The cloud was a few minutes away, there was a sound on the wind, a chattering, clicking, like seeds being poured.

"Shit," Will's eyes were round. "What in the world?"

Will and I ran to the soddie and closed the door. I shut up all the windows and Will peered through the shutters as the cloud came closer. The sound of clicking grew louder and was followed by soft sounds, lots of them, all at once. Something tapped on the roof, falling like heavy rain. Rachel and Beth sat on their tick, clutching each other's hands, Thomas stood by the wall, eyes wide.

"What is it?" I asked.

Will turned to me, his face stunned, "Grasshoppers. Hundreds of them."

"Where did they come from?" Rachel said.

"Out of the sky," Thomas told her.

William had returned to his place at the window. "They're in the garden, in the fucking corn!" He turned to me. "They'll eat everything!"

It was like being hit in the chest with a lump of ice. That was our entire future growing out there. Every shoot, every slowly growing ear was needed to pay for our winter supplies.

"Get sacks," I said, gesturing for Rachel to go through the supply chest. "We'll cover the garden."

"Cover the well too. Boy, load up the tub with chips and any wood that's left. We'll smoke them off."

Leaving Beth inside with Nora we ran out into the fall of grasshoppers. The ground was already covered in them and as more fell they bounced off of our shoulders, scrabbled on our backs, getting caught in our hair. Rachel screamed and I squealed despite myself. Under my feet the insects turned to green-brown sludge, I could feel them crunching under my boots.

The well cover was a handful of planks nailed together, but I lifted it over the hole in the ground and weighted it with stones. Rachel and I threw our sacks over the small plants and tried to shield them from the clicking, leaping insects. It was no use, the grasshoppers were too fast, there were too many. I could see the green sprouts being eaten up before my eyes. Everywhere their shiny eyes bulged, their jaws worked and the sounds of their chewing, of their hopping only grew louder.

Rachel started to wail, and I saw that she had several of the things, each as long as my forefinger and twice as thick, tangled in her hair. I scooped her up, hurrying back to the soddie. With shudders running down my spine I pulled the grasshoppers from her hair and threw them down on the ground, then pushed her inside and slammed the door.

There were grasshoppers in my skirts, and my underskirts. I pulled each one off and threw them into the stove, where they smoked and popped in the flames.

"I don't want to go out again Ma." There were tears on Rachel's face.

"I won't make you, there's no point." I rubbed my hands over my face, then looked at them, they were stained with juice, like tobacco spit. I screwed my nose up. There were brown stains on my clothes and Rachel's too.

The smell of smoke crept into the soddie. I peered through the window to see a fire at the edge of the corn field. There were more grasshoppers than there was bare earth, the whole ground was crawling with them. I watched between the shutters as they continued to land, tumbling over each other in their search for food.

William and Thomas ran through the door a little while later, both streaked with sooty smuts and grasshopper blood. I helped beat the insects from their clothes, threw them into the stove.

"There's nothing to do," Will said, scrubbing his smoke reddened eyes with one hand, "Too many to keep them off the corn. They're eating it right down to the ground." He cast about him, looked at me - we both knew we were ruined.

He sank into a chair and put his head in his hands.

Rachel was holding her sister like a doll and we all looked about us, listening to the march of the army outside. We all knew there was nothing we could do.

I had Thomas play cards with the girls, read them what he could from the Bible, just so they wouldn't be too frightened. Myself, I was terrified. Without the corn and wheat, there'd be no supplies to get us through winter. Without the grass, without the turnips, what would we feed the oxen? Our money was being eaten out of the ground, every last cent.

The only times that the grim cloud on us let up was when a grasshopper squeezed under the door, or through the window shutters. Then Thomas would run to snatch it up and burn it before it could hide under a tick, or between the chest and the wall.

William went out into them to fetch back a bucket of well water at noon. We had to fish nine of the insects out of it, but it was clean, so there was that to be thankful for.

That night I lay awake to the sounds of grasshoppers everywhere. It felt like we'd been dropped straight into hell.

*

With the invasion outside, work came to a standstill. I was restricted to what little fuel we had in the house, so we ate corn mush made quickly over a tiny fire and potatoes baked in the ashes. For three days I tiptoed around William, feeling his mood gather and darken like a storm on the horizon.

I worried for Cecelia, alone and without experience. She had no well of her own, and I knew that since she'd built her home she'd been relying on snow and rain water. She had some kind of water barrel, but how long would that last? How was she coping, alone with the sound of the insects? We had no idea how Jamison and Hattie were fairing. Their crops, planted so late, were probably in better shape than ours. The grasshoppers couldn't eat what hadn't sprouted yet.

On the morning of the fourth day William snapped. I'd just cooked up some mush for breakfast, as I was stirring the salt into it a grasshopper fell from the ceiling and plopped into the thickened corn. I spooned it out, looking at its claggy body for moment, before William grabbed the spoon and flicked the insect into the fire.

"God fucking damn it!" he threw the spoon down on the table, making Beth jump. Rachel took hold of her sister's hand and shushed her. Like me they'd been waiting for him to go off. Thomas watched his father from his seat on the tick beside Stick, who whined.

William kicked the leg of the table, the whole thing tipped sideways. Beth started to cry, choking on her own sobs in an effort to keep quiet. I went to her and picked her up, ushering Rachel away from the table with my other hand.

"Fucking grasshoppers. This. Fucking. Place!" He grabbed the empty water jug from a shelf and threw it at the wall, a shower of dirt hit the floor. I jumped, clutched Beth tighter, pushed Rachel behind me.

"Will, please."

He stopped, chest heaving as he drew breath, his face mottled with rage. He was sweating, and dropped into a chair and covered his face with his hands.

"There'll be nothing left," he said, finally.

I put Beth down beside Thomas. "We'll manage, somehow."

"We'll starve," Will spat, "every single one of us. There's nothing we can do. Nothing."

I said nothing. He was right. By the time the grasshoppers left, if they ever intended to, there would be nothing left of our crop.

"I'll get the water," I said. "You shouldn't have to go out there every day."

William didn't respond, just sat and glared at the rough wood of the broken table.

Outside, the clicking, humming sound of the grasshoppers was far louder, like a thousand mouths chewing tobacco and sharing gossip. Almost at once I felt the insects hopping against my skirts, dropping onto my shoulders from the roof of the soddie. I walked quickly, shaking my body slightly to rid myself of them.

All the grass was gone, some brown wisps blew here and there over the soil like hair on an otherwise bald pate. The new green of the garden had been eaten up, leaving only sticks that I'd put in for the vines to grow up. Even those had been chewed. The turf on the soddie had been gnawed bare.

Pulling aside the well cover, I tried to keep the grasshoppers out of the water below. It was an impossible task, as they'd already eaten holes through the cover itself. When I hauled up a bucket of water it was tinged brown. The bodies of grasshoppers floated in it. I fished them out. It was the only water we had.

Hauling the bucket back to the house, I looked out towards Cecelia's soddie and saw only a dull brown brick against the parched dirt of the prairie. There was no time to linger outside.

Back in the soddie I shook out and burnt a handful of insects that had clung to my clothes. The water tasted foul, even after I'd boiled it, but we drank it anyway.

Chapter Thirty-Two
Cecelia

I'd thought that I'd experienced the very worst of what Indian Territory had to offer, from wolves at my door to howling snowstorms, blistering heat and crushing loneliness. What else could the prairie have in its arsenal of unpleasant tricks? It was only when the grasshoppers fell from the sky that I realised how stupid I'd been to tempt fate, to make plans. I felt as though I was being punished for thinking that I could have a new life, after running away from my old one.

Punished for everything I'd felt and done since meeting Laura.

They ate everything. Not just the crops and the grass, but the sacks I'd put over parts of the field, trying to save it. They ate the bristles from my broom, the boards of the smoke house and the paint from my schooner. When I battled my way through the thick layer of grasshoppers to get to the barn, I found the remains of the shirt I'd put out to dry; barely more than a collar and some buttons clinging to a frayed piece of shirtfront.

The worst thing was the thirst. The barrel I'd set up for catching water in the winter was less than half full by that time. I had to ration out the stagnant water, one cupful at a time. One cup at breakfast, one at dinner. I couldn't mix up mush or cornbread because I didn't have the water to spare, and there was so little around to burn in the stove anyway. I ate smoked venison in strips, which only made me thirstier. When those ran out I chewed dry meal mixed with a little preserve.

The mustangs got a cup each, morning, noon and night. Missy was thirsty too, and I gave her one cup a day of water to drink. She still whined for more and lay by her bowl with glazed eyes, staring at nothing.

I waited for rain, waited so long that I thought I'd go mad; weeks passed but none came. I thought of going to Deene, to his well, but he'd been so enraged when he last came to my door. I thought he might shoot me on sight. I watched my water running out, too hungry to think straight, knowing I would die if it didn't rain soon, fearing I would be killed if I crossed the prairie to beg for help. I worried about Laura a great deal, but I knew William was made of harder stuff than me. He was cruel, but he would see to it that she survived.

A week passed and the grasshoppers showed no signs of leaving. The dirt outside started to swirl in the wind, too dry to stay packed down with no grass to keep it there. The wind swept the grasshoppers too, piling them against the side of the soddie up to two feet deep. The level of water in the barrel dropped day by day, until there was barely any left.

I didn't have enough water in me to cry, even when I carried Missy's limp form outside, laid her on the ground. Screwing up my eyes I hit her in the head with the stock of the rifle. She made no noise, but blood ran out over the parched ground. I would have stayed by her body, but the grasshoppers were already swarming.

There was no way to bury her, the dirt was light but under it the soil was baked to a brick. It was the grasshoppers that picked her clean, leaving only bones and a few strips of furry hide, weathered to a no-colour under the sun.

Twelve days after the grasshoppers came, I walked into the barn and stroked the dry noses of the mustangs.

"Hey, shhh now," I said, as one snorted and stamped. They were thirsty, hungry. The grasshoppers kept getting into the barn and eating what was left of the fodder. There was no grass outside for them to eat. Grasshoppers leapt at their legs and onto their backs and they twitched all over, ears rotating to take in the relentless chirruping whirr of the grasshoppers' noise.

Leading them out into the sunlight for some exercise, I felt my legs shake. Their eyes were big and scared in their thin faces, and we'd taken but a few steps when the smaller of the two, my private favourite, stumbled and fell to the ground. Grasshoppers were crushed by her flailing body and others jumped onto her twitching hide. She screamed and rolled in the dirt.

I couldn't do anything, backed away and covered my mouth with my hand. The noise was terrible. The other mustang shied from the body of its partner and whinnied, sidestepping on its weak legs. My body ran with cold sweat as I went to the house and fetched out the rifle.

I didn't do it right. The mustang whinnied shrilly, eyes big and white. Blood gushed into the parched soil from her neck, seeping away almost immediately to leave a black stain. I shot again, and this time her body went limp, save for a twitch in one hind leg. Most of her soft face was gone, fragments of bone and pulped brain speckled the dirt.

I stood and retched, but nothing came up.

The other mustang was rolling its eyes to the whites, pulling on the tether that held it to the edge of the barn. I was scared to go near her, and just stood under the hot sun, looking at the bloody dust. When I led her back into the barn, she was quiet and laid down immediately, exhausted.

With nothing else around for them to feast on, the grasshoppers swarmed over the mustang's body and the bloody dirt around it. I had no food left. It had been days since I'd last eaten, and I had only a little water. I took a knife to the body, carved off pieces to cook over my stove. Broken wood from my empty smoke house made a good fire, it was drier than hay. I could hardly wait for it to be cooked and ate some bits bloody. I cooked and ate as much as I could, knowing the rest would quickly rot in the heat.

The next day I heard rifle shots from the Deene farm. Looking from my window I saw the small form of Laura standing by the brown shapes of the fallen oxen. I wanted to go to her, to them, and beg for water, but my legs were almost too weak to hold me up. As it was I could barely stand at the window.

My legs were so weak, I sank to the floor and crawled to my tick, lying with my face turned into the rough sacking material. All around the grasshoppers whirred and clicked. The water had run out. I wasn't strong enough to go and get more.

I was going to die.

I'd been so stupid to put off going for help. So Deene may have had it in him to shoot me; nothing would be worse than thirsting to death, I knew that now, but I couldn't bring myself to get up. My body might as well have been dead already.

It grew dark, then light again, I couldn't keep track of the days. I slept for parts of them, not sure if the light I woke to was the same day I'd closed my eyes on. All the time the grasshoppers made their din. I half-slept, cried with dry eyes and no sound. It got harder to think, harder to find words to think in. My tongue was swollen and dry, my eyes sore. I started to wish for it to be over.

At one point I heard knocking. Frantic little taps at the door, my name, my real name. I tried to sit up, when that failed I tried to call out, but my voice was gone. A tiny sob came out through my nose, was someone there? Laura? It sounded like her, her voice rougher and cracked. I looked up at the door, which I'd bolted from habit out of the fear that wolves might come upon me as I slept. It swam before me.

There was a thumping at the door, scraping at the shutters. I tried to move even my fingers, but they hardly twitched. My lips were cracked and blood a welcome wetness on my tongue. I mouthed her name but couldn't make a sound, heard hoarse sobs and footsteps stumbling away.

Silence came and swallowed me up.

I tried with everything to make some sound, to lift myself, but however long it'd been since I lay down, several days at least, my body had given up. I couldn't even stay awake. I closed my eyes for an instant to the bright light and opened them to total darkness. The world was already moving on without me. Day to night, night to day. I couldn't stop them rushing past.

Then the voice came back, saying a word that I didn't immediately recognise as my name. Please let it be her, even if it was only an illusion, it would be better than nothing at all, than the blankness and the grasshoppers.

I realised it was a man's voice, felt a soul deep rush of fear. Charles had come at last to punish me. Why hadn't I died already? Was God really that cruel?

"Cecelia?"

I saw the wink of sun on a knife blade slid between the door and the frame. The latch lifted.

I was dead. It wasn't real. The face above me was claimed by a black cloud, streaking in from the distance until it swallowed everything.

*

I woke up on my tick. For a moment it seemed that the whole thing had been a fevered dream, but when I opened my eyes he was still there.

Franklyn was above me, spooning water to my lips. When he saw that I was awake he sat back on his heels.

"Cecelia?" he had on travelling clothes, trousers in a hard wearing black fabric. "What have you been doing out here?"

I tried to sit up, grabbed for the wall as my strength failed me. Franklyn leapt forward and helped me to lean against the sod. He took a flask from beside my bed and held it up.

"Drink. Don't worry, I brought plenty out with me. You're lucky I thought to buy a wagon to sleep in. I think the poor people in town were selling it off in a hurry. I felt quite bad over the price, though I didn't haggle, and they threw in quite a lot of dry goods to get a few more cents out of me."

It was water, not cold and certainly not fresh, but the best that had passed my lips in days. I gulped it down.

"Christ," I heard him murmur, "Cecelia..."

I put down the empty flask and wiped my mouth with my hand. "There's no water here."

"I know. There's nothing here. Only those insects, over everything. I've got another flask here. Drink all of that. Do you even have food in this place?"

I shook my head. "All gone."

"I've got some." I saw for the first time the two bundles on the floor. "I'll get you some and then you can tell me what on earth brought you here."

"A stage," I said, "then a wagon...and then me. I walked."

"Very funny. You know what I mean." He went and opened one of the bundles, pulled out brown paper parcels and made a disgusted sound. "I've been out here almost a month now and this is all they've been giving me to eat. Mush. Beans. Cornbread. Has no one here heard of pastry?"

His continuous mutterings were as familiar to me as they were strange in the soddie.

"Cecelia?"

My head has started to droop, but I raised it again. "Mmm?"

"I'll make the mush, just hold on. Eat this." He pressed a strip of jerky into my hand. "It's the last of it."

While he swore and growled at my stove, the added heat of which made the soddie almost unbearable, I chewed up the strip of jerky and leant against the wall, trying to calm my nerves.

"You should know, I left Charles in town. He didn't want to come all the way out here on a bit of gossip. Not with those grasshoppers getting into everything. You're lucky we even came this way at all; if the bank hadn't responded to the description of your jewellery we wouldn't have gone looking for the 'man' that sold it." He looked over at me, blonde hair sticking to the sweat on his forehead. "I mean, it's like the plagues of Egypt out there, another day and you might have..."

"Died. I know." I was feeling more myself with a little food in my belly, even if knowing Charles was nearby made me feel like casting the whole lot up again. He was going to take me away. It would've been kinder to let me starve.

"Exactly." Franklyn sighed, bringing the pot from the stove and dishing out portions of cornmeal mush. "When I saw that horse outside, I thought the worst."

"She fell. I had to shoot her."

"You know the other's dead in the barn? Of thirst." He brought me a bowl of mush and sat on the edge of my tick. "Why didn't you try to contact me, or Father?"

"I've been managing on my own," I said, looking at the steam coming off of the yellowish mush, he hadn't put enough water in. "Building this place, surviving the winter, the wolves..."

"Wolves?" Franklyn blanched under his traveller's tan.

I nodded. "Anyway...I couldn't go back...how long has it been, since the grasshoppers came?"

"I got here two weeks ago and I've been riding out searching for this 'Clappe' character ever since. In town they said it'd been about two weeks again since all this started."

A month since the grasshoppers came. Three weeks of rationing and despair. Almost a week since I ran out of water.

The smell of the mush was too much, I started to eat the dry mess quickly, feeling it settle in my stomach, heavy and solid.

"Cecelia, no one's angry with you," he caught my eye and then looked away. "Well, Charles is very caught up in the humiliation of it all, and you know how I hate him but...if it was me, if Kate were to run off and leave no clue of her reason for doing so, I might feel the same as him."

"I wasn't thinking when I left."

"But there was something? Something that pushed you to run away, in the middle of the night?" he said, face set for the worst. "Cecelia, did he hurt you?"

I shook my head. "He never did anything to me."

"Then why? Why all this..." he gestured to my cropped hair, which had started to grow out, "I almost didn't recognise you. What have you done to yourself?"

It was almost funny. Hadn't I imagined him over and over again as I'd built the soddie? Hadn't I looked at myself and wondered what I was doing in those first few months? It was as though I was seeing myself and my home again, for the first time; dirty and plain and poor. I couldn't recall exactly when I'd dispensed with binding up my chest and layering my clothes to hide my girlish frame. If I'd ever been a convincing man I was certainly not one now; only a foolish girl in his eyes, dressed in rags and half-starved.

"I wanted to write to you, to let you know I was safe, but I couldn't stand the idea of being found and taken back."

"But if Charles didn't do anything-"

"I didn't run away because he hurt me. You don't understand! I was afraid and I knew, I knew you wouldn't believe me if I told you-"

"Told me what?"

"That he killed Charlie." I was took a breath, my head swimming. I'd never said it aloud, so bluntly before.

Franklyn looked aghast. "Cecelia, Charles isn't what I'd call compassionate, but even he couldn't-"

"I saw him," I said, reaching out and grasping Franklyn's hand. "I came into the nursery and I saw him do it. He smothered Charlie, with a pillow, when he thought everyone was asleep. When he saw me he said that, if I told anyone it would be the asylum for me until I was 'myself again'. He kept me prisoner after that. I tried to get a note to you but he found it and said he'd send me away. I had to run then, or be locked up until Charles saw fit to take me back into his custody.

I saw pity in Franklyn's eyes, but only the smallest sliver of understanding. Probably he thought me hysterical, but he hadn't seen Charles, or heard him say that Charlie would have been better off never being born. I'd tried to convince myself that he would never hurt me, he wouldn't have been able to hide that so easily, yet I hadn't been able to make myself believe it. Killing me wasn't the worst he could do.

"Franklyn, you have to believe me. Why else do you think you never saw me? Why I never came to visit? Did you think I was just grieving? How could I do that without you and Mother? You know how much I love you, how much I would have needed you. You can't take me back to him. Please."

"I'll take you home, to Mother and Father." Franklyn promised. "Cecelia, Mother is sick with worry over you, and Father has aged so much in the past year. I hardly recognise him."

"But if I go back, Charles-"

"Charles will have a claim on you, but you should stay with Mother and Father until you're well enough to discuss the future."

"I don't think I can go back, not even to them."

I had not grown to love the prairie, but I had come to understand it, and to view my life before as something that was beyond me forever. I had let Cecelia go. Whoever I was, I couldn't be her any longer, at least not the her that Franklyn had known. There was something different about me now.

There was Laura.

My thoughts, still sluggish and laboured, were filled with her. Where was she, and how long ago had she come knocking frantically at my door?

"When you came, did you see anyone at the other house? The one south of here?"

"No one outside," he said, "but what do you mean you can't go back? It's like the end of days out here. I've spent a year and half a fortune to find you and now it's time to give up on this...mistaken attempt at playing the peasant, and come home with me."

I waved him off. "Help me up, we need to check on them."

"Who?"

"My neighbours, my friend."

He took my arm but still hesitated.

"Help me up now! God dammit, it might be too late already."

Chapter Thirty-Three
Laura

I was throwing out the pot when I heard horses. Looking up I saw a wagon coming across the dirt, wheels brown and thick with crushed insects. For a moment I thought I'd lost my mind. I hadn't been more than a few steps from the soddie in three days, or maybe four. I didn't dare step outside for longer than it took to throw out the slops.

Cecelia hadn't answered me, and I knew it was because she was dead inside her house. Why else would she not even call out for me, or come to the house?

I was sure I'd gone mad when I saw who rode the wagon seat - though in our months apart she had grown thin I still knew her. She was dirty and thin, save the trousers and shirt she was unmistakeably female, her hair had grown out a little and she hadn't attempted to bind her breast. She stumbled from the wagon and ran to me, clutching me tightly. I held her back, my tongue tied by relief and sorrow. Grasshoppers leapt onto my skirts but I didn't care.

"Laura…" she pressed her nose to my cheek.

I couldn't say a word, only hold on to her, so hard I thought my fingers'd break.

"We have to go," the man behind her insisted, "Miss, I'm sorry but we have to be back in town before evening if we're to set off for Ohio in the morning."

"Cecelia…is this him?"

"No, he's my brother. Franklyn." She took a step back from me. "But Charles is in town. He doesn't believe me, Laura. I tried to tell him."

She took my hand and looked at my dirty shift, loose hair and my hard, rounded belly.

"Are the children alright?"

I shook my head.

She squeezed my arms. "Tell me."

"Beth and William both took ill a few days ago, now they're too weak to get out of bed. Rachel and Thomas are sick from the well water, I've been trying to help them but there's no more water, no food." My voice was like an old crow trying to sing.

"Franklyn has food, maybe quinine…what about Nora?"

I shook my head, couldn't seem to stop once I'd begun. Couldn't say how I'd come home believing I'd lost Cecelia forever, love rotting in my chest, to find Nora in her cradle box, dead as a doll. Cecelia let me rest my head against her shoulder, stroked my dirty hair.

Franklyn offered me a watchman's bottle. "Drink something."

I took the bottle and drank. The water was warm and tasted like metal, probably drawn from a pump in town, but it was better than tainted well water. Better than the last days of having nothing to drink at all.

The sun beat down on us like a rain of hot coins. I could feel my skin getting tighter, dryer, the smell of vomit and piss and sweat from my shift growing stronger with each moment.

The yard was covered in ash, swirled up from where I'd built my fires for boiling soiled clothes and sheets. I'd burnt the clothes themselves when the water looked to be running out, to stop the spread of sickness. The carcass of one of the oxen lay in the heat, its ribs poking up like sticks. I'd hacked the meat off of it days ago and now it was all eaten or spoiled. From the barn came the cries of the remaining oxen, tied up in the heat and calling in vain for water, for food.

"Sit down," Cecelia said, leading me to the stump we split logs on, "It's alright, I'll look in on them. Rest."

Stepping away from me she stumbled a little, weak as I was from lack of food. Still, she gestured for her brother and walked toward the soddie.

Inside I knew things would be as I'd left them. Thomas and Rachel lying on the tick nearest the door, Beth on her tick, bundled in several blankets despite the heat. William on our bed, naked under a sweat soaked sheet.

I waited outside while she checked on them, shifting to keep the insects off me. I tried to gather my scattered thoughts, to pull myself together. I heard her say, "Franklyn, find any wood around and build up a fire where the ground's scorched." Then she was back by my side.

"Laura?"

I looked at her, knew before she said it that another one of my babies was dead. I took her arm and dragged myself to the soddie, knelt down by the tick. Her hand touched mine where my fingers rested on Beth's vomit crusted cheek, feeling the stillness between her lips, where air should have flowed.

Cecelia took hold of my shoulder, squeezed it. "Give the water to the others."

I didn't move. No matter what I did it didn't do any good. I couldn't save Nora, or Beth. What was the point in fighting when nothing I did could help anyone? They were all sick, dying. I was going to lose them no matter what I did. Only days ago I'd stood with the rifle and thought of ending it. If I had Beth wouldn't've suffered so.

"Laura, they're still alive. There's nothing we can do for Beth, not right now...where did you put Nora?"

"The barn," saying the words made my chest squeeze. I turned away, bad as I wanted to give up I couldn't fight the need to carry on. I took the bottle, stumbled as I returned to the doorway and knelt beside Rachel.

"Ma?" Rachel's mouth moved in the shape of the word, her voice a bleat. I smoothed her hair from her face and put my arm under her shoulder to lift her up.

"Drink this, sweet pea."

Holding the bottle to her mouth, I watched her drink. I felt Cecelia behind me, heard her wrap the blanket around Beth and lift her. I didn't look. Couldn't.

"Slowly now," I said, easing the bottle back. "Don't make yourself sick."

Thomas pulled himself upright, one hand clinging to the wall. "Ma, Beth stopped crying."

"I know," I said, passed him the bottle, even though Rachel whined at its loss. "Drink. Thomas, share with your sister. I have to take care of your father."

I picked up the sheet that William had thrown off and covered him over. He groaned, tried to fight the thin material, but weakened quickly. His bloodshot eyes stared at me without really seeing anything.

Cecelia came to crouch beside me, a bottle of castor oil in her hand. "Tilt his head."

I tipped his chin up and his mouth fell open, Cecelia wrinkled her nose at the foul smell of his breath, but she poured the castor oil into his mouth and though he choked, he swallowed it down.

Cecelia put her arms around me and for a few seconds I allowed myself to crack while she was there to hold me together. Then that moment of relief ended, with Franklyn at the door, brushing grasshoppers from his clothes.

"The water's boiled now."

Cecelia let me go and turned to face him. "Steep the quinine. Then we need to get some food into these three."

"He looks half dead, should we take the children out..." Franklyn trailed off as William stated to jerk in front of us, twitching and twisting on the tick. His head twisted to one side and the cords in his neck standing out. His legs kicked and pinkish spittle leaked from the corner of his mouth.

I reached out and grabbed his arms, trying to still him. Every muscle was tense, his eyes rolled.

"Will! Will can you hear me?"

Cecelia took hold of both sides of his head, holding him down, but it made no difference, he continued to shudder and jerk. Grasshoppers that'd come in when Franklyn opened the door were jumping over his body.

"Franklyn, we need that quinine, soon!"

He went to brew it, shutting the door and leaving us in near darkness. I heard the lid of the pot being slammed back on to keep the insects out.

William went suddenly still, his eyes closed and his mouth falling open. Blood oozed from the corner of his mouth onto my hand.

"His tongue," I tipped his head so the blood could run out of his mouth, "he's bitten his tongue."

"Ma." It was Thomas, I turned to see him propped against the wall, Rachel leaning against him as he fed her small sips of water.

"Thomas," Cecelia said, leaning on the wall for support. "Help your sister outside. Franklyn will find you food and more water." She looked at me. "You should go with them, sit, eat something. There's so many bugs in here it hardly makes a difference."

"Will-"

"I was there in town when…" she stopped, and I knew we were both thinking of Beth. I wondered why God had not taken her then, to spare her the days of heat and hunger and thirst. "…I know what to do."

Still I didn't move.

"Go," she said gently, "I'll watch him." Her hand crept to mine and squeezed, "As soon as he can be moved, we'll put him on the wagon and leave here. There's water in town, we can find somewhere for you to stay."

I gripped her hand in mine, never wanting to let go.

"Rest, I'll see to him," she said, releasing my hand, stroking her thumb across my palm. I nodded, picked myself and went out into the blinding light, still feeling her touch on my hand.

Rachel was in the shade of the soddie, lying on a blanket. Thomas sat beside her, swatting the grasshoppers away if they jumped onto her. I knew they'd seen Cecelia go by with Beth. Thomas had already held Nora as she died. I went to them, held both their hands, leant and kissed Rachel, then Thomas. There was nothing to say and I couldn't have said it even if there had been. I only held them and let them cling on to me.

"Ma," Thomas said, after a while. "Mr Clappe's a lady."

I squeezed his shoulder. "Yes, sweet pea. She was a very scared lady, and she was hiding here."

"Is she still going to help us?"

"She and her brother are going to help us get away from here. Soon as Pa can be moved."

"Did you know she was a lady?"

"For a little while."

"Why didn't you tell Pa?"

"She was afraid of anyone finding out. Otherwise I would've told you, and Pa."

"And then he would've let you be friends."

"Yes, maybe he would."

"Pa doesn't like her," Rachel said, suddenly.

"Pa doesn't like strangers."

"She asked me about Stick once," Rachel said, "She doesn't act like Pa does she? Not like Uncle Jacob or Mr Jamison. She's odd."

"Ma likes her. And she's nice," Thomas said.

"That's what I said," Rachel said.

They were quiet after that, and I knew I had to get up, get them fed. I couldn't be any kind of protection to them if my thoughts were only with their sisters. Refreshed by the water, Rachel and Thomas could cry real tears for Beth and Nora. Mine would come have to come later, if I could help it, along with them would come the teas of relief that my children had found Cecelia out, and still trusted her. Trusted me to know good from bad.

The brother, Franklyn, was standing in the shade, swatting and stamping on grasshoppers, looking back towards Cecelia's soddie with a frown on his face. He left off staring and turned to me as I came over.

"Where's my sister?"

"Still with my husband," I said, then looked at the brewing quinine. "Give it a few minutes, then she'll need that." I pulled an insect out of my hair and threw it down. "I wish I could burn every one of them."

"This, everything out here, I find it hard to believe," he said. The grasshoppers were massed all over the hard baked ground, Thomas was continually plucking the insects from himself and his sister, while Franklyn batted them off of his clothes and stomped them into tobacco spit in the dust.

"What will you do, when we leave?" Franklyn asked.

"Cecelia said you might be kind enough to take us to town, they've got pumps there so there's at least water. From there..." I considered, there were no options, not real ones, for us. We had no money, no possessions worth a damn. "I expect my husband will decide where we're to move on to. It's likely we'll end up working somewhere while we save to start over."

Franklyn nodded like he wasn't really listening, I didn't try talking to him anymore. He had jerky and bread, which I gave to Thomas so he could share it out with his sister. I sat in the heat and thought of Beth's pale blond hair and how it looked in the sun, of how she'd made big rosy prints on her dress with a pudgy hand covered in jam, grinned up at me with her small teeth. Even that dress was gone, burnt with the soiled sheets and clothes.

Franklyn ladled out quinine and took it to the soddie.

That night we cleared as many grasshoppers from the house as we could and tried to sleep. I'd grown almost deaf to their noise by that point and no one else mentioned it, or the stink of the soddie. William lay on our tick, Cecelia and I slept on Rachel and Beth's bed, turned over to give some protection from the stains of sickness. Thomas shared his tick with Rachel. Franklyn offered to take the floor and no one argued with him, so he put down a bed roll from his wagon.

I didn't sleep to start with, just looked up at the dark roof and listened to the breathing of my children. They'd eaten and drank lots of water and though Rachel's bowels were still loose, she was not as weak as she'd been that morning. Thomas, already mostly over his sickness from the bad water, was shaky on his feet, but had been alert through the day. Neither of them were speaking much. I thought they must have seen too much in the past few days to be set right with a little food and water. The soddie felt so empty without Nora's cries and Beth's snuffling breaths. Rachel was holding Beth's doll against her chest tightly in her sleep, as though scared it would be snatched away.

Cecelia shifted onto her side and I felt her forehead on my shoulder. She didn't say anything about Beth, or Nora. I think she knew there was nothing she could say. She was there. Her hand stroked my arm and finally, I felt tears gather in my eyes.

Chapter Thirty-Four
Cecelia

I woke throughout the night and, leaving Laura to sleep, administered quinine and castor oil to her husband. It was hard to tell in the darkness of the soddie, but he seemed to be resting. When I put the metal spoon to his lips he drank the contents with a shudder and took sips of water from the cup I offered. I don't think he even knew who was tending him.

I tried to shut out thoughts of Charles, though at times the fear would come so strongly that it made me want to run into the dark, never to be found again. Laura and her children needed me, that was all that kept me tethered to that place.

Thomas and Rachel slept peacefully, exhaustedly, but water and food had stoked their fires well and I was filled with intense relief. Laura couldn't lose any more of her children, she'd suffered more than enough to satisfy whatever God was bringing these plagues down on us.

Lying awake at Laura's side, I listened to her breathing. The silent tears that had shaken her had run out in the small hours, leaving her exhausted. My hand curled around her wrist, tethering us together. All the months of frozen loneliness I'd dreamed of this, whether I admitted it to myself or not. To have it, now, like this, was the worst of tricks the prairie had yet played on me.

When the dawn light crept under the door and through the tightly closed shutters, I got up and went out to clear grasshoppers from the fire site and boil up water for cornmeal.

Franklyn rose ahead of the others and came to join me, yawning and scratching the sanding of blond hair on his jaw. He found me sitting by the fire, watching the grasshoppers jump stupidly into the flames.

"We don't have enough water to stay another day," he said.

"Good morning to you too."

"Cecelia, we have to leave, today. And if you insist on bringing that woman with us we don't have time to delay."

"If we ration the water, there's another day in it, and that's all that's needed to see if he'll be fit to travel." I poked at the old ashes. "I'm not leaving them."

He sighed and looked at me, long and hard for a moment, I knew then that we were almost strangers, or at least, I was strange to him.

"Alright, we'll wait another day, but tonight we'll pack up and tomorrow morning I want to set off without delay." His voice turned soft, the tone he'd used a long time ago, when he'd tried to teach me the kings and queens of England; slow, encouraging.

"That's fine by me. Though, we have other neighbours, they might be in bad shape too."

"Cecelia, I'm not rescuing every settler out here!"

I smiled, teasing him. "After you rode in, a one man grocery store with water enough for a whole damn family?"

His brows drew down. "I wish you wouldn't talk like that."

"Like what?"

"You sound like one of those women, from town, like-"

"Like my friend, Laura?" I put the kettle down on the ground.

"It's just not something they'll appreciate at home."

I hadn't noticed my Clappe voice bleeding into the way I thought and spoke as myself. Then again, who was to say it was him? Perhaps it was Laura. I'd grown to like the way she spoke, simple and dry, her smile showing in her words, even when she was too tired to paste it on her mouth.

"I'm not the same as I was a year ago, and I'll not pretend that I am." I said, moving past him to the soddie. "If you'd ever seen anything beyond home, you'd understand."

I didn't mean to be cruel to him, but he was treating me like his little sister and I felt as though I'd aged beyond him, as though time had moved faster for me in the past year. My husband had murdered my son in front of me. I'd survived a winter bad enough to bring wolves to my door, because I was too afraid of Charles to ask for help from my family. I'd seen grasshoppers falling from the sky, had nearly died out of fear – fear of William Deene and his rifle. I was more scared than ever knowing that Charles was waiting in town, knowing that Franklyn didn't believe my story. The most frightening thing of all was that I was in love with a woman and would be condemned for it if anyone ever found out.

I couldn't make myself forget all that. Whatever the future held, it scared me, but I couldn't run from it or hide in ignorance as I'd once done.

As I stepped around Laura to get to the cornmeal, she sat up and rubbed a hand over her face. She turned to look for her children and, finding them sleeping peacefully, she looked back at me.

"You should've woken me," she whispered.

"I've not been up long," I whispered back, so as not to wake the children.

"How's..." she glanced at Will, "I felt you get up in the night to see to him."

"He's keeping the quinine down, it's all gone now though so, if he's going to get better, now would be the time."

"I've been trying to think of what's to come, once he's well and you've taken us back to town. What we'll be doing. What I'll need to take. Not that there's much to take."

"Where will you go?"

"There's logging camps, mines, places he could get work. I'd most likely be taking in washing and mending, try and earn a little to bring back and start the farm over again."

Something of my dismay must have shown on my face, for she cupped my cheek and tried to soothe me.

"Hey now, I'll be fine. I'll have Thomas and Rachel to help, and we'll be settled somewhere soon. You'll be safe and I'll think of you. Always."

My eyes welled. "I don't want you to be alone. I don't want to be without you."

"I know...but you know as well as I do, we don't get to do what we want."

I was going to be without her for the rest of my life, however long that was. It seemed like a long, long time just then. I raised my hand to hers where it rested on my cheek, held it there. I moved forwards and touched my lips to hers, felt them give. She traced her thumb over my cheek and I moved back, released her and looked into her eyes. Laura let her guard down, and she wrapped her arms around me tightly. Closing my eyes I fought to memorise the feeling and kissed her again, knowing it might be the last time.

Sudden light and the scrape of wood on dirt made me turn around. In the doorway, framed in the searing light, stood Franklyn.

I sucked in a mouthful of air, but couldn't move or make a sound.

Laura was already pulling away, stepping in front of me. Franklyn drew back from the door and vanished into the brightness outside.

"I have to..." I started after him, "oh God."

Laura was at my side, following me as I crossed the dusty, ash strewn yard and found my brother studiously untying and re-knotting the ropes that held down the cover on his wagon, angrily lashing out at the insects on the canvas cover.

"Franklyn?"

He turned and I saw that his face was reddened, brows drawn close together. I'd embarrassed him, made him angry and ashamed of me.

"Don't tell me I'm mistaken, I saw you kissing her." He said, looking from me to Laura and back again.

"Franklyn, keep your voice down, the children," I begged.

"Children? You're concerned for their innocence, now? How long have the two of you been-" he broke off, shook his head, "All this time I thought you might be in trouble, that you were alone and naive amongst all these men. That you might get hurt. I thought you were a good woman."

"I am." I said, my insides quivering with hurt at his anger.

"You ran away from your husband, from your family, to let some foolish drudge lead you into sin. Can you imagine the disgrace you'd cause if anyone at home were to find out? Cecelia, this pretence has gone far enough. You're not a man, and you cannot act like one."

"I'm not acting, and I'm telling you that if you call her another name, I'll get a rifle and shoot you." I let the threat sit in the hot air between us. "And as for what Laura and I have done...I've made my peace with it."

Franklyn's mouth was a thin line as he looked between me and Laura. Even the grasshoppers seemed to go silent, waiting for him to speak.

"Tomorrow morning-"

"Tomorrow morning we'll be off back to Ohio," I said, cutting him off. "It's likely that I'll never see Laura again. I certainly won't be able to talk about her. So if you could refrain from taking what time we have left, and turning it into a sermon, I'd be grateful." My voice cracked and I felt my eyes start to well up. "And if you could still love me, even a little, I'd be-"

Franklyn stepped towards me and put his hands on my shoulders. "You're my sister. Of course I love you. I just...I want you to be well."

"I'm only well because of her," I said, "Franklyn, I would have died if she hadn't been here."

Laura was still at my side, as solid and unmovable as a pillar of earth. I pulled back from Franklyn and took her hand in mine, endlessly grateful that she was with me and not running to hide in shame.

"Thank you, for helping my sister," Franklyn said, grudgingly.

"It's not as though you didn't help save me and my family," she said. "If thanks are owing, I think they're due to you."

The three of us stood there a moment, as the heat of the day grew stronger, and the grasshoppers leapt at our legs and landed on the thick cover on Franklyn's wagon. It was strange, to stand there with Laura and Franklyn, unbidden came the thought of my wedding day, when I'd stood before my family with Charles at my side. I knew that Franklyn didn't, and likely wouldn't ever, understand what Laura meant to me. I knew that to him it was as foreign as the idea of a house made of dirt, or a woman in trousers, but I couldn't help that. I only knew it felt right. It made sense to me.

"I should get some things together, start packing up," Laura said, turning away, "if you want to talk to your brother..."

"We can talk plenty on the way to town," I said, "you should...there's time now for you to pay your respects."

Laura glanced towards the barn, nodded.

Franklyn said nothing, but he gave me an uncertain look and followed us back to the soddie. I felt the weight of my old life starting to settle on me. How long would it be before I was bathed and laced into a dress, sitting before my parents in the drawing room of their house? How long until my life on the prairie faded like an old print, until I forgot the sound of Laura breathing beside me as she slept?

Thomas was asleep, propped against the wall to keep the insects off. Rachel sat nearby, watching the fire as it burned. They looked so tired and dirty, I wondered what would become of them once we'd left them behind. Would they forget the cruel sun and vast nothing of the barren prairie, or would they soon long for it, as life brought them nothing but hardship and poverty? If I could have taken each one of them onto my lap and held them, I would have, as it was, I only looked at their dusty faces and felt all my grief for Charlie over again, in their name.

"Are you feeling better?" Laura asked, crouching between her children in her dirty shift and putting her hands out to them. Rachel was crying but she hugged her mother, Laura's arm holding her tightly. Thomas took Laura's hand in his and nodded sombrely.

"We'll be leaving here soon," Laura soothed. "Tomorrow morning, we'll be leaving for good."

On the ground I saw the doll Rachel had slept with, picked it up and shook the dust and grasshoppers from it. I went over to them and held it out to her, her little hand closing around my fingers briefly as she took it. Her palms were red raw and blistered, as though she'd been pulling up the well bucket by herself.

"Your hands," Laura said, touching the welts lightly.

"I'll fetch some liniment," I said softly.

I couldn't watch them, couldn't let Franklyn see my face as I watched them. I went to the soddie, intent on finding liniment to soothe Rachel's hand. Grasshoppers had already started to get into the house; it wasn't as though there was anything in there that needed protecting, Laura had burnt most of the blankets and clothes.

William lay on his tick and I cast my eyes over him as I went to the supply crate. I froze, my foot just touching the floor. William was motionless on the tick, his eyes open and bulging up at the ceiling, a red halo around his throat.

On the floor beside him was a coil of rope.

.

Chapter Thirty-Five

Laura

Cecelia came out of the house. I felt Rachel stiffen, her hand holding tightly on to mine.

Cecelia looked at me, at all three of us on the ground, "William, he's...he died, Laura."

Once, when I was very young, I'd stepped on the rotten cover to the cellar door and fallen straight through. The moment I realised that I was falling was far, far worse than hitting the ground below. For days I'd been afraid of his death, scared that I would be alone under the strain of the work before us. Now William was dead I felt only a sharp pain, which was gone almost as soon as it came.

Thomas jumped up and ran for the house.

"Thomas!"

He froze, turned back to me wild-eyed. "He was getting better. You said."

"I was wrong," I said, "I'm sorry."

I'd always known that despite his meanness Will mattered more to Thomas than I did. Pleasing him, or trying to, was the reason he'd gone doggedly into the fields, never complaining. His sisters had died while he was watching over them, now he'd lost his father too. I had no words for him.

I'd been chained to Will for so long that I could hardly believe he was gone.

"Laura," Cecelia crouched in front of me. "There's no sense waiting now, we should set off while we still have supplies."

"I know," I said.

"I don't want to be heartless-"

She stiffened in surprise when I put my arms around her and held her.

"You'd never be that," I said.

She patted my back and I squeezed her tightly before releasing her.

"Hadn't we better..." Franklyn looked at the soddie, "I mean, shouldn't we bury him?"

"The ground's too hard," I said, "we'll have to do something for them, before we go, but now-"

"I know, we should pack things up," Cecelia straightened and looked at Rachel. "I know you've done a lot to help, but I need you to do just a little more, alright?"

To my surprise, Rachel nodded. She'd changed so much since the coming of winter. It seemed only a few months ago she'd been set on the fact that Clappe had killed our pig. Now Cecelia had her chest unbound and wasn't speaking as a man anymore, I'd though that would upset Rachel more, but she didn't seem vexed, only tired. I wondered what questions she would have after this, about Cecelia, about 'Clappe', about all of it. The past year full of deception and pretending, what would she make of it? For now at least she was too grief stricken and ill to ask me questions I had no answers to.

Cecelia sent Thomas and Rachel to fetch out the old tools we still had in the barn. She looked at me, "I'll empty a tick. We can wrap him up."

I nodded, thinking of the shirts I'd sewn him, the food I'd made, the coffee and pipe tobacco and whisky that had gone into him. The rows he'd planted, the sod he'd hauled, the things he'd built, and now there was nothing to him that couldn't be wrapped in a tick cover and stowed away with my poor children. Half my life wrapped up in sheets and laid out on the barn floor.

"Franklyn, can you pack up the supplies and then help Thomas with the stove and the furniture once the tools are packed up- it all has to come with us."

"I thought you were set on going to see how your neighbours were faring?"

Cecelia looked over at me and I felt a stab of shame. I hadn't thought of Jamison and Hattie at all. 'Course they hadn't come to see us either. I'd been shut up in the soddie, they could've driven right by and I wouldn't have seen.

"Why don't we ride past there on the way back to town?" I said.

"That adds miles to the journey," her brother pointed out.

"Better a few miles onto the journey than a wasted trip there and back on a horse. If they're in trouble we'll all end up riding out there to help anyway," Cecelia said.

We all stood quietly. I watched Rachel as carried a basket of tools to the wagon. The doll was tucked into the waist of her skirt, her eyes were dry. I'd thought losing Will would have brought more tears.

I tore my gaze from Rachel and straightened my back. I wasn't about to break, not while there was work to do.

"I just want to get away from this place," I said. "We'll all go."

"Franklyn, pack up your supplies, then help us with the stove," Cecelia said. Her eyes were full of sadness, but her voice held none of it. I was grateful for that. I couldn't take any more pity.

"The stove?" His voice was incredulous. "Will there be room?"

I looked at him. He really had no idea. "Most everything else's been eaten or burnt. There'll be plenty of room." I turned and headed for the soddie, hearing Cecelia's steps behind me.

"I'm sorry about him, he means well enough. He's just not used to this. To how things are out here. I must've been the same when I came here."

"But you know what it's like now. And what it's like to lose what I've lost."

Only she'd never seen her baby grow up to speak and run and laugh at jam prints on his clothes. I had a lock of Beth's gold hair, tied with a piece of twine and pressed between the pages of my Bible. Nora had barely sprouted a single curl, but I'd trimmed that too and kept it. I would not forget what the prairie had taken from me.

In the soddie William lay on the tick, completely still, a soiled sheet drawn up to his chin. I brushed grasshoppers from him and looked at his face for a moment. That face had spewed hate at me, hovered over mine as he forced himself into me, sweat dripping onto my cheeks. That face had been the first face I'd seen every morning for over ten years. The man who'd bought me flowers, who'd struck my children as they hauled turnips. I put my hand on my belly. I had his child in me still, and it would never know him.

Thomas came to my side and looked down at his father. He tucked his pipe and empty tobacco pouch between Will's arm and his chest. He looked at Will for a long moment before going outside, where I heard him heave a shuddery breath. Rachel didn't come and I didn't look for her.

I heard Cecelia emptying out the dry grass from a tick outside. I could only look down at William, wondering why I felt so sad. Hadn't I thought of killing him a hundred times in the past year? Still, I felt an ache. He'd died a bad death, the same as Beth and Nora. I'd wanted to spare him that.

"Laura?"

Cecelia was at my side, the empty tick in her hands.

"I'll do it," I said, taking it from her.

I knelt down beside him and raised the sheet to cover his face. I felt that I should say a prayer, but nothing came to mind. Instead I eased Will's body over by his shoulders, rolling him until the sheet lay beneath him. The tick cover I draped over his naked back. Once the loose fabric was twisted around him and knotted firmly, I stood and nodded to Cecelia.

We moved him to the barn. Cecelia led the starving oxen out onto the parched dirt, then helped me to carry Will inside. Beth and Nora were lying in the far corner, separated from where the oxen lived by a low wall of sod that had once protected the fodder.

She laid her hand on my arm for a moment, then squeezed gently and let her arm fall. She gave me a minute to say goodbye, and after a few moments Thomas and Rachel joined me in the barn. I ignored the ripe smell of rot and knelt by my babies, whispered to them and touched their hands through the sheet wrappings. Rachel put her ribbons in the centre of their bundled up bodies, along with the gold buttons she'd cut from her dress before we burnt it.

Thomas touched his sisters' feet, gentle squeezing as he had when he was just a tiny boy, meeting his first baby sister, now his only sister. He had no trinkets to leave, but stayed at their feet for a while, as if watching over them.

We walked into the sun together, leaving the dark and the dead behind

The wagon was barely half filled, even with the brother's supplies and our remaining things. It was hard to believe that we'd come from Ohio with a wagon heaving with goods.

"Ma, what should I do now?" Rachel asked as I put her up inside the wagon.

"Stay out of the sun, we'll be going soon," I said. She was still so thin and weak looking. I worried that at any moment the fever might set in and take her too.

"Where are we going?" she asked.

I didn't know. My mind had only taken me so far as filling the wagon and leaving the stinking soddie behind. Without Will my instinct was to return to Ohio, where there was some part of our family. But what then? Could I present myself to Jacob and ask that he honour his brother by paying my passage back to England with the children? The thought of seeing my parents, Will's mother and father, made me feel tired and helpless. But what else was there for me to do? I couldn't imagine myself marrying another man, at my age, and feeling as I did for Cecelia. I'd have to go on alone, taking care of my small family.

"Why did that lady lie about being Mr Clappe?" Rachel asked.

There seemed no point in continuing the lie. "Mr Clappe is a person that Cecelia made up. She was just pretending to be a man so she could live here and farm."

Rachel's dark brows drew together. "I thought he was too pretty to be a man."

I felt my heart ache for her innocence, still there after the death that had come so close to taking her.

"I'll be back in a while, don't go off," I said.

"I won't."

I went around the house and found Thomas just outside the barn. Both the oxen were tethered out of the way while he struggled with the last thing to be loaded, our sod cutting plough. It really was such a rusty old thing. He looked up as I came closer and I saw the strain in his face, the paleness under the dirt.

"Take a rest Thomas, you're still sickly."

"I need to get this on the wagon."

"I'll do it, with Franklyn's help."

He looked at me, as though we were meeting for the first time. "He's that lady's brother, isn't he?"

"Yes."

"Pa thought you were sweet on her, when she was all dressed up, acting like a man."

"Pa was just worried," I said, because Will wasn't with us anymore and all the unkind, true things I'd known about him didn't matter.

"You're sweet on her," Thomas said, "I saw you."

He must have seen us kissing. I'd been too relieved to have her back to keep my wits about me. That was how Franklyn had caught us, and now Thomas knew as well. I'd never really thought about what it'd be like if the children found out. Only in so much as I'd imagined having them taken from me by their father or some God fearing town's people. I guess I'd thought if it got that far Will'd kill me before it mattered. I should've been afraid, at any other time I would've been scared out of my mind at what Thomas thought of me, about who he might tell. But the normal world, where nails were ten cents a sack and seeds sewn in spring would come up by fall had stopped existing for me.

"She's a good woman," I said.

Thomas had gone red in the cheeks and I wondered how much he understood of the things Will and I had done to make him and his sisters, how much he understood of what I was still only beginning to grasp. About Cecelia and I.

"She's sweet on you," he said and bolted for the wagon as if he expected me to cuff him across the back of the head.

For a moment my heart thudded guiltily, then I looked into the darkness of the barn, and saw the white shapes, wrapped in sheets. That was how much good love was at holding back the bad in the world. At least when I lost Cecelia I'd know she was home with her family. Who would take care of my girls here?

Chapter Thirty-Six

Cecelia

It saddened me to see how little Laura had to take with her; but not as much as it broke my heart to see all that she left behind.

One we'd put the rusted plough onto the wagon, Laura took a shovel, and so did I. The walls of the barn were strong and baked hard as brick under the sun, but with Franklyn helping we levered a few pieces of sod loose near the top and the roof began to fall in. Though it all, Laura's face wore only an expression of effort, and we pushed and hacked at the walls until they toppled and fell down on top of the crumbled roof. No part of the shrouded bodies was exposed, but I looked at the pile of dead earth with a shiver. Grasshoppers were already jumping over the dirt and scraping out their infernal song.

Charlie had been buried in a tiny coffin of polished wood, with flowers and candles in the church as we prayed for him. I didn't even know if Nora and Beth had been baptized. They deserved better, and I was appalled that we could offer them no better.

Franklyn walked to the wagon and I heard him climb up on to the seat. The two children were inside already, under the wagon cover, sheltering from the sun and the insects. After a moment I joined my brother, leaving Laura to her grief.

Looking back into the wagon, I saw a wooden supply crate with their few odd possessions in it; candles, soap, boot polish and tooth powder. Tucked to one side was the family Bible, its leather cover worn to a shine, tied closed with a blue hair ribbon.

There was a crushed insect on almost everything that had been loaded into the wagon, and a few of the pests remained alive to hop around until Thomas caught them and flicked them through the small hole in the cover. The wheels on either side of us were caked in grasshopper pulp, dried brown and mixed with dust. Behind the wagon the two surviving oxen trailed listlessly on long ropes, too tired and thirsty to do more than put one foot in front of the other. I hoped that they'd make it to the creek in the ravine, and that there'd be water there when we reached it.

Laura climbed up onto the seat beside me and was silent as Franklyn brought the horses to order and started us in the direction of Jamison's house. Her body was stiff and unwelcoming as a bit of spiny brush. I knew she didn't want me to reach for her hand and I bore my sadness at not being to offer that comfort. I knew from losing Charlie that there were no words that could take the pain away, no touch that could go to deep enough to sooth the raw place inside where that bond was torn out. I could only offer her what I'd wished to hear at that time, and pray that it would help, even a little, like lighting a candle in the longest night.

"You did everything you could," I said softly, "you were a good mother to them while they were yours, and you will never forget them, or love them any less for being gone. They will always be your children."

Laura only nodded stiffly, as though to do more would undo her entirely. The time for tears, for breaking, would come, I knew. Now she had to be strong, until danger was behind us, and she could cease her watch over her children, and close her eyes to grieve.

I had no way of articulating what I'd seen in the soddie; the marks on Deene's neck, the coiled rope, Rachel's raw palms. I kept telling myself that I must have been mistaken in what I'd seen, yet I couldn't get the image of it out of my head. It made me feel cold all thought the centre of myself as though I had witnessed the crime myself. Crime was what it was; murder, patricide. A murderer not yet out of girlhood, and not by some easy, impersonal means, but by the savage use of her own hands.

Desperation wasn't a foreign thing to me, but to be so desperate to be free of hardship, of a father's harsh will that I would strangle him in his sickbed as he showed signs of recovering? I could not imagine such despair, or how it might feel to carry such an act on shoulders so young. I could not let myself imagine, for sheer horror prevented me.

I was only glad that she had done it and wished that I'd had the strength to do it myself all those months ago, as he'd thrown Laura into the snow. Perhaps without him keeping her in the soddie she would have come to me for help sooner and we could have left the prairie behind.

Maybe if I'd been braver and gone to her, Beth and Nora would have survived.

None of us looked back at the ruined barn or the soddie that still stood beyond it.

It took a good while to reach Jamison's soddie, the constant weight of the sun on us, the knowledge that we had very little water, the presence of the grasshoppers that leapt up at the wagon, landing on Laura's shift, striking Franklyn's hands as he held the reins. I was filled with dread at the thought of the long journey back to town.

The house was shut up tightly, its shutters closed and no sound coming from anywhere around. Even the barn was silent. We wasted no time on wondering what was inside. I climbed down after Laura, Franklyn followed us to the door. I found myself at the front of our small party and knocked on the splintery boards. No answer came.

"Hattie, Jamison? We're coming in." I called, glancing at Laura, who looked as tense as I felt.

Inside, a crudely made table and two chairs were standing by the tick that still lay on the floor, piled with dirty sheets. Everything seemed in order, down to the pipe sitting on the table by a glass, sticky and covered in flies. There was a pot on the stove, reeking of spoilt meat and the smell made my eyes water.

Laura stepped into the house, while I held my nose and Franklyn coughed. "There was a tin up here," she said, gesturing to a small shelf on the wall, "Jamison kept money in it. Will told me."

"Maybe he took it and figured they didn't need any of the things here?" I said.

She lifted the lid of a small box at the foot of the tick.

"His clothes are gone." She dipped her hand in and pulled out a handful of skirt, covered in lace and ribbons. "Hers are still right here."

"Maybe Hattie's wearing his spares? If they were going on a long journey it might have suited her better." It was logical but still I felt uneasy, Jamison hadn't seemed the kind to lend his trousers to his wife, whatever the circumstances. "Franklyn, go check the barn and see if the horse is there."

He went and I joined Laura, looking at the box of women's clothes.

"She's not here," she said, "whatever happened...she has to be somewhere."

We both looked around us, and seeing nothing amiss in the living area, I pushed open the door to the lean-to at the back. The smell intensified, and I could see it had nothing to do with the pot on the stove. Lying between the washtub and a clutch of tools was Jamison's body. The sudden stink of him billowed up and made me cough, my eyes watering. There was broken glass all over the floor, it looked as though he'd been struck with a bottle while he was bent over seeing to some task. I shut the door quickly, knowing even as I did so that I would be seeing that grasshopper-gnawed face in my nightmares for the rest of my life.

My hand flew to my mouth and I must have made a noise because Laura was at my elbow in a second. She thrust me back, opened the door and closed it quickly with a short intake of breath. With all she'd seen I doubted there could be fresh horror left in her. She squeezed my hand for a moment, then went to the supply chest and started to look through it.

"What are you doing?" I asked, but I knew already.

"He's gone, and so is she. Whatever they left here isn't going to do them any good now." She glanced up at me. "Don't look at me like I'm some thief."

The sting in her words wasn't aimed at me, I could see the self-disgust all over her face.

"I know. You're right," I said, "I'll see if there's anything on the shelves."

As it turned out, there wasn't much. The food had all been packed up and taken. The only thing I found was a paper sack of flour with a hole in it. There was no sign that mice had gotten to it, or that insects had found their way into the course power, so I took the bag and wrapped it in an apron before putting it in the supply box.

Franklyn returned just as we were carrying the box to the wagon.

"There's no horse in the barn," he said, "no body either."

"We found it," Cecelia said. "It's Jamison."

"It looks like his wife took his money and his clothes and ran away." I said, my voice so quiet even I could hardly hear it. The smell was still in my nostrils, I could almost taste it on my dry lips. More than anything I wanted to scrub it off of me.

"Where do you think she's gone?" Franklyn asked.

"Maybe she went off to find some other fool to marry her," Laura said.

"When we reach town we should get word to the marshals. She killed her husband," Franklyn said, keeping his voice low. "Why on earth would she-"

"She's a whore, not a homesteader," Laura said, "the drought, the grasshoppers...if I could barely manage she must have been desperate. Desperate people can do terrible things to survive."

Franklyn closed his eyes briefly, then returned them to the prairie ahead.

I glanced back at the wagon. "We should start back now. We'll need to stop at my house as well."

He didn't ask me for a reason. I wondered how much the last few days had affected him. He had lost the bluster and self-righteousness of a man on a rescue mission. He was sunburnt and tired and I knew he would never forget the amount of death he'd witnessed, as I wouldn't.

"Shouldn't we bury him?" Franklyn asked.

Laura swallowed and glanced at me.

"There isn't much of him to bury," I said.

We left Jamison's body behind us and headed for my soddie. For most of the way we could see back to the Deene house and I saw Laura cast her eye to it frequently. I couldn't imagine the things she must have felt, leaving her children with no grave marker aside from their empty house, a house she'd weathered so much in.

We drew up at my house and I jumped down, taking grim pleasure in crushing insects under my boots.

"Thomas, can you help us carry things, you'll have to wake your sister and get her to move." I turned to Laura, who was watching me with a guarded face. "You were right, you'll need whatever you can get. Everything in there, you can take it. I want you to have it. If it wasn't for you I never would have lasted long enough to own any of it."

She watched me for a long moment, then nodded. "Thank you." She paused, looking at me, then sighed. "Would you...do you think your brother would mind taking us as close to Morrow County as he can? Will's brother's there and...well he's the only family we have left here."

I could see how much pride it had cost her to ask, and I would not refuse her. Whatever it took I would make Franklyn bring her back with us, to her brother-in-law's porch step if necessary. Anything that I could do to ensure her life was somewhat better, I would do it, without a second thought.

It seemed like weeks since I'd laid on my tick, waiting for death, but the soddie was exactly as I had left it. Between us, with Thomas and Rachel carrying the smaller bundles and Franklyn helping with the plough, we packed everything into the wagon, including the stove. I suppose it helped that we weren't burdened with food or seed, otherwise we never would have been able to load it all, and the horses wouldn't have been able to pull it.

While Laura settled the children and tied up the back of the wagon cover, I took Franklyn to one side and told him of our changed plan. Laura would not only be accompanying us to town, but all the way back to Ohio, where she would, I hoped, be safe with family. I could tell he didn't like it, but he said nothing, only nodded and took his seat on the wagon. I sensed that he was biding his time until Laura was further out of earshot, but I would deal with that when it came to it.

At last we were seated on the wagon, and for the last time, Franklyn set us in motion. All around us the grasshoppers chirped and hopped, the unending motion of their brown-green bodies nauseating to witness. I remembered my arrival, the first time I'd seen Laura amongst the waving, sighing grasses. I could no longer remember where on the Deene land we'd been, any hint of a landmark; a particular clump of grass or scattering of flowers, had been eaten away.

The drive was long and arduous. The heat alone made me feel ill, and my mouth was dry, lips cracked where they weren't sticky with dried spit. We took sips of water as infrequently as we could. None of us had eaten a thing; there was nothing to eat besides cornmeal, and for that we'd have needed to build a fire, only there was nothing to burn. I remembered the watermelons of the ravine, and could have killed for a taste of their cold, crunching flesh.

As the sun passed its peak and started to sag, slowly sinking in the sky, I began to feel the pull of Ohio, and a sense of great desolation filled me. It had seemed to me that Franklyn and his wagon were lifeboats, saving us and taking us somewhere safe. Thinking of my parents, of Charles and the life I'd left behind, of Laura and her collection of dirty, damaged goods headed off to God knew where, I began to feel as though I was on a prison ship.

I looked behind me and saw that Thomas and Rachel were both asleep in the narrow space between the wooden crates and packed up tools. Turning back around I saw that Laura had looked over her shoulder as well. Our eyes caught and it was then that I knew she'd been waiting for them to sleep; even before the first tears rolled down her face, I knew she'd been holding onto her grief for hours, ever since we'd buried her daughters, and her husband.

She leant against me and let out the first of many sobs, stifling it with one hand as her whole body shook with the force of it. I held on to her helplessly, keeping her on the seat, with me, as she sobbed out her bitter loss.

Chapter Thirty-Seven

Laura

After I'd cried myself hoarse, Cecelia had me climb into the back of the wagon with my children. I don't know how, but I slept.

I woke when the wagon suddenly shifted down, following the trail into the ravine. With Rachel and Tom I climbed out of the wagon and eased my aching legs. We stopped for a while to relieve ourselves behind a large, dead, tree. Everything was dead down there. Even the creek was barely a trickle, hardly enough to wet the stones in its bed. Franklyn scooped up what little he could and offered it to the horses that pulled the wagon and the oxen that trailed behind it, equally used up. We all drank from the cask of water, which was nearly dry by then.

I was too thirsty to be hungry. I think everyone felt the same, because no one mentioned food. To get the wagon up the other side of the ravine we walked along side, then climbed back in once we'd reached the flat prairie again.

Usually the journey to town took from before sun up to just past noon. That was with two yoke of well rested and heartily fed oxen pulling. We'd set off so late that by the time we were past the ravine the sun was already on its way down.

I heard Franklyn and Cecelia talking as I lay in the rear of the wagon.

"We should make camp," she was saying, "we could lose a horse, or worse, driving in the dark."

"We're following a track now, we'll be fine."

"But-"

"Cecelia, it can't wait any longer. We barely have water left. I am driving us to town, and then I am making arrangements for us to get back to Ohio."

"Us and Laura."

There was a short silence.

"Franklyn?"

"I was perfectly happy to go along with your plan, but now...her husband is dead, Cecelia. I mean, is there any benefit in her going to his family; three more mouths for them to feed and no prospect of her husband being able to support her? Depending on their circumstances they might not even take her. Perhaps she'd be better off finding herself a new husband here. There can't be any shortage of men."

"Quiet, or you'll wake her," Cecelia muttered. "Anyway, she doesn't want that."

"How do you know? Have you asked her?" he sighed, and I heard the seat creak as he shifted on it. "Cecelia, I know you...care for her, but you understand that she has to do what's best for herself and her children. Without a man she cannot prosper, there's precious little work a woman can do, decent work anyway, and it does not pay enough for a family. How will she cope with the legalities of claiming land? Buying supplies? She'll be cheated and preyed upon without a husband to defend her."

She was silent, and I thought of my own muddled plans. What was I going to do?

I didn't want a new husband, but Lord, how impossible it felt, lying there on the jolting planks of the wagon box, surrounded by the few things I'd managed to hold on to. Franklyn was right. Having a man meant being respectable, being accepted. There would be people that thought my children bastards without a husband by my side. Who would trade fairly with a desperate widow? I would be dependent on charity.

I rested my hand on Rachel's shoulder, careful not to wake her. Rachel and Thomas, I would try my damndest to keep them safe and well, but how would I make money to keep us? Mending or washing until my hands bled, all for cents, I supposed. A long hard road stretched ahead of us and one on which I would be alone, scraping together coin a day at a time.

It was still night when the wheels under me lurched and eased themselves from rough dirt to the well-trodden and cindered main street of town. Even the saloon was dark and quiet. I climbed through to the front seat.

"I've never seen it so still," I said. My breath came in a white cloud, it had grown so cold overnight, with not a cloud in the sky. The only sounds were the grasshoppers and the nickering of the horses.

"There's a pump just down the street," Franklyn said, already climbing down from the seat as we slowed. "I'll be back with some fresh water for us, and the animals."

I took his seat. Cecelia was only inches from me. I wanted to hold her again and tell her that I needed her to stay with me. I couldn't bear leaving her with her husband, and I didn't want to be without her in the tough times coming my way. God knows what she'd say to that, knowing already the life I led. No, at least back in Ohio she'd be safe from hunger and heat, from cold and disease. Franklyn would keep her safe. He had to.

"He can't wait to get me back to Ohio," Cecelia said.

"You not excited to be going home? Hot bath, good meal, back in your own bed in your own room?"

She shook her head.

"Liar," I said, nudging her. "If it was me I'd have gone back as soon as the grasshoppers came. Think of it, grass and trees and windows with glass in, someone else to do the washing and the cooking." I heard my voice go flat. "Sounds like heaven."

She hunched over and peered out from under the wagon cover. "Charles is in one of these buildings, asleep probably. I told Franklyn what I remembered…he didn't believe me. Even hating Charles like he does he can't see him like I do. If I hadn't been there I wouldn't believe it either. So, when Father says I have to go back to my husband, there'll be no fighting it. Franklyn told me that in Ohio I'd have to forget about you. About this. He was right."

I felt like a bullet had gone through me, my lungs seemed suddenly useless, my heart like the rotted shell of a pumpkin.

"I don't think I could stand it out there, thinking about you all the time," she said, her eyes were lowered, and under the moon her skin looked pale and fine, rather than rough and sun scorched, as I knew it to be. "So, I've decided, I don't want to go back."

Something was squeezing my pulpy heart. "Cecelia..."

"I want to go with you," she said, "I want to live with you."

As soon as she said it, I could see it in my mind. Us in another sod house, Cecelia tired and bent over a pile of sewing work, me parcelling other people's laundry. Her voice in the dark, next to me on a scratchy tick, in a rented shack that was bleeding us dry, saying 'I wish I'd never gone with you, Laura. I wish I'd gone back to my family.'

"You can't," I said.

She looked up at that, her eyes big and wide. She was still so young and full of romantic notions, even a year on the prairie hadn't completely knocked that out of her, not if she was proposing that we live together as Will and I had. The talk would be one thing, the hardship of being without a man quite another.

"Laura, I know it'll be difficult, but I want to go with you. You don't have to do this alone."

"I know that. I'm a good bit older than you and I know it'll be difficult to find a place for me and the children - just like I know you don't really want this to be your lot in life. And I won't let it be."

"It's been my life for a year."

"One year out of how many? This has been my world since I was born. In the end, you'd hate me. Just like I hated him."

I heard the clash of buckets, loud in the cold silence of the street. I could just see Franklyn walking back with his arms weighed down.

"I wouldn't hate you," she said, stubbornly.

"You would. You'd see this life for what it is and you'd be cursing me. Your brother can keep you safe back east." I looked her firmly in the eye, refusing to be swayed.

"There's a sign saying one bucket per day," Franklyn said, setting down his two pails of water. "No one's watching it though, and I thought the animals could use it after the drive." He looked up at us on the wagon seat. I hadn't moved and neither had she, we were both facing each other, her hand on the seat between us, like she wanted to reach for me but couldn't quite bring herself to.

"You two alright?" he asked.

"I've very tired," Cecelia said. "Do you have a room here? One we can go to?"

"Just over there, above the stables behind the saloon," Franklyn searched his pockets and came up with a key on a piece of string. "There's some stairs by the gate into the yard, climb those and you'll find the door at the end of the walkway. You two need a chance to wash and get some rest. Take the children and I'll send someone for you once everyone opens for business."

At the back of the wagon I looked in on Rachel and Thomas, shook them gently awake and helped them down from the box. Perhaps in days gone I would've left them to sleep, but I'd lost two of my children. Now more than ever I wanted them by me.

There were grasshoppers clinging to the board siding of buildings and hopping in the street, but the night-time coolness had them a little slower than under the full heat of the sun. On the prairie the grasshoppers had destroyed everything, but here people at least had pump water and the store for food. When harvest time came they would probably feel the loss of custom and goods, but for now they only had to shut themselves up inside with canned food and wait it out. It wasn't like the insects could eat up dimes and dollars.

I carried Rachel in my arms and Thomas walked beside me with the water bucket. Cecelia was angry, I could see it in the set of her shoulders as she strode along in front.

The back stairs were creaky, the wood popped and sighed as we climbed. Along the walkway were a few doors, and the one that Cecelia unlocked led to a small room with a table chairs in it. There was a lamp on the table, with some matches beside it on a chipped plate. Cecelia lit it as I crossed the room and opened a door into the next room. There was a bed in it, a brass framed thing with a proper mattress sagging through the old slats. I laid Rachel down on it, she was practically sleeping already. What were a few bedbugs now?

"Thomas, come and lie down. Try to get some sleep."

"Are we going to Ohio tomorrow?" he asked.

"I don't know yet. Perhaps."

"I don't want to live with Uncle Jacob."

"I haven't made up my mind yet, go to sleep now."

He frowned, looking back at Cecelia. "She's going to Ohio, why can't we stay with her?"

"She has her own family to live with," I said, not looking at her. "It'd be rude to press ourselves where we're not wanted. Don't embarrass me now, Thomas."

He ducked his head and went into the bedroom. I stroked his hair as he passed and closed the door softly behind him. Alone in the room with her, I looked at the prints on the wall, the small stove, the cracked dresser, anywhere but her face.

"Is there anything to eat in that?" I gestured at the dresser.

"There's a bit of jerky, and half a tin of coffee."

"No firewood," I said, pulling out a chair and easing myself onto it. There was a little cushion on the seat, which made it the most comfortable chair I'd sat on in over three years.

She brought over the jerky, wrapped in brown paper. Two cups were strung on her fingers, and she dipped water out of the bucket with them. For a while the only sounds were the paper rustling and us chewing the dry meat.

"You can't stop me, you know, from not going back," she said.

"Franklyn would have something to say about it."

"I've been thinking about it," she said, twisting a piece of jerky in her fingers, "and I think he'd let me go. I don't think he has it in him to force me."

"And Charles?"

"If we're gone before he sees me he doesn't have to know Franklyn found me. He'll keep looking, then give up, there's only so long he can stand it out here. Even if he did suspect Franklyn of helping me escape, there's nothing he can do to him. It'd be his word against my brother's and my parents would side with him."

I could feel something in me wavering. I wanted to be steel against her thistledown dreams, but they were so tempting.

"And go where? Back to the prairie?"

"Anywhere you want."

"That isn't an answer."

"Anywhere, further west? Or we could go south, north. There's all that country out there to settle. No one need see us or hear from us again, if that's what bothers you. The talk."

"And when we get there, we build a house and plough some land and plant up?"

"Yes. You know we can do it."

"And when the next drought comes? Or maybe a flood, or grasshoppers, or the whole damn list of plagues straight out of Egypt, what then? Your brother won't come on his white horse with food and water to save us."

"You think I don't know what it means, the hardship?" Cecelia said.

Furious tears blinded me. "What if you come, if we go together and then you get the fever and die? There'll be you with a rusted plough and two children that aren't yours. Would you take care of them?"

"You know I would."

"But you don't know what it's like." I squeezed my hands into fists on the table top. "Nora and Beth, my...they're dead, and I don't know what to do, how to keep the others safe. I don't know a damn thing, and I have to think of them, only them. I can't think about what it would be like going off with you, because it's them I have to care about."

Her hands, warm and dry, curled around my fists. I bent my head and closed my eyes to the sight of the table's scarred surface.

"Laura, I was there with you. I saw what it did to you. I know what it's like to lose a child, but I can't imagine what the last few days have felt like. I can't imagine the years you've spent, not thinking of yourself, and I'm not asking you to be selfish now."

I looked up at her.

"I'm asking you to let me take care of things. I'm asking you to let me take care of you."

I shook my head. How could she take care of me? She was so young, so soft at heart. I had to take care of myself, of my children.

"Laura, if you say you'll let me, I swear to spend the rest of my life watching over your children, like they were my own. I already know them a little, and I will love them." She was crying now, the tears running down her dusty cheeks, leaving tracks. "Laura, please don't make me leave you behind. Please tell me you don't want me to go, tell me you meant it when you kissed me."

I couldn't look away from her tears, made brown by the dust, dripping from her chin.

"You wouldn't have done it if you didn't want to," she said.

"And what does that mean?"

"That you don't want me to go. That you want a house with me in it, a bed for the both of us," she said, her face flushing a lively red. "And even though it's like nothing I've ever even thought of, it's what I want too."

I hadn't let myself hope in years, that was the price of carrying on. You couldn't let yourself think it would change, that it would get better, because you'd do nothing but wait for it. Wait for the sun to shine and your heart to lift.

With two of my children in the ground, no home, an empty purse, half a wagon of broken things, and a heart swollen with a terrifying love, hope was all I had.

"North," I said, freeing a hand from her grip and raising shaky fingers to brush away her tears. "Let's go north."

Chapter Thirty-Eight
Cecelia

I swear that hearing her say those words, those three words that spoke of a future for us, was more of a relief to me than Franklyn's gift of water days before.

I took her hand from my face and held it as I rounded the table and dropped to my knees on the wood floor. I laid my head in her lap, against the stained and dusty cloth of her shift. Her hand fell to my hair, brushing through it and making my neck prickle with heat.

"Somewhere with trees," she said, "where we can build a proper wood cabin with a floor." Her fingers traced the lobe of my ear, sending a shivery thrill over my skin. "I heard a man once talking about tapping maples and boiling the sap for sugar and syrup. Sounds like it can't be too hard to learn how."

I looked up at her, and her face was smoothed out, save for a crease of concentration between her eyebrows. She was considering the path before us, and I saw that it had her interest. Her mouth lifted into a small smile, tempered by uncertainty.

"You're sure you'd like to go? It means travelling hard, and we've no money, we'll have to work for someone to get a piece of land, and it'll be a struggle to get an even deal."

"I want to go, with you," I said, "I can work, and help you take care of Thomas and Rachel."

"Will you be dressed like a man still?"

I shrugged. "I can't see being able to keep it up, not now that Thomas knows, Rachel too. It'd be better to be honest, wouldn't it? Or as honest as we can be."

"What'll we tell them, that we're sisters?" She laughed her brittle stick laugh, "there's no one that'll believe you and I are cut from the same cloth."

"But we are," I said, because we were the same; she wanted me as I wanted her.

She smiled a little. "Perhaps we'd make good widows."

"The world's no kinder to widows."

"True, but at least they're decent and can hold their heads up in town."

"What about the children?" I asked.

She looked towards the closed door, behind which Thomas and Rachel were resting. "Thomas said you were sweet on me, I think he knows part of it, though I doubt he can understand it. Rachel might have guessed a little of it." She sighed, her shoulders slumping under the rough shirt, "if they could tolerate being brow beaten and struck for not picking a turnip right, they can grow to tolerate life with two women for a family."

My throat felt tight, hearing that. In her bed. I thought about her in bed, without her shift and with her hair down. It wasn't the first time I'd pictured it, but having my hands on her, looking up into her face, made my heart beat wildly. I didn't know what I'd do, in a bed with her, our skin free to touch all over. It scared me, but it drew me too.

"North then," I said.

"North."

I stood and refilled our cups with water.

Unbidden, the image of William's bruised neck and slack face came to me. I would carry that with me for the rest of my days, I knew. How could I tell Laura that her daughter had blood on her hands? She'd lost so much, and the millstone of William Deene was finally gone from around her neck, I couldn't place the weight of Rachel's guilt in its place. I hadn't realised until I'd seen Beth's still body how much I'd grown to care for the children.

Rachel had seemed so hard to me, but I'd seen her desperation and the rope burns on her hands. I understood her. I swore to myself that I would take what I knew of William's death to my grave; that I would do it for love, of Laura, and of her children.

Outside the sun was reluctantly rising, the gradual lightening of the sky painted shadows on the wall opposite the window. When the lamp ran out of oil there was enough daylight to see by. I had my hand in Laura's on the table, we both held on as if afraid the other would fade like dew if we didn't. I doubt either of us could have slept for fear and excitement.

Too soon there came a rap on the door and I rose to open it. There was a small boy, perhaps ten years old, clutching a piece of brown paper, which he thrust at me.

"Mr Ellis says the wagon's almost ready," he said, when I took the note.

"Could you let him know we'll be down soon?"

"I will," he darted off, already rattling down the wooden stairs as I closed the door.

The note was grease pencil on a torn paper packet.

Cecelia,

I hope you've rested. I'll be speaking with Charles before we leave today. I've paid off the man I rented the wagon from, you can let Mrs Deene know that it's hers once we've reached Ohio. If she isn't coming all the way with us, you and I can take the stage rather than take her out of her way. I've also withdrawn some funds and am prepared to give her fifty dollars for being such a good neighbour to you while you were away.

Come down as soon as you can, I'm having supplies for the journey packaged as I write.

Franklyn.

"What does he say?" Laura asked.

"He says the wagon with your things on is yours when we part ways. He's got fifty dollars for you as well."

There was a short silence, then I heard her chair creak as she stood.

"Could be a thousand dollars, it wouldn't change anything."

"Fifty dollars buys a lot of land. A lot of maple trees. You won't get the wagon or the money if I don't go with him."

"Then I don't want either," she said, and I turned and found her looking at me with her hands on her hips. "I took you at your word. From this point on, nothing comes between us."

"Nothing," I agreed.

"Could be getting out of this town's going to be harder than getting off the prairie," she said, "if he's got your husband backing him up, plus any men around who're itching to get involved in a struggle...I don't know what's going to happen." She glanced at the bedroom door, "I only hope they'll be safe."

"Franklyn would never let them get hurt. Charles either. They're not brutes."

She didn't look convinced, and I couldn't blame her. In truth I didn't know what Charles would do when he saw me.

"We'll have to speak to Franklyn," I said, "I think I can convince him to let us go, keep Charles from us for long enough that we can get together some food and water from the wagon, then be on our way. If he can take Charles to look for me further south for a time, we'll be able to outrun him. Once we get north of the territory there'll be nothing to lead him to us."

"If you can convince him."

"I believe he doesn't want me to go back with Charles, he just doesn't know what else to do with me. This gives him an option other than taking me back to our parents, where Charles could still force me to go home. He might not like me going off again, but he can't deny that I stand a better chance with you than with Charles. I'll make him see that."

Laura eased open the door to the bedroom, stirring Thomas and Rachel from their exhausted sleep. The four of us left the room and took the stairs down to the yard behind the saloon.

There weren't many people about on the street, only a pair of men taking barrels off of a cart and hefting them into the saloon, grasshoppers smashing under their boots. Our wagon was where we'd left it and Franklyn was standing by the back, lifting large brown sacks up to a boy balanced in the box. He turned his head, looking first at me and then at Laura's children. Laura reached for my hand and held it. I saw his face go still and hard at that.

"Franklyn," I said, as we came up to the wagon, "I need to speak to you, privately."

Franklyn took a few coins from his pocket and handed them to the boy, who leapt down into the dust, his boots crushing grasshoppers.

"Right, sir," the boy, the same one who'd come up to the room, stuffed the coins into his pocket. "Need anything else?"

"No, that's all, boy," Franklyn took my elbow as the boy rushed off, "Cecelia, I have to go and speak to Charles-"

"Don't."

He glanced at Laura as I spoke, tugged on my arm a little more forcefully. "Cecelia, you agreed."

"I can't leave her," I said, "I won't. I don't expect you to tell me it's the right choice, or even to wish me well, but I'm going with her today, and we'll be walking all the way if you see fit to keep the wagon for yourself, but I hope you don't. I think that's the one gesture of brotherly love I can expect from you, but I can understand if you can't bring yourself to make it."

I said it all fast, not looking in his eye. He was my brother, I didn't want to see what the thought of me and Laura together made him feel inside. I didn't want my last memory of his face to be tinged by his disgust.

"What do you expect me to say?" he asked, "that I'm happy to see you go? That you have my blessing? Cecelia, this is foolish."

"Pretending I'm the same woman I was a year ago would be foolish," I said, "Franklyn, if I couldn't stand being in Ohio then, how could I stand it any better now? You're asking me to live with a murderer and give up the woman I love."

He glanced around us as if expecting a torch wielding mob to surround us. Twenty yards away the men were still struggling with their barrels.

"I still can't believe that of Charles," Franklyn said. "And he's still looking for you, what would you have me do about that?"

I'd believed Franklyn wouldn't take my word for what Charles had done, it was part of what had driven me from Ohio in the first place, but having it confirmed to me was like a heavy stone in my belly. Only Laura would ever believe me, I could see that now. I wished there was some way to show him the side of Charles I'd seen, to prove it to him once and for all. But there was no time. I could stay and make my case, or I could escape.

"Tell him I'm dead," I said. I'd imagined my death often enough since the grasshoppers came, it hardly gave me a chill to say it.

"You'd let Mother and Father think that?" I looked at him and his expression was a mixture of surprise and horror. "It'll break their hearts."

"You don't think seeing me like this would be worse for them?" I said. "The shame of them knowing about me and Laura? Because I will not forget her, Franklyn, and I will talk about her. They'll see the truth of it on my face."

"Are we leaving now?" Thomas was asking his mother.

"Soon," Laura said quietly, her hand still in mine.

"But she's coming with us?" Thomas said.

"Yes."

I looked at him and found him nodding at me. Franklyn was watching the boy when I turned back to him.

"I've chosen. I'm sorry, Franklyn."

His jaw was set, and in that moment I could see just how much he'd aged in the past year. His eyes weren't hectic with youth anymore, his mouth had grown thinner, more anxious. I was sorry, very sorry for all I'd put him through, but I was not about to give up the rest of my life to making amends. I wasn't selfless enough.

Franklyn's eyes shifted from my face to the street behind me, and in one motion he pushed my head down and hauled me around to the side of the wagon.

"Take your hands off her," Laura demanded, her hand closing like a manacle around his wrist.

"Charles is over there, coming out of the store," Franklyn said. "There's a table in the back where he eats in the mornings. I didn't think he'd be awake so early."

"Franklyn?" I said.

He lowered his voice to a hiss. "If it were only a matter of taking you home to Mother and Father I would, in a heartbeat, but Charles will not willingly let you live apart from him. Much as I think you're confused about what happened to Charlie, I know he hasn't treated you well." He glanced at Laura, "If you'd been alone-"

"I'm not alone."

"She has a family," Laura said, "she has me and..." she looked to Thomas and Rachel, standing together to the side of her.

"She said she'd come and take care of us," Rachel said.

I saw Franklyn's face soften and I felt for him. How long had he and his wife tried for children and failed?

"Franklyn," I said, seeing my chance, "please, let me go."

His hand left my arm, reached up and plucked my hat from Laura's head, clapping it onto mine and pulling it down low.

"Get in the wagon."

My heart froze. Was he telling me it was over, that he was taking me home?

"Both of you," he said.

Laura released him, grabbed my hand and squeezed. "Come on Thomas, Rachel, up into the wagon now."

Thomas climbed up into the box and helped Rachel up beside him. Rachel clambered up the tail board and stood under the canvas, looking down at me and my brother.

"Franklyn-"

He pulled a canvas bag from his pocket. "There's about two hundred dollars here, it was supposed to be for travel and for Laura but, take it." He held it out to me. "It should get you far away from here and pay for paper and mailing." His eyes held mine, "when you get wherever it is you're heading, I want a letter, you hear me? Telling me that my sister is alive and well, and much improved in her house building skills."

I snorted a laugh, but my eyes were wet. The money was heavy in my hand and his palm was warm through my shirt as he touched my arm.

"I love you Cecelia."

"Franklyn...I love you too."

I threw my arms around him and hugged him close, his shirt soft under my hands. I kissed his cheek and he brushed his lips against my forehead.

"Go," he said, releasing me. "Go and...I hope you don't regret it."

"I hope so too."

I circled the wagon, climbed up onto the seat with my heart between my teeth. What if Charles saw me, came running across the street and dragged me down? I took up the reins and looked at the gleaming backs of the horses. Ahead of us the street was mostly empty, a few people were on the boardwalks but the rutted road was clear.

Laura climbed from the wagon box onto the seat beside me and I glanced behind us, down the length of the wagon, to where Franklyn was standing in the street. I tipped my hat at him and flicked the reins. The wheels under the wagon gripped the dust and rolled, crushing grasshopper bodies under their metal treads.

No one would ever lock me up again. Though I might face danger, even death, I would never have to look on Charles again, or feel that fear. The weightlessness of relief made me giddy and I could not make myself sombre and serious in the face of our long journey north.

Laura's hand covered mine on the reins and I turned and smiled at her. We were leaving town, heading north with money, goods and provisions enough to start again, or rather, to start for the very first time, with each other.

Thanks to the Reader,

Thank you for buying a copy of *Night Fires in the Distance*. I hope you enjoyed it, and would really love to hear from you if you did, especially if you have any suggestions or comments on my work.

I regularly check Goodreads and Amazon for reviews so please feel free to feedback to me there. I'm also on twitter @JollySnidge or on Instagram as JollySnidge if you want to keep up with me, events I'm at and what new things I'm working on.

As a self-publishing author, your feedback is invaluable to me.

I have various other novels on Amazon, and if you'd like to check them out, they are all published under Sarah Goodwin. Whilst they do not have the professional input of a literary agent, which this novel benefitted hugely from, they are all works that I put a lot of love and hard work into – and they are a bargain at only 99p each.

Special Thanks,

My heartfelt gratitude goes out to everyone on my MA course for their input into this novel, to my Mum for reading me all the 'Little House' books as a child, and to my agent Laura Williams for all her hard work and input into getting this book as damn near perfect as it is.

Printed in Poland
by Amazon Fulfillment
Poland Sp. z o.o., Wrocław